# one fell down

OTHER BOOKS AND AUDIO BOOKS
BY RONDA GIBB HINRICHSEN:

*Betrayed*

# one fell down

A Novel of Suspense by **Ronda Gibb Hinrichsen**

Covenant Communications, Inc.

Cover image: *Maori Face Tattoo* © alekup, courtesy of shutterstock.com.

Cover design copyright © 2017 by Covenant Communications, Inc.

Published by Covenant Communications, Inc.
American Fork, Utah

Printed in the United States of America
First Printing: February 2017

23 22 21 20 19 18 17     10 9 8 7 6 5 4 3 2 1

ISBN 978-1-52440-140-5

Dedicated to
Katrina and Jenny—
you've blessed my life

# Acknowledgments

WHILE MANY AMAZING PEOPLE HAVE guided and supported me through the development of this novel, I want to specifically thank Carolyn Hansen for her factual insight into New Zealand and the Maori culture; my critique group—Josi Kilpack, Nancy Allen, Jody Durfee, Becki Clayson, and Jennifer Moore—for their unfailing wisdom, friendship, and generous feedback; and my "beta readers" who helped me fine-tune my manuscript before submission. Big thanks to my editor, Stacey Turner, and all those at Covenant Communications who've put so much time and effort into turning my story into a book. And finally, as always, my never-ending gratitude goes to my family and most especially to my loving husband, Rolin.

# Chapter 1

"Lucky to be in love with . . ." The singer's voice crooned through Mikaela's car stereo speakers with the same warmth and romance it had held last night when she and Trevor, her fiancé, had snuggled in front of his parents' fireplace and listened to "their" song. At least Trevor insisted the song belonged to both of them, and she supposed he was right, but in her heart of hearts, Mikaela thought only of him when she heard it: his quiet smile, the sparkle in his green eyes, the gentleness that rippled through his voice whenever he spoke to her. Mikaela sighed. Trevor was the man she'd loved every moment of her life since she was a sophomore in high school—*five years ago!* She glanced at the clock on her dashboard. And next week—no, in six days, fifteen hours, and thirteen minutes—she would marry him.

Mikaela leaned against her headrest. The barrette she'd clasped at the back of her straight, light-blonde hair poked into her scalp.

"Is something the matter, babe?" Trevor asked.

"No. I'm just happy."

They crested the first hill of Sardine Canyon, the four-lane highway that crossed through the Wasatch Mountains and connected Logan and Brigham City, Utah. The last time she and Trevor had driven it had been an early October weekend, when thick-needled pine trees, red maples, and yellowing underbrush lined much of the road, but today, snow buried all but the trees' upper and outlying branches. It would be a white Christmas.

"You're not still upset at me for driving your new car, are you?" Trevor said.

Mikaela held back her smile. Sometimes her law-student fiancé took things a little too literally, and she couldn't help but tease him when he did. "Actually, now that you mention it . . ." She lifted the collar of her sports jacket higher up her neck and faced her side window.

"You really are upset?"

That time his voice husked through her like slow warmth. She looked back to him and squeezed his knee. "Just kidding. It actually feels good to relax a bit. I owe you one."

"One what?"

Heat crept into Mikaela's cheeks. *Blast!* How could she ever keep anything to herself if her blush always gave her away? "Will a big kiss do?"

"I won't accept less than two big kisses."

"Deal! But seriously, thank you. I hadn't realized how tired I'd be after that last final. My brain feels like it ran a marathon." She leaned toward him and gave him a quick peck on the cheek.

"Anytime. But that doesn't count as one of those two kisses."

They started down the other side of the second hill. Mikaela yawned.

"You've got a good twenty minutes till we reach Brigham City," Trevor said. "Why don't you take a nap. I'll wake you when we get to your grandparents' house."

"I'd better not. I'll probably just dream of landscape details and the proper use of space, and right now I'd rather not think about anything architecture related until after the holidays."

"Yeah, right. How much do you want to bet the first old building we see in town, you'll say, 'Can I just tell you how cool that gingerbread window trim, or whatever, is?'"

Mikaela pursed her lips into a fake pout. "I'll bet you a scoop of chocolate brownie ice cream I'll say no such thing."

"The ice cream and *three* big kisses. That's my final offer."

"I'll take it. But, sadly, you're going to lose this bet." To prove her point—not to mention make certain she wouldn't even *see* any of Brigham City's Gothic Revival homes—Mikaela reached for the stack of mail she'd set on the backseat. She'd grabbed it from her mailbox on her way to pick up Trevor from his apartment. One of the envelopes had fallen to the floor on top of her hiking shoes. She maneuvered in her seat, reached behind her, and finally found it. As she pulled it and the other mail between the two front bucket seats, the back of her fingers brushed Trevor's hip.

"Not while I'm driving, please," he said.

"You wish."

He laughed and pulled into the passing lane to get around a slow-moving semitruck.

Mikaela flipped through the mail—water bill, the local newspaper, an American Express advertisement, and a pale-blue envelope with no return address. They weren't a lot to look at, but if she read slowly, she could make them last until they reached her grandparents' house.

"An early wedding card?" Trevor said.

"Or Christmas." Mikaela inched her forefinger through the opening of the blue envelope's upper corner and slowly slid through the stickied seal. She peeked inside.

"Which is it?" Trevor asked.

"Neither. This is really weird." Furrowing her brow, she pulled the card from the envelope. The words *Thinking of You* were written in swirly, dark-blue letters across the top, and a bird with its wings spread out and its legs extended like it was about to land filled the center. The picture was embossed with silvery-white ink. Why would someone send her a sympathy card? No one she knew had died recently.

Mikaela opened the card and searched for the signature. Finding none, she looked to the handwritten words at the top of the page. *Jack and Jill went up the hill to fetch a pail of water. Jack fell down and broke—*

Trevor gasped.

Mikaela looked up at him. "What's wrong?"

His eyes rounded wide, and his knuckles clenched white around the steering wheel. "Hold on."

Mikaela looked out the windshield. The car ahead of them grew closer . . . closer. "Slow down."

"We've lost our brakes."

Her stomach dropped. She slammed her feet on invisible brakes. "What? The car's brand new."

Trevor shifted the automatic into third gear. He swerved into the passing lane. "Call 911."

Mikaela yanked her purse from beneath her seat. She scrambled through its contents, grabbed her phone and pressed *9*.

Trevor locked the drive into second. "Why won't this thing slow down?"

"-1-1." *Please answer!*

"Oh, my—Mikaela!"

Mikaela winced.

"9-1-1," the dispatcher said. "What is your emergency?"

"We've lost our brakes. There are two cars blocking the lanes ahead of us, and—"

Trevor yanked the emergency break. He swerved toward the mountainside. Mikaela pressed her hands against the dashboard. The car spun once . . . twice . . . plowed into the mountain. Was it her voice or Trevor's she heard screaming?

\* \* \*

Hunapo stared out his rain-spotted living-room window at the heaps of rundown, beige houses across the street. In all the years after he'd retired that he'd lived in this part of San Francisco, he'd never once crossed that street to visit any of his neighbors. Uneducated *bogans*, all of them. Bogans who didn't want to know him any more than he wanted to know them.

His phone buzzed too loud. A text.

Hunapo adjusted his hearing aid to a lower volume and scowled at the dark clouds hovering over the neighborhood. "You can get as black as you want," he said to them, "but this is gonna be good news." *At least it better be.*

*Buzz.*

Why hadn't he kept that phone with him? He pushed himself up from his rocking chair and lumbered across the sparsely furnished room to the kitchen. He picked up his cell phone from where he'd left it on the table next to his unfinished foil dinner.

*Jack died. Not Jill.*

He swore and slowly punched in his reply.

*Get it right next time.*

# Chapter 2

ATTENDING TREVOR'S VIEWING AND SUBSEQUENT funeral had required more strength than Mikaela knew she had, more tears than she thought existed in the world, and innumerably more times telling herself that God knew she could bear the loss of yet another person she dearly loved. *He that endureth to the end shall be saved.* That was the scripture's promise, wasn't it?

And yet there she was, barely a year after Trevor's death, enduring another funeral. Only this time, rather than sitting near her grandparents and hiding from well-meaning mourners, she stood in the same place Trevor's mother had at Trevor's funeral. And it was Mikaela who squeezed hands or nodded to friends and neighbors as they moved down the family receiving line. It was also her grandfather who now stood next to the casket—her grandmother's casket. Was he holding up okay?

Mikaela looked his direction. His lips quavered when he spoke to the person in front of him, and his shoulders slumped so far forward that he looked much shorter than his six feet. His tight, blank expression twisted through Mikaela's emotions. If only they could run away from this place. If only they didn't have to pretend everything was all right.

Mrs. Olson, the gray-haired woman who'd lived across the street from her grandparents for as long as Mikaela could remember, stepped in front of her and held out her hand. Mikaela reached for it, but rather than clasping it, Mrs. Olson moved closer and wrapped both arms around Mikaela's shoulders. "She was a good friend. Always brought over the best homemade chicken soup when I was sick."

"Grandpa said it tasted so good because she seasoned it with compassion," Mikaela said. "He called it Grandma's *Thinking of You* soup."

*Thinking of You.* Mikaela stared at the woman, but she saw only the memory of Trevor and herself hanging upside down from their seat belts when her car had rolled in Sardine Canyon. The *Thinking of You* card she'd received that day had lain flat against the shattered glass in front of her face.

Mikaela's thoughts returned to the present as Mrs. Olson released her and said, "She looks good, doesn't she?"

*No! Grandma never looked that pale or bruised or expressionless in her life.* "Thank you for coming," Mikaela said.

Mrs. Olson's slow nod and quick glance away from Mikaela told her the neighbor hadn't really believed her own words about Grandmother's appearance either, but she'd said them, and now it was time to move on. Mrs. Olson stepped in front of Aunt Maureen, the tall woman standing next to Mikaela. Aunt Maureen was Mikaela's mother's only sibling. She'd never married and never had any children. Had she, perhaps, also lost someone the way Mikaela had lost Trevor?

Next a man shook Mikaela's hand. She didn't recognize him, but his frown reminded her so much of the way Trevor's father's face had looked during Trevor's funeral that she clenched her fists and dropped her gaze. *Breathe. Don't run. I can get through this. Grandpa needs me.*

"I'm sorry," the man said.

Mikaela nodded and swallowed. "Thank you."

When he moved toward her aunt, one of her grandmother's closest friends stepped in front of Mikaela. She had dark eyes. Grandmother's dark eyes had always glowed with warmth, especially when she'd said, "You have more beauty inside you than you realize." She'd first said that phrase the night Mikaela stayed home from the junior prom because Trevor, her unrequited crush at the time, had invited another girl. Her grandmother had written those words on a card and placed it on Mikaela's bedroom mirror. The card was still there.

"I wish Marge could have made it back to New Zealand before this happened," the friend said. "She was so looking forward to the trip. Talked of nothing else."

"I wouldn't be surprised if she's there now," Mikaela said. "Or been there and come back."

Tears welled in the woman's eyes. "That would be like her."

Mikaela took a fresh tissue from the Kleenex box she'd put on the small round table behind her and dabbed at her eyes. If only her grandmother hadn't been so anxious to get back into nature after the long winter. If only she'd waited for Mikaela to get home for spring break. They could have hiked up Perry Canyon together. Mikaela could have kept her from falling down the mountainside.

"Grandma always was an adventuress." Mikaela dropped the tissue into the small trash can on the floor beneath the table and numbly glanced toward the open door. A young funeral director in a neatly pressed black suit stood somberly next to it. He barely moved and hardly blinked, seeming more like a royal British guard protecting Windsor Castle than a compassionate host. But then, maybe emotional restraint was how he'd learned to cope with his job. Maybe showing no emotion was how he took care of his clients.

"If I die first, you must take care of your grandfather," her grandmother had told her when they'd returned home after Trevor's funeral. "He'll take care of everyone but himself."

Mikaela wiped new tears from her face. Had her grandmother had a premonition of her death?

"You must be Mikaela York."

Mikaela looked up at a tall, dark man with a full head of starkly white hair. His black-brown eyes crinkled downward, he leaned heavily against his yellow-and-black striped cane, and he had an open-vowelled English accent similar to her grandparents'. Was he also from New Zealand? "I am," she said.

He handed her a blue envelope and looked down the line. "Him and me, we were mates years ago. When I heard 'bout his wife, I could not stay away."

Mikaela followed his gaze toward her grandfather. She couldn't see his face because a large woman stood in front of him. "I'm sure he'll appreciate seeing you. Thank you for coming."

He pressed his lips into a hard line and glanced between her and her grandfather the way so many others had done when they were trying to keep their emotions in check. *He must really care for him.*

Mikaela gave him a sad smile, placed the card he'd given her on the table behind her in the stack of other sympathy cards, and turned back, but a short, thirty-something woman stood in his place. Had the line moved already?

She scanned the people between her and her grandfather. The large woman still stood in front of him, and several others she'd already spoken to stood behind her, but where was the man who had handed her the card?

# Chapter 3

IF HER GRANDMOTHER'S FUNERAL MEANT good-bye, her burial felt like a final farewell. But it wasn't. It couldn't be.

Mikaela hugged her coat and huddled next to her aunt beside the grave site. She cried as the bishop spoke of heaven, but her grandfather, his face twisted in anguish, kept his face bowed toward the ground. Occasionally he wiped his cheek with the back of his hand, but he didn't look up until "amen." Nor did he speak more than a few words to those who offered their good wishes and "I'm sorrys" until after they'd finished the luncheon their neighbors had served at the church.

Mikaela slid her arm through his, Aunt Maureen took his other arm, and the three of them left the building and plodded across the parking lot to Grandfather's silver sedan.

Aunt Maureen hugged him. "I wish I could stay longer, Dad. I wish work would have given me more than three days off."

"No worries." It was her grandfather's usual phrase, but the quick, rounded way he said it always reminded Mikaela that his homeland was not the United States.

Aunt Maureen's lips quivered. She looked at Mikaela over the top of his shoulder. "You'll take care of him?" she mouthed.

Mikaela nodded.

"Thank you." She stepped back from her father and looked him fully in the face. "I'll call when I get home."

"I'll look forward to it."

Mikaela's gaze drifted toward Trevor's nearby grave site. On this day, nineteen months ago, Trevor had taken her to a park, dropped to one knee, and, staring into her eyes, proposed. Trevor had always been so much more romantic than she'd ever thought to be.

Her grandfather squeezed her elbow, pulling her from her reverie. Mikaela turned her gaze back to his. She lowered her hand, which she'd involuntarily touched to the narrow, bright-red scar that ran vertically from the corner of her left eye down to her jawbone. She'd received it during the rollover.

"I love you, Dad," Aunt Maureen said. They pressed their cheeks together in an almost kiss.

"Back at you, my girl." He stepped slightly away from her. "Looks like a storm is coming. You'd best get to the airport before the roads turn bad."

"I suppose you're right." She hugged him again, said a hoarse good-bye, and headed for her white rental car on the opposite side of the parking lot.

Mikaela helped her grandfather in then walked around to the driver's side. She sat in the gray bucket seat next to him and automatically reached for his seat adjuster. But she hesitated. This was his car, but he hadn't trusted his emotions enough to drive. She gripped the steering wheel.

He wiped his nose with a handkerchief her grandmother had given him. She'd embroidered his name, *Joseph Parker*, in the corner of it. "How are you holding up, sweetheart?" he said.

"Not very well, but I'm trying. You?"

He inhaled a long, slow breath. "Empty."

"Is there something I can do to help?"

"Yes, but it's too important to talk about in the car. Let's wait until we get back to the house."

His voice was so serious, his gaze so intent, that Mikaela's stomach turned over twice as she started the ignition. In the past, talking about something *later* with her grandfather always ended up being something she did not want to do.

*Take care of your grandfather.*

Mikaela inhaled a deep, pained breath over the sound of her grandmother's voice inside her mind. Her grandparents had left their home and business in New Zealand to take care of her after her parents had died—they hadn't wanted Mikaela to have to move from the only home she'd ever known. How could she refuse what he needed her to do? No matter what it might be?

Too soon, she and her grandfather stood on her grandparents' front doorstep.

Holding the sympathy cards they'd collected at the viewing, Mikaela turned the cold brass doorknob and pushed open the door; the pair walked into the small living room. Red-and-black poi balls, tiki statues, and wooden bowls—traditional New Zealand knickknacks she'd seen so many times she could describe them in her sleep—and white upholstered furniture filled all but a narrow, mazelike path through the room. Mikaela scanned from one end of it to the other. Too quiet.

Her grandfather must have thought the same thing because he just stared as if he didn't know what to do.

"Why don't you try to get some rest," Mikaela said.

"Not until after we've talked."

Mikaela swallowed, slipped off her shoes, and crossed to the living room couch. She placed the sympathy cards from the viewing on the coffee table next to the stack of mail neither she nor her grandfather had felt like opening over the past few days.

Grandfather slouched into the armchair across from the couch and lowered his chin against his chest. Mikaela watched him, waiting for him to speak, but when all he did was stare at the mail, she said, "I suppose we ought to go through these."

He shrugged, and she set about sorting them into five groups: junk mail, bills, newspapers and magazines, miscellaneous, and sympathy cards.

When she finished, he said, "I haven't had a chance to ask you how things are in Logan."

"My boss gave me time off, so that's good."

"I wasn't talking about work."

*I know.* Mikaela glanced away from his bloodshot eyes and to the miscellaneous pile. There were three letters in it; two were addressed to her grandfather and the third to her. She picked that one up.

Her grandfather wiped his nose with his handkerchief. "Whenever your grandmother and I had to be apart because I was on a business trip or something, I missed her terribly. But this is different. I hurt. Both inside and out."

Mikaela closed her eyes against the moist heat gathering behind her eyelids. "I know. I'm sorry."

"I had forty-seven years of marriage with your grandmother, and I need time alone to mourn. I don't know how long it will take." His eyes wavered slightly, but he didn't look away. "With you, it's different. You're young. You need to get on with your life. No—hear me out. Of course you still hurt over Trevor. I understand that. And I don't have any idea how long it'll take you to finally accept what's happened. He has moved on, Mikaela, and you need to as well. You've got to face this head on, to quit running from your feelings. Let yourself get over him."

Mikaela gripped the letter in her hand. *How can Trevor have moved on? I feel like he's right here.* "I'm doing fine."

"No, you're not." He looked across the room to his wedding picture on the wall. His eyes clouded. "You're a good girl, Mikaela. A gifted girl. But you've quit school—"

"I'm waiting for my arm to heal."

"We both know it healed months ago."

Mikaela touched the scar on her face then quickly lowered her right hand to her left arm, where it had broken just above the elbow. Couldn't he see how much progress she'd made? It used to take every ounce of her strength just to get up in the morning. And now, some days, she didn't even cry. "I'm getting along."

"You're wallowing." His voice turned monotone. "You're only going through the motions. It's like part of you has died."

Part of her *had* died. She folded her arms across her chest. "That's not true."

"Oh? Tell me one thing you've drawn lately. It doesn't even have to be a building."

Mikaela winced. She hadn't drawn anything since the final she'd taken before the accident. "I haven't found any good subjects."

"Not one face? A tree? The mountains? Those used to be your favorite subjects." He leaned toward her. "Have you even doodled a flower while talking on your phone?"

Mikaela stared at him. Though she didn't feel cold, she rubbed her hands up and down her arms. Why was he throwing these questions at her now? Didn't he care about how much she also hurt over Grandma's loss? How much she, too, simply wanted to be left alone to grieve?

"Don't struggle for an answer. I already know."

"I'm not struggling. It's only—lately I've been thinking maybe I'm not meant to be an architect. Maybe I should just, I don't know, take a break from school for a while so I can figure it out."

"A break? You haven't been in school since Trevor died."

"I haven't been able—"

"No. I'm sorry. You don't have to be an architect." He rested his arms on his knees and leaned toward her. "But, Mikaela, whatever you choose, I've never known anyone to have as much of an artist's heart as you do. You love lines, shapes, shadows. You light up when you see historic buildings. You study people's faces. That's who you are. Pushing that part of you away won't bring Trevor back."

Pain welled inside Mikaela's chest. She would not cry.

"All of us, we're like your pencil drawing there above the mantel," he continued. "You told us White Rock stands like a beacon on our mountainside, but look closely. Without the shadows you've blurred behind it, it's just a shape on a piece of paper."

"I know."

"But do you understand?"

"Of course."

"Enough to do something for me?"

A sudden March wind crackled against the south side of the house like a bad omen. *So here it was. His request.* She sat up a little taller, bracing herself. "What is it?"

"Your grandmother and I were supposed to fly to New Zealand this weekend."

Mikaela nodded.

"But now that I have so many legal ends to tie up, I have to stay here until they're finished. I would like you to go now, in my place, until I can get there and take over."

"But—" She shook her head. "The airline will give you your money back under these circumstances, won't they? Or let you postpone it? Take your trip later. When you feel better."

"I can't postpone it, my dear. Kotuku Inn needs some renovations completed before winter hits in a few weeks. The contractors begin work next weekend. I need someone I trust to be there, to make sure everything is done my way."

Mikaela clasped her chilled fingers. "I—I've already had to take off so much time from work. And to ask for another week—"

"—three weeks—"

"Three weeks for a sudden trip. And with Easter and spring break coming—those are some of the restaurant's busiest days. And anyway, the bed and breakfast's manager, Tui, will be there, won't she? She's been at Kotuku Inn for so long, I'm sure she'd be better at overseeing everything than I would be."

"Tui is a jewel, but she's not me."

"Neither am I."

"You know my tastes much better than she does. And she doesn't have your eye for structural beauty." He pressed his handkerchief to his eyes. "I'd also like you to get something out of the safe for me before the renovations begin. Please, Mikaela, will you do this?"

*Take care of your grandfather.* Her grandmother's voice filled her thoughts, but in the end it was the emotion in his eyes that made her say, "I'll see if I can get the time off from work."

"You will. Your boss was one of your grandmother's best friends. She'll do anything for you."

Oh yeah.

# Chapter 4

BY THE TIME MIKAELA'S FLIGHT landed in Auckland, New Zealand, she could hardly see straight. She'd only slept about six of the past twenty-four hours, spending most of it upright in a narrow seat sandwiched between the airplane window and a talkative stranger. Worse, her muscles felt like they hadn't relaxed since she'd last climbed out of her bed. She'd been too worked up over the thought of acting in her grandfather's behalf despite only looking at his building plans and contracts. How could he believe she was up to such an assignment?

After finally getting through New Zealand's border customs, Mikaela walked through international arrivals and entered the main hall. The corridor wasn't as large as the Salt Lake City airport's, but its shiny white floor and white ceiling gave the wide strip, lined by shops of all sorts, a roomy yet welcoming look. *Hmm.* White on white. She kinda liked it.

Mikaela quick-scanned both directions for the information desk where her grandfather had said Tui would meet her. *Ahh. There it is.* And standing in front of it was a forty-something, buxom Maori woman with short, curly black hair. She wore a red dress beneath a black cotton jacket and held a sign saying *Mikaela York* in front of her. She smiled too. A little sympathetically, it seemed, but that could be because she knew of Mikaela's grandmother's death. Not Trevor's. Mikaela had made her grandfather promise he wouldn't tell anyone in Rotorua about him. She didn't want everyone tiptoeing around her emotions any more than they already might because of her grandmother.

Mikaela walked toward the woman. "Tui Davies?"

"Mikaela York? But of course you are." She set her sign on the floor and, holding Mikaela's gaze, warmly clasped her free hand warmly. "You all right?"

Mikaela blinked. *All right?* Did she look sick or something? But even as she wondered on that, she bit her lip to keep her smile in place. The warmth in Tui's eyes and the low, round-vowel way her voice lilted like music reminded Mikaela of her grandmother, and for a moment her heart ached with missing her.

Tui stepped back. "It's good to finally meet you. Let me help you with your luggage."

"It's nice of you to offer, but there's no need. I can manage."

"Nonsense. Hand me that suitcase." Tui took Mikaela's rolling suitcase and motioned down the aisle toward the glass doors between the parking shuttle service booths and car rental stands. "Come along," she added.

Outside, Tui and Mikaela followed the covered sidewalk along the length of the building to a crosswalk. Mikaela, shading her eyes from the brilliant sunlight with her free hand, stepped off the curb.

Tui grabbed her arm and pulled her back onto the sidewalk just before a car horn honked. When the vehicle passed, she said, "Look right, not left."

Mikaela winced. "Oh, yeah. Sorry." *New Zealanders drive on the left side of the road.* Mikaela looked right while Tui waited for another shuttle bus to pass then followed Tui to the other side. Mikaela's instincts took over. She looked left, right, left, right, all the way across the street to the uncovered, short-term parking lot, where Tui had parked her blue sedan.

The older woman stowed Mikaela's luggage in the trunk—er, the boot—and unlocked the left-side passenger door. Mikaela climbed inside and waited until Tui sat beside her in the driver's seat.

"How far is it to Rotorua from here?" Mikaela asked.

"Near 'bout three hours." Tui slid the key into the ignition. "I know you must be knackered, but I'd try to stay awake a while longer if I were you. Your grandfather said you like to draw nature, and you'll see heaps of it along the motorway."

Mikaela rubbed her hand down her spine at the back of her neck. Her grandfather had told her New Zealand was a beautiful and varied country that "might reawaken your artistic eye." She should try to see as much of it as she could, he added, especially after he arrived later on. Mikaela had made herself agree, but the truth was, no matter how beautiful or varied the landscape might be, her "artistic eye" had buried itself next to Trevor. "I'll do that. I'm hoping to stay awake anyway. Trying to beat jet lag."

Tui gave her a quizzical look, pulled out of the parking lot, and turned into the line of traffic. Mikaela scanned the large, curved *City of Sails* sign that hung over the terminal then looked out toward the harbor.

"I'm guessing everything's ready for the contractors to begin work tomorrow?" Mikaela asked.

"It is. I'm sorry to say all our moving around does make the inn look a bit disorderly, but it doesn't seem to have hurt business at all. We'll have a full house by tomorrow night. That might be because of Rotorua's first ever Tolkien convention this weekend. One of our guests, a young bloke named Brentin Williams, is even coming all the way from the States to help with it. He arrives tomorrow."

Mikaela focused on the road ahead of them. Though the airport was located on the outside of the city, there were still enough cars driving toward them from the absolutely wrong side of the road that Mikaela's muscles tensed. She clutched the door brace. "What will Mr. Williams be doing at the convention?"

"He's a videographer. Perhaps you've heard of him, eh. Amiria, my daughter, tells me his films from previous conventions in other countries have gathered heaps of followers on YouTube."

"Sorry. I haven't heard of him. But I've seen the Tolkien movies."

"No worries. I haven't seen his films either. But I do enjoy Brentin's company when I have a chance to chat with him."

"It sounds like he's more than just another guest to you."

"More like a son. His mother and I grew up together. We stayed in touch after she married and moved to the US. Brentin stayed at the inn with me and Amiria the summer he turned seventeen. I'll be certain to introduce you to him—though I doubt you'll see much of him. He's a bit of a loner."

They'd driven far enough outside of the city now that the traffic had eased. Mikaela released the door brace. Growing up, people often told her she was a loner because she spent so much of her time in her bedroom, sketching and such. But what they never seemed to understand was that when she worked on her art she didn't feel alone. Her art was a living thing to her. At least it used to be. Was it the same with Brentin? "I understand," she said, "about being a loner."

"You do? Maybe you can explain it to my Amiria. No matter that she and Brentin have a bit of an understanding; she's never understood why he keeps to himself so much of the time." Tui entered a roundabout.

"What kind of understanding? Are they engaged?" She hoped her voice didn't sound as tight as it felt in her throat.

"I suppose that was the wrong term. I do indeed wish it were the case. Amiria does too, but no. Though they've kept in contact over the years through e-mail and such, they've never spoken of a long-term commitment. Amiria says when he gets here, she hopes they'll pick up where they left off." Tui smiled. "His mother and I do too."

"I see." Mikaela settled back in her seat and turned fully away from Tui. She didn't want to be rude, but she wasn't yet ready to hear about others' romantic relationships. "You said you know his mother?"

"We grew up together, were closer than some blood-related sisters, so it was only natural that when she married and moved to the States we kept in touch."

They continued south on the highway, and though Mikaela had no idea how much time had actually passed, it seemed like in less than a half hour the urban landscape changed into a quiet countryside. There were groves on groves of trees; lush green fields that covered the acreage like a soft, billowing blanket; and quaint farmhouses surrounded by log fences and grazing animals.

"If you ever decide to paint a picture of this landscape, I'd sure like to see it," Tui said.

Mikaela closed her eyes. "I'm not much up to painting anymore."

Tui gave her an odd look but said nothing.

Two hours later, Mikaela leaned forward in her seat. She stretched out her lower back and shoulders and forced her eyes to stay open. Normally she'd love watching the lush green countryside flash by like a National Geographic video of the world's most beautiful places, but after sitting all night on an airplane in front of a mother with a fussing baby, Mikaela found the tall, thick-needled pines, winding rivers, and even the occasional herd of sheep more like hypnotizing sleep aids than stunning scenery.

Seeing her stir, Tui spoke. "We should reach Kotuku Inn 'bout five o'clock. Since it's your first day, I suggest you take it easy tonight. Maybe walk around the grounds before you head to bed. Or there's the Redwoods of the Whakarewarewa Forest just across the motorway. Heaps of guests and locals go there to unwind. I've found it to be a great place to be alone but not alone, eh."

"A walk sounds wonderful. Maybe I'll do that, but first I'd like to empty the safe. Grandpa said you can show me where it is?"

"No worries. I expect he wants you to get the doll?" They rounded a long bend in the road that ran alongside a fast-flowing creek.

"He said you didn't know about it." *And not to show it to anyone*; he didn't want to cause conflicts.

"What a thing to imagine," Tui said.

* * *

Hunapo set his cell phone on the Formica tabletop and leaned over it, palms flat on the gray surface. He read the new text.

*Granddaughter went to NZ. Not Joseph.*

Hunapo scowled. Partly because Joseph still lived amid all his finery and partly because it had taken Hunapo a full day to recover what was left of his strength after returning from Marge's too-silent, too-short funeral. Couldn't he have included at least one mournful chant out of respect for Marge's homeland?

But then, maybe Joseph had forsaken all the old ways. Maybe that was why Hunapo's *tupunas*, his ancestors, had been so slow to answer his petitions; they were waiting. They wanted the blood of all those Joseph had wronged to cry out in vengeance against him, proving his guilt without excuse, before they approved the called-for recompense. Besides, Mikaela was supposed to die before Joseph. Maybe the tupunas were simply guiding things to their rightful order.

Hunapo exhaled, exhaled again. Maybe. But whatever the reasons, his tupunas had finally heard him and would now help him exact their ancient justice against Joseph. *Utu*, the law of restitution for good or bad deeds, of blood for blood when blood was the only way to satisfy, of the full restoration of balance. Finally, fortune would be with Hunapo and not with the other guy.

He clenched his hands, pushing his knuckles into the tabletop until his joints felt numb. *The other guy.* When the fiancé had died instead of the granddaughter, he'd worried his tupunas would again let the other guy win. But then—THEN—Marge Parker's death had come so easily. Trusting to a fault, she probably hadn't even realized the other hiker had pushed her off the tiny trail. That she hadn't, as the *Box Elder News Journal* had reported, slid on a patch of ice before falling down the mountainside and hitting her head on a boulder in the creek. It was perfect. Her death had come after nothing more than a few moments of fear. It was how all the deaths would be. They'd be going along, living their lives, then—dead.

Hunapo yanked up the phone. He scanned the keys beneath the screen and pressed one. The screen changed. Another button and a new screen came up. Why couldn't he ever remember how to reply?

He slowly walked around the table to the drawer beneath the micro-wave, opened it, and fumbled through the papers and notepads until he found his cell phone instructions. After glancing through them, he located the REPLY button.

*Plan B. No mistakes this time.*

He pressed SEND, slid the phone in his loose slacks pocket, and shuffled over the smooth linoleum onto the carpet that looked more the color of gray dishwater than the rich, earthy brown his landlord had claimed it was.

His cell phone buzzed again.

Hunapo reached his recliner and lowered himself into the chair's worn softness. He tapped the text icon and read the response.

*Working on details. Wait for update.*

"I don't have time to wait," he yelled. "Tomorrow's my next round of chemotherapy." *My final one.*

# Chapter 5

SINCE *KOTUKU* WAS THE MAORI word for a rare white heron, Mikaela had imagined the inn would be located near Rotorua Lake. Instead, Tui drove a few miles south of the sulfuric-smelling town of Rotorua along a two-lane highway that bordered the dense, mountainous Whakawerawera Forest on the west and the expanse of rolling green hills on the east.

"It's a nice, secluded area for a bed and breakfast," Tui said, "but I often wonder how Caroline Evans, the original owner, got along out here after her husband died."

"My grandfather helped her, I understand."

"I'm sure he helped her a great deal, but outside help can never make up for the lack of family."

They turned off the highway onto a paved lane that led east into the hilly countryside. A wooden fence and groves of bushy, tall trees with narrow, gray-barked trunks lined both sides of the lane for about a hundred feet before climbing an open, low-lying hill. So beautiful. And yet all Mikaela thought of was the last time she'd sat in her backyard and drawn the tree swing. She'd been eighteen, preparing to leave for college the next week, and had rearranged many of her responsibilities to get that one hour to herself.

Mikaela forced herself back to the present. "Maybe Caroline was the quiet sort. A loner, like that Brentin Williams you mentioned. Maybe she didn't mind being on her own."

"She might have been a loner," Tui said, "but she was not quiet. She was rich and generous, they say. But she signed her name to every penny she gave away."

They reached the manicured property of Kotuku Inn, and Tui parked in front of the now-empty, attached carport. Kotuku Inn had at one time been a simple, rectangular, colonial-style building of timber and yellow stucco, but a previous renovation had added both a second floor to its southern half and a bay window and front porch to the other. Tui climbed out of the car. Mikaela did too.

"*Nau mai.* Welcome to Kotuku Inn," Tui said.

"*Tena koe.* That's *thank you*, right?"

"Right enough."

Mikaela took a deep breath of pine-fragrant air, still tinged with sulfur, and glanced across the extensive, newly mown lawn, across the green hills, and toward the distant, tree-covered mountains. *I'm in New Zealand!* "This is such a lovely spot of ground, Tui. You've kept it up beautifully."

Obviously pleased, Tui opened the car's trunk, er, boot, and pulled out Mikaela's luggage. "I'm glad you can see the front before the workers tear it up. But the backyard they started on last week. The flower garden is still intact. Perhaps you'd like to look at it, eh, before they change it." She handed Mikaela her backpack, pulled out the large suitcase, and stacked the smaller one on top of it. She pulled out the extended handle. "Your room is one of the smaller suites, but it's also the quietest. I thought you'd prefer a bit of peace since—"

"The funerals." Mikaela blinked. *Idiot.* She'd not only finished Tui's sentence—a habit she was far too prone to do—but she'd also said *funerals* rather than *funeral.* Had Tui noticed? "I'm sure the room will be perfect."

Tui wheeled—clacketed—the suitcase across the cobblestone walk to the cement stairs that led to an approximately six-foot-square landing. A large, bronze fishhook hung above the door frame.

Tui must have noticed Mikaela's gaze. "It's a symbol of good luck," she said. "Keep an eye out for the moldings and such. Caroline Evans had fishhooks built throughout this house soon after her husband drowned. A bit ironic, if you ask me. Anyway, that's the one thing I wish your grandmother could have convinced your grandfather to do—to carry that fishhook theme into the new additions." She opened the door and stepped aside, allowing Mikaela to enter. "I should have said this before, but I'm truly sorry about your grandmother. She was a good and fair woman."

Both her grandmother's and Trevor's faces filled Mikaela's thoughts. "Me too."

"You were close?"

"Yes." Mikaela ignored the emotion that burned behind her eyes and stepped farther into the wide entry hall. Its wood floors were the color of mahogany. A decorative wood door of the same color led to an office at their left. A staircase lined the wall on their right, and a large arched doorway at the end of the hallway opened into what looked like a kitchen and informal dining area.

Tui poked her head into the office. "I'd hoped to introduce you to Amiria, but it looks like something took her away."

"Maybe her young man arrived early."

"Brentin? Mehbe." Tui took a quarter-sized, pale green stone attached to a key ring from her pocket and motioned to the staircase. "Your room is at the top of the stairs. Number five. I'll call for Amiria to come and help you with your bags. She can't be far away."

"That's kind of you, but I'll manage in a couple of trips."

"All right. If that's what you'd prefer. Go ahead and settle in, my dear, while I hunt down the key to the cellar. Look for me in the kitchen when you're ready."

"Thank you." Mikaela pushed her large suitcase against the wall and hefted her backpack and small suitcase up the narrow stairs to the first landing, turned, and climbed the remaining stairs. The second floor consisted of a short hallway with one door on either side. Her room, number five, was directly to her right. Decorative fishhooks, painted a bright red in full contrast to the creamy white walls, hung above both doors.

Mikaela unlocked her door, set her luggage inside, and returned downstairs for her larger suitcase. Finally alone in her room, she clicked the door closed behind her and set her things next to the closet. She sat on the queen-sized bed. The top comforter, patterned with orange and purple daylilies, felt thick and soft, and though the mattress wasn't quite as plush as her bed back home, it felt firm and comfortable. Mikaela fell backward, took a deep breath, and closed her eyes. If only she could sleep—

But not yet. She brushed the tired from her eyes; sent a quick text to her grandfather, telling him she'd arrived safely; and forced herself up from the bed. Minutes later, she found Tui in the kitchen behind the counter, along with an older man and woman. The couple sat at a small dining table next to the glass door that opened onto a large deck. A white cane leaned against the back of the man's chair. He looked to be in his sixties, wore sunglasses, and spoke close to the woman's ear. She, rather than having gray hair like his, had dyed hers black. She typed on a laptop computer.

"That's Ira Lawrence, one of New Zealand's best-selling authors," Tui said to Mikaela under her breath. "He went blind 'bout five years ago.

Vicky Robison is his aide." Tui hung her green apron on a wall hook. "The cellar door is around the back of the house."

Ira's voice grew louder. Mikaela couldn't hear what he said, but all at once, he flung his pencil across the floor. It landed next to Mikaela's right foot.

"There's no need for you to make such a fuss, Ira," Vicky said. "The scene's just about right."

Mikaela picked up the pencil and set it on the table in front of the author.

"Who's there?" he demanded.

"Mikaela York. I just arrived."

He grunted.

"That's very kind of you, Miss York." Vicky's voice had a small, mousy sound, but her brown eyes were large and bright.

Ira took hold of Vicky's hand and moved it to the keyboard. Vicky blushed, and when he again spoke close to her ear, she blushed even redder. Mikaela had no idea what their full relationship was, but whatever the case, Vicky clearly had feelings for her employer.

Mikaela walked to the door and looked over her shoulder at Tui. "Ready?"

Tui held up a key and smiled.

The two stepped onto the wide, plank deck, climbed down a stairway on the right, and followed the carport to the cellar door. About twenty more yards of lawn led to a line of tall pine trees at the back of the property. Mikaela's grandfather had told her of a creek back there. He'd called it his *thinking place.*

Mikaela stepped to the side, allowing Tui to pass in front of her. "Go ahead. You have the key."

Tui wiggled the key in the lock a few times before it finally opened, and Mickaela followed her inside.

The cellar smelled of stale, moist dirt. It was almost like the sour odor that permeated the abandoned mine up Perry Canyon back home, only the mine also smelled like leftover death, like a raccoon or skunk or maybe even a mountain lion had crawled inside and died. And rotted. At least nothing had died in this cellar. As far as she knew.

Mikaela flicked on the light switch to their left. Two single bulbs about ten feet apart provided dim light for the narrow room. The floors and walls were made of cement, and the white wooden shelves that lined those walls were covered with clean, jar- and box-shaped patches surrounded by thick dust.

"Where'd you put all the stuff that used to be in here?" Mikaela asked.

"In boxes in the lounge. Guests don't often use that room." Tui walked farther inside and pointed at the large silver safe built into the back wall. "You have the combination, eh?"

"I do." 04-19-46. Her grandmother's birthday.

Tui lifted her hand—her fingers trembled—to a white fishhook pendant hanging on a silver chain around her neck. When had she put that on? Mikaela wondered. She hadn't worn it to the airport, had she? Or had she kept it tucked beneath her dress?

"Is something wrong?" Mikaela asked.

Tui flinched slightly. "I'm all good."

Mikaela shrugged, crossed the room, and opened the safe. Inside, she found a stack of manila folders, several thick envelopes, and a pile of documents held together by a thick rubber band. A small, yellow shoe box sat against the back wall.

"Probably the doll," Tui said.

"That's my guess too." Mikaela handed the folders, envelopes, and documents to Tui and pulled out the box. She slid her finger beneath its lid. "Grandpa said it was a rare Maori doll."

Tui's voice lowered. "I've heard that. Some of the rumors say Bessie Murray made it."

"Who's Bessie Murray?"

"A famous doll maker. She died over fifty years ago; her dolls are still valuable. Especially to collectors. I saw one in the Museum of New Zealand a few years back."

Mikaela opened the box and peered inside. The ten-inch doll was a traditionally dressed Maori woman holding a bone out to a small dog, whose eyes and nose were as intricately detailed as the doll's. The doll wore a red tie-dyed silk dress, a black-and-white checkered shawl made of rough fabric, and tiny pieces of green glass made to look like a beaded necklace. Her hair and eyes were as dark as Tui's. Her lips were just as full too. Vertical, zigzagged lines decorated the doll's chin.

"What do you think?" Mikaela asked. "To me, she looks like a Maori Old Mother Hubbard." When Tui didn't respond, Mikaela looked up. The older woman's complexion had paled like cream-dolloped coffee. "What is it?"

Tui, her lips quivering, hugged the folders and envelopes against her body and back-stepped to the door. "Evil. *Kotiri!*" She charged up the steps.

Mikaela closed the safe door, put the lid back on the box, and hurried after her. Tui was already halfway up the stairs by the time Mikaela stepped out of the cellar. "What are you talking about? What's evil? You don't mean the doll?"

Tui didn't look back at her. "You must get rid of it."

"Will you please tell me what's upset you? I'm sure we can work it out, whatever it is."

Tui folded her arms in front of her and lifted her face to the sky. At last she faced Mikaela. Her expression was tight, her lips pursed; she tromped back down to Mikaela and set the folders and envelopes on top of the closed doll box in her arms. "Either the doll leaves or I do."

"I—I, of course, don't want to upset you, but where else can I put it? My grandfather asked me to take care of it until he gets here so it isn't damaged in the remodel."

Tui's left cheek muscle twitched before she once again touched her fishhook pendant. "I know that doll's important to your grandfather, but he does not know 'bout . . . I had not seen its face before. I don't think the fishhooks' powers are strong enough to hold off murder."

Mikaela gaped as Tui charged through the deck door and disappeared beyond the kitchen. What had just happened? How could Tui possibly believe a doll could cause a death? Would Grandfather know the answers?

Hoping he would, Mikaela hurried up to her room, set the documents and box on the desk, and clicked through her phone to her Skype account. She slid her finger toward DIAL but hesitated. Her grandfather was on the other side of the world and wouldn't wake for about five more hours. Surely this problem could wait until morning—his morning. Besides, Tui had to have realized by now that the doll couldn't be *that* dangerous. It had already been inside this house longer than either Mikaela or Tui had been alive. And no one had been murdered during all that time. Right?

Mikaela closed the Skype screen and logged on to her e-mail. She'd already received a message from her grandfather. As usual, he'd typed his note as if he were writing a formal letter.

*Dear Mikaela,*

*I'm so glad that you made it safely. I know I gave you work to do, but please try to have a good time. New Zealand is a beautiful country, and its people are among the best I've ever known. I hope you'll find new friends among them.*

*Love,*

*Grandpa*

Mikaela frowned, brushing her fingertips down the length of her scar, and composed a new message:

*I'll try to enjoy myself if I have time, but something has already come up. Tui said she already knew about the doll, so I showed it to her even though you'd asked me not to, but now she's upset. She says I need to get rid of the doll because if I don't, someone will die. Do you know what she's talking about? Please advise.*

She pressed SEND just as someone knocked on her door. She got up from the bed and opened the door. Standing in the hall was a young woman close to Mikaela's age and height. The girl had long, wavy brown hair with blonde highlights, but her oval face and voluptuous lips were almost replicas of Tui's. She had to be her daughter, Amiria.

"Gidday, Miss York," she said.

"It's Mikaela, please."

She smiled and handed Mikaela a folded piece of paper. "Mum asked me to run this up to you."

"What is it?"

"I don't know. She's gone to bed. But I'll be in the office until ten o'clock if you need anything."

"Thanks."

After Amiria left, Mikaela opened the handwritten note.

*Miss York,*

*I am sorry for the way I acted earlier. As your grandfather's granddaughter, you have a right to know why you cannot keep that doll in this inn. Three nights ago, I dreamed my spirit flew like a bird above Kotuku Inn and met up with another spirit, one who looked like that doll. She chased me. I tried to get away, but she caught me and pointed to a small man who poured red juice from the deadly tutu plant on the driveway. When I woke holding my breath, I could only remember pieces of it. I'd thought it was a nightmare I was happy to forget, but when I saw that doll, I remembered it and realized the dream and the doll are Kotiri, evil omens. According to ancient traditions, a dream where your spirit is flying along, pursued by another and is captured means evil is in the dreamer's path, but to also see a man spilling tutu juice is even worse. Tutu juice symbolizes blood, and spilling it as that man did means someone will soon be murdered.*

*Mikaela, I've had dreams such as these before. My mother did too, and their predictions have always come to pass. Please, I beg you to get the doll out of this inn. Hopefully, that will appease the ancestors, and this time the evil will not come true. This time no one will die.*

*Tui*

Mikaela frowned. How could she discount Tui's fears? Tui's belief deserved respect.

She slid Tui's note inside the desk and glanced at the black-and-red fishhook that hung above the interior doorframe. Mikaela's mother and grandparents had told her about a few Maori traditions, and how, even after all these years, some Maoris still clung to many of them. But they'd never told her of such strong superstitions.

Mikaela lay back on her bed and stared up at the motionless white fan blades above her. She couldn't remember her grandmother as having had any superstitions, but Trevor . . . On December 1, he'd hung mistletoe above the front doors of both their apartments.

*"It's a sign,"* he said. *"A reminder that neither of us must leave this place without kissing the other."*

*Mikaela laughed. And blushed. "What happens if we forget?"*

*He turned to her, wrapped his arm around her waist, and pulled her against him. He kissed her. "If we forget, I'll die." His lips smiled against hers. "Of a broken heart."*

The memory burned. Mikaela rolled onto her side and squeezed her eyes closed until they no longer felt wet, only ached for the sight of Trevor. *Rest,* she told herself, *in peace.*

Her thoughts paused. Good thing Tui hadn't heard that last thought.

# Chapter 6

Cold, like ice, like death, shivered through Mikaela's bones the moment she opened her eyes. It was an unsettled feeling, the kind that made her feel like someone was watching her—no, worse than that—like someone was creeping up on her. No one was, right? Barely daring to move, she searched the shadows surrounding her bed and listened. All remained as quiet and still as it had been when she'd turned out her lamp last night, so why did she feel out of sorts? Had she had a nightmare?

Mikaela closed her eyes again and tried to remember the last images that had crowded the back of her eyelids, but all she saw was thick, empty blackness. Maybe she'd slept too long? Or not enough?

She focused on the sliver of moonlight that seeped along the inside edges of her heavy curtains and rolled onto her side, facing the bed stand next to her. The red numbers of the digital alarm clock showed *6:08 a.m.* She'd slept for more than her typical seven hours. That had to be why her senses felt like they were on overdrive. Messed up sleep always messed with her mind. What's more, it was late-morning back home. Her body was probably just trying to adjust to the fact that she was in Rotorua. She sat up. Had her grandfather responded to her e-mail?

She jumped out of bed, clicked on the desk lamp, and checked her phone. *Dang!* No new e-mails. Frowning, she sent him a quick text, asking him to check his e-mail, and then went to the bathroom sink. She splashed water on her face then looked up, staring at her reflection in the mirror. Dark circles hung beneath her eyes like bruised streaks on pale skin; her thin, straight hair stood out from her head as if she'd rubbed a balloon over it. *Lovely.* Not exactly how she wanted anyone to see her. True, it was early enough she doubted anyone was awake, and with the inn as quiet as it was and her body as anxious to get moving as it was, maybe it wouldn't matter if she left for a bit. Maybe take that walk Tui had suggested last evening before the doll fiasco. She could go to the forest across the highway, or—what about the creek at the back of the property? It had helped her grandfather think through his problems. Maybe it'd help her.

She glanced at her large suitcase, where she'd tucked the doll box, and walked to the large, curtained window behind the desk. She peeked through the slit. It was too dark outside to see the grounds, but Tui had said the renovators wouldn't be there until eight that morning. She had time to kill before then.

*Kill—murder.* Mikaela closed her eyes. She touched then pulled back her hand from her scar. *Stop thinking about death!*

She heaved her suitcase onto the armchair, set aside a clean pair of jeans and her favorite black T-shirt, and transferred her remaining clothing to the armoire. After that, she returned to the en suite bathroom and closed the door.

Fifteen minutes later, she'd dressed, pulled her hair into a ponytail, and smoothed a bit of foundation over the dark circles under her eyes. She again checked her phone. Still no messages from her grandfather.

Her stomach rumbled like it was lunchtime, which it was back home, and she opened her curtains. The rising sun had lightened the backyard enough that she could make out the green-black shadows of the treetops at the back of the property. She'd been so physically and emotionally drained last night that she hadn't noticed how spectacular that grove really was, but now . . . Her fingers tingled slightly then dulled. Before the accident, it would have required all her willpower not to sketch the wide-fanned, lime-green ferns, the dense hedges, and the few remaining flowers that still dotted the landscape—the deep purple petals that clung to their orange stigmas as if winter would never come. But now the mere thought of her pencil and art book brought tears to her eyes. She hadn't packed them, but somehow they'd wound up inside her large suitcase beneath her shoes. *Grandpa.*

A stream of light from a car's headlights flashed toward the grove at the back of the property. Had the contractor arrived already? It was barely seven o'clock, but if it was him she'd like to talk to him before his crew started their work.

She grabbed her dark-blue hoodie and headed for the door. No noise touched the hall, but light seeped beneath the door of the other room.

Tui had mentioned on their drive from the airport that Sara and Frank Kendrick, honeymooners, had rented that room the day before she'd arrived.

Not wanting to disturb them, Mikaela tiptoed downstairs to the brightly lit kitchen. Bowls of fresh fruit and plates of sliced bread filled the center of the counter. Again, her stomach growled, but she ignored it, skirted past the counter and dining tables, and walked out the back door. Cool, humid air—*sulfur again!*—wisped over her cheeks. Tui and a forty-something-year-old man wearing a yellow hard hat headed up the deck stairs toward her.

"Good morning, Mikaela." Dark circles as thick as those Mikaela had seen on her own face draped beneath Tui's eyes. "This is Mr. Norris, the contractor your grandfather hired."

"Gidday, young lady," he said.

Mikaela shook his hand. "I hear you're the best in the business."

He grinned. "You're all good. Your grandfather told me you're here to act for him. I look forward to working with you."

"I'll just go inside now and leave you two to your work," Tui said. She nodded to both of them, obviously uncomfortable, and hurried into the inn.

Mikaela sighed. Hopefully her grandfather would respond soon so she would know how to work things out with the woman. "Is there anything you need my help with?" she asked Mr. Norris.

"Yeah, nah, sis. Most of it's good, but there's one thing I need your help with. Your grandfather, he wants a sculpture added to the back property. Something Maori. He said you'd know best what it should be. He said you have an artistic eye."

*Had* an artistic eye. Mikaela slid her hands in her pockets, clasped her phone, and held his gaze as steadily as she could. "He wants me to pick it out?"

"That he does. The only thing is the sooner I can get it ordered the better."

*Grandpa! First my art supplies and now this. You're pushing me too hard. My talent's dead.* "I'll let you know as soon as I can."

"If you think it'll be too much," he added, "let me know that too. I'll see what I can do to keep the cost down." Three new sets of headlights streamed, one after the other, across the backyard, and Mr. Norris stepped onto the first stair. "Will you be about this morning?" he asked. "Or should I call you if we have any questions?"

"I'll be back there in the trees for a while, but if you can't find me, go ahead and call. Do you have my cell number?"

"I do." He nodded, said, "Gidday," and headed along the sidewalk toward the distant voices and closing car doors at the other end of the carport.

Minutes later, Mikaela stood in the grove at the back of the property. A brook that couldn't have been much wider than two feet meandered back and forth between the trees like a large snake, hidden beneath the wild undergrowth in some places and glittering with the white light of the rising sun in others.

She took a deep, relaxing breath. Pine and wet grass. She closed her eyes. Such a beautiful place to think, just as her grandfather had said.

Brambles snapped behind her.

Mikaela turned. A tall, dark-skinned Maori man in a blue jacket and a yellow hard hat stepped toward her. He half-smiled, but his jowls hung downward. "Miss York? The boss told me I could find you out here."

"Is something wrong?"

He shook his head and reached inside his jacket pocket. "Yesterday when I was out here diggin' about a bit, I found this here earring in the hedge there, just beyond the rock staircase. We thought you should see it."

Mikaela took the earring and turned it over in her hand. It was made of an opaque, grey-green stone. The setting and hook looked a bit corroded, but its shape was unmistakable. "A fishhook."

"Made of greenstone."

She frowned. The only person she knew to have such an affinity with fishhooks was Kotuku Inn's previous owner. "I'll make sure my grandfather gets it." She slid it in her jacket pocket. "Thank you."

He nodded, looked back and forth between her pocket and her face, and turned and walked away.

When she could no longer see or hear him, Mikaela strolled along the edge of the stream for several more minutes until she reached a log lying against a wooden fence. Fingering the earring inside her pocket and wondering if it had, indeed, belonged to Kotuku Inn's previous owner, she sat on the log and inhaled. The wet pine scent now mixed with a heady, floral fragrance, and her senses relaxed even more. She had so many responsibilities there was no way she could just stay here and let her heart heal, but for that moment she was grateful. *I'm sorry I was angry at you a minute ago, Grandpa. Thank you for sending me to this place.*

Shortly after eight o'clock, Mikaela left the grove and headed back to Kotuku Inn. The trees must have blocked the sound more than she'd realized because the grounds were already humming with activity. Pickup trucks and small cars were parked near the carport, several men in hard hats hauled equipment, and two pounded stakes into the earth at the bottom of the staircase near the hedges where the man had said he'd found the earring. Mikaela took it out of her pocket and held it in her open palm toward the sun. In the shade, it had looked opaque—out here, almost translucent.

She continued on toward the inn. It wasn't until she reached the deck's staircase, until she heard a soft giggle, that she saw the young couple wrapped together in a blanket. They sat together in a two-person bench behind a round, white outdoor table. On top of it was a camera, and something steamed from two cups, but neither the slight, dark-haired girl nor the muscular, copper-skinned man seemed interested in any of those objects. They were too busy kissing each other and staring into one another's eyes. They had to be Sara and Frank Kendrick, the newlyweds.

Mikaela felt the blood drain from her face. She shouldn't look, shouldn't climb the stairs toward them, shouldn't let herself remember the emotions and excitement that had rushed through her when Trevor had looked into her eyes that very same way and asked her to be his wife.

"Hello," a man's deep voice said from behind her.

Startled, Mikaela slipped backward onto the lower stair and, while trying to regain her balance, dropped the earring. It skidded through the empty riser space to the ground.

"Watch it!" The young man caught her elbow.

She looked up at him. He was unshaven, wore thick glasses, and had an American accent. "I'm all right, thanks," she told him.

"Sorry. Didn't mean to scare you." He climbed back down the stairs and crouched close to the ground. He whisked his hand through the grass. A thick strand of his dark blond hair, which was cut longer on top than at the sides, fell in front of his face. "Ahh." He pulled the earring out from under the stairs and dangled it in front of her. "Is this what you dropped?"

"Yes, thank you, Mr.—?"

He handed it to her. "Williams. Brentin Williams."

*Amiria's guy.* Mikaela quick-scanned the length of him: forest-green T-shirt, blue jeans, brown loafers, and a blue canvas camera bag. She'd expected someone as exotic-looking as Amiria to be attracted to someone a bit more extraordinary. "That's right. Tui mentioned you'd be here. She said you're helping with the Tolkien convention."

"Guilty."

Mikaela followed his glance to the newlyweds, whose noses were so close to each other she couldn't tell if they were kissing or still staring into one another's eyes. She looked quickly away. "Tui also said you were a bit of a celebrity."

"I'm hardly a celebrity. Not yet, that is." He grinned and motioned for her to climb the stairs ahead of him. "I've done a few films for past conventions, but I'm hoping to do more."

"Good films, I hear. At any rate, you're a celebrity in Tui's world. And in Amiria's, I understand." When he didn't respond, she looked back at him over her shoulder. His brown eyes narrowed slightly, watching her. "As for me," she continued, "I figured you were a celebrity the moment I heard you were filming the convention. I love *The Lord of the Rings* movies. I'd have tried to get tickets to the convention if I'd known it was in town." *And if I'd known before a few days ago that I was coming here.*

He followed her up the stairs. When they reached the deck, he said, "*The Lord of the Rings*, huh? I bet you have a crush on Aragorn."

She turned to him. He was only a few inches taller than she was, but his sudden nearness overwhelmed her personal space. That had to be the reason that blasted heat instantly rose to her cheeks. She inched backward. "Nope. I'm partial to Ents."

He smiled. Not widely, but enough that through his glasses she saw his eyes crinkle upward at the outer edges. "I'm at a bit of a disadvantage here," he said. "It seems you know about me, but I know nothing about you. Your accent says you're an American."

"From Utah."

He opened his mouth as though about to say something more then closed it again when Amiria stepped out the glass door. Her long, thick hair draped softly over her yellow, short-sleeved blouse. "Brentin!" She ran to him and threw her arms around his waist.

Brentin grinned and briefly hugged her back.

"You should have called," she said. "Mum or I would have picked you up from the airport."

"I knew you'd be busy. Besides, I wanted my own rental."

Mikaela tried not to notice Amiria's hand slide down Brentin's arm and into his hand. She'd often greeted Trevor in just the same way, and he'd always entwined his fingers through hers. Brentin didn't do that though. He only squeezed Amiria's hand then released it.

Amiria sidled in closer to him and looked back at Mikaela. "Oh! I haven't introduced you two, have I? This is Mikaela York. Her grandfather owns Kotuku Inn."

"Ahh," Brentin said. "That's two things I now know about you. Anything else so we can call it even?"

"There's nothing even remotely interesting about me." Mikaela didn't notice when it had actually happened, but sometime between their first meeting and when Amiria had arrived, Brentin's words had rounded out into a soft New Zealand accent that was similar to her grandfather's. Tui had said Brentin had spent at least a summer here. That must be why. "Well, thanks again for your help," she said, turning away from them and heading for the door.

"Sure," Brentin said.

"Oh! Wait a minute, Mikaela," Amiria said.

"Yes?"

"I'm sorry. I wasn't thinking. Mum said you liked *The Lord of the Rings*. And anyway, the opening ceilidh for the convention's tonight. Why don't you come to it with Brentin and me?"

Mikaela bit her lower lip. Amiria was grinning, and Brentin looked, well, like he didn't care one way or the other. "W-what's a kay-lay?"

"A celebration," Brentin said. "This one's mostly a banquet. Come. That way you can attend at least some of the convention."

"It might even help you stop thinking so much about your grand-mother," Amiria said.

Mikaela winced, and Amiria clapped her hand over her mouth. "I'm so sorry! I promised your grandfather I wouldn't bother you about that, and there I go doing it anyway." She looked at Brentin and lowered her hand. "Mikaela's grandmother died a couple of weeks ago."

Brentin's gaze at Mikaela narrowed. His expression drooped.

*Great! That's all I need. More pity.* "All right. I'll go. It sounds like fun. When should I be ready?"

"Will five work?" Brentin said. "The ceilidh begins at six, but I need to go early."

"I have a couple of formals you can try on for the cosplay," Amiria said. "And we can do your hair up like Aowen's or anyone else you'd like. Who are you going as, Brentin?"

"I'd planned on being a dwarf tonight, but the airline lost my luggage."

"Not even!"

"No worries," he said. "It should get here tomorrow. I'll go to town after breakfast and find something to get me through."

Amiria squeezed his lower arm. "I know just where to go. Actually, Mikaela, why don't you come with us there too?"

Mikaela frowned. The last thing she wanted was to be a third wheel. Her cell phone buzzed. *Finally.* "Sorry. I've got to take this." She pulled her phone out of her pocket and turned away from them, starting for the door.

"You'll come with us into town, won't you?" Amiria asked. "After breakfast?"

Mikaela made herself not roll her eyes. "Sure. Yeah. I'll go. Thanks." She gave Amiria a quick wave and, heading for the door, read the text from her grandfather:

*Move the doll. I will make the arrangements. Details in e-mail.*

In the kitchen, Mikaela took the nearest booth, sent her grandfather a quick reply, and logged on to her e-mail. Her grandfather had sent a lengthy letter.

*Dear Mikaela,*

*I should have told you about how superstitious Tui is, but I'd thought most of it was connected to that fishhook pendant of hers and wouldn't cause any trouble. She thinks it gives her good luck. At any rate, the best you can do is respect her fears and take the doll to the King's Hotel. It's a guesthouse near the Government Gardens. I've spoken with the previous owner. He used to mentor me and my partner when we first bought the inn. I told him you needed help. His son now runs the business, but he'll tell him to keep the doll in their safe deposit box for you. His son will be out of the office until 5:00 p.m., so you'll have to wait until then. If you need to contact the hotel, the number is +6473460811.*

*You will be happy to learn I finally made it through the stack of sympathy cards. I appreciated the well-wishes of so many good friends. Knowing how much people will miss Marge makes me even more proud and grateful to God that she was my wife. But one of the cards was quite odd. It was in a blue envelope and hadn't been mailed. It wasn't signed either, and the message was only two lines from that nursery rhyme about Humpty Dumpty. It said: "Humpty Dumpty sat on a wall. Humpty Dumpty had a great fall." I wish I knew who gave it to me. I'd know better what to do with it. Any ideas?*

*Grandpa*

Mikaela stared at the last few lines before replying with:

*Grandpa,*

*Thanks for the info about Tui and the doll and how to manage the situation. I'll take it to the King's Hotel at 5.*

*I don't know what to think about that sympathy card either. I received one like it just before my car accident. It's hard to believe it could be a coincidence. Maybe it's a mean prank? Some people can really be jerks. If I knew who sent them, I'd either report them to the police or tell them how NOT funny they were. Or both!*

*Sorry. I'll stop ranting now.*

*Something odd happened here too. One of Mr. Norris's workers found an earring on the property. The setting's a bit rusted, but it's in the shape of a fishhook. He said it's made of greenstone and might be valuable. I'll send you a pic, and if I don't hear differently from you, I'll put it in the safe deposit box with the doll.*

*Love you. See you soon.*

*Mikaela*

# Chapter 7

MIKAELA REMOVED HER NEWLY PURCHASED blonde wig and craft supplies from the plastic shopping bags and laid them on the bed. Before she'd left that morning for her three-hour shopping trip with Amiria and Brentin, she'd met Amiria in her room and chosen the ice-blue, princess-cut dress to wear to that night's ceilidh. It had a modest, rounded neckline that draped about an inch below her clavicle, just as her bridesmaids' dresses would have done.

"*Choose the blue one,*" *Trevor said.* "*It's my favorite color on you.*"

"*That doesn't matter. I'll be wearing white.*"

"*Can I help it if I want everything about our wedding to remind me of you?*"

Mikaela hugged her arms as if they were a blanket and told herself to breathe, to swallow, to stop—*Please, Father in Heaven, help me stop thinking about Trevor.*

Somewhere outside, hammers pounded over the whippor of a songbird. She closed her window, but still she heard a tractor engine roar to life. Trevor had grown up on a farm and had always liked the rumbling sound of a large tractor engine.

"Stop wallowing," she whispered, but it was her grandfather's voice she heard inside her head. *Move on. Think about something else.*

She looked through her window and clenched the windowsill so hard her knuckles turned white. Mr. Norris stood on the pathway just beyond the flower garden, talking to one of his crew. Perhaps she should go down and ask how things were going. Watching over the renovations was the reason her grandfather had sent her.

Mikaela drew back her shoulders, absolutely did not think about the blue dresses her bridesmaids would have worn, and left her room.

"There you are," Tui said when Mikaela entered the kitchen. She stood behind the wrap-around counter, wearing a red-and-black apron. "Sit yourself down, and I'll get you some lunch. I hope you don't mind fish. A friend stopped by this morning with heaps of trout he'd caught and grilled this very morning. It's too much for Amiria and me to eat on our own, and though it's best right off the grill, it's still good rewarmed." She pulled a black platter from the refrigerator, took off the plastic wrap, and lifted the lemon slices from each of the eight large fish steaks.

Mikaela glanced through the back windows. Mr. Norris still stood where she'd last seen him. "It looks and smells delicious," she said to Tui, "but I'm not yet hungry. Not after that big breakfast you made."

"Don't be silly. You need some meat on those bones." Tui's words were similar to those Mikaela's grandmother would have used, but her voice sounded so tight that Mikaela did a double take. Chills shot along the back of her neck. Tui clutched her fishhook pendant.

"I have some good news," Mikaela said. "I spoke with my grandfather, and he's arranged for me to have the doll out of the inn by five o'clock."

"Ta." Tui, still clutching her fishhook, glanced at the one hanging above the door. "There are several more hours before that dinner tonight. Are you sure you wouldn't like a bit of lunch?"

"I better not." Mikaela grabbed the back door handle.

"Very well. I'll just go and get Amiria's dress ready for you then. You can pick it up when you come back in."

"That's"—Mikaela made herself not swallow, not think about Trevor and the color blue—"very nice of you. Thank you."

"No worries." Tui took the large fruit bowl from the corner of the counter and placed it in front of her. "I'll at least cut you up an apple. Or would you rather have a pear?"

"A pear, but really, you needn't bother. I'll only be a few minutes, and like I said—"

"I'll have it ready."

There was nothing left for Mikaela to do but smile her gratitude.

As it turned out, the few minutes she'd expected to be with Mr. Norris became only a moment. He was directing the movements of a fully extended backhoe. She called out to him, and he responded with an *OK* hand signal, but that was the extent of their exchange. Mikaela returned to the kitchen.

Tui finished arranging the pear slices on a white saucer and slid it across the counter. "I'll get out the dress for you while you eat." She bustled from the room, and Mikaela bit into the pear. Sweetness squirted throughout her mouth. *Delicious.*

The front door opened and closed, and a moment later Sara and Frank passed the kitchen doorway. Both nodded to Mikaela before starting up the stairs. *They're just a couple like any other couple.*

Mikaela had just swallowed her fourth pear slice when Tui returned to the kitchen. She held the dress, still on its hanger, in front of her. The blue silk swished with the movement like a gentle whisper, and it glistened in the bright kitchen light more than it had in Amiria's room. So *beautiful.* But now, looking closer at it, she realized the shade wasn't quite the same as the dresses she and Trevor had—

"You chose this one, right?" Tui asked.

"Yes, thank you. Amiria's lucky to have so many lovely dresses."

"She's never been one to stay home from school dances or anything else she could get herself invited to. And since she earned the money for them, I figured she had a right to them." Tui's gaze distanced. "I imagine she'll want her and Brentin's wedding to be quite the formal affair."

Mikaela pictured Amiria wearing an elaborate wedding dress and holding onto Brentin's arm, but in her imaginings, Brentin wore a green T-shirt. "Is everything settled between them then?"

"Neither has said anything to me, but I always say it doesn't hurt to be prepared."

"Does Brentin want a formal wedding too?"

"Crikey. I don't know as how anyone's even asked him."

"Well, I suppose he'll get used to the idea." Mikaela held Amiria's gown up to herself then hung it over her arm. "Thank Amiria again for me, will you?"

"Of course, but—"

"What is it?"

Tui twisted her pendant between her fingers. Her gaze drifted to the glass door behind Mikaela, and Mikaela couldn't help but look over her shoulder. There was nothing there.

"Would it be all right if you took a taxi to the ceilidh rather than riding with Brentin and Amiria? That way you wouldn't have to leave as early." But when Tui glanced up at the fishhook above the door and again twisted her pendant, Mikaela knew Brentin wasn't the reason at all. *The doll.*

"You don't need to worry," Mikaela said. "I've already called for a taxi."

"Bless you, my dear."

Just then, someone pounded on the back door. Mikaela whirled and opened it. Mr. Norris, his face pale and his eyes wide, stared at Mikaela.

"We found a skeleton," he said. "Human. In the back. Beneath the hedge at the bottom of the staircase."

Tui gasped.

\* \* \*

Mikaela stared out her bedroom window toward the bottom-of-the-staircase-turned-possible-crime-scene. She'd sent her grandfather a text, and as before, he hadn't immediately responded. But when it came right down to it, what could he say? Or do? After Mikaela had talked with the detectives and given them the fishhook earring the worker had found in the vicinity, the police blocked all access to the backyard and cordoned off a square area around the hedges with red-and-white crime-scene tape. They'd also halted the renovations until they could fully recover the remains and photograph the area. They had given Mikaela a bit of information— albeit unwillingly and with the caveat that it wasn't yet substantiated— that they believed whoever had been buried there had died years ago. Not recently. And not because of Tui's warning about the doll.

Mikaela turned away from the window and tucked her sweaty palms inside her crossed arms. She had to quit looking out there, had to quit thinking about the body and wondering who had died, or at least had been buried, in such an obscure place. Those thoughts only made her think more about Trevor and her grandmother.

*Focus on something else.* Her gaze traveled to the wig and craft supplies she'd purchased for the dinner that night. It was a ceilidh. A celebration. The perfect diversion from death. And she only had a little more than forty-five minutes to get ready and meet Brentin and Amiria in the lounge.

She hurried to the bathroom for a quick shower. Minutes later, she bobby-pinned her wet hair up from her face and shoulders, put on the dress, and slid on the long, straight blonde wig. After that, she draped a fake diamond necklace across her forehead and wrapped a long strip of silver-gray fabric around her shoulders into a makeshift cape. Finally she slipped on her everyday shoes; she'd switch into the silver slippers after she arrived at the convention.

Mikaela examined herself in the mirror. Just as she'd hoped, she looked like an ordinary Middle Earth Elf. Even her scar didn't stand out quite as much as usual.

She crossed back to the bed, where she'd placed the box containing the Old Mother Hubbard doll, slid her slippers in the box—she'd wrapped the doll in packaging paper—and tucked it under her arm. She then left her room and headed to the lounge. When she reached it, she stopped in the arched doorway. She scanned past the beige English sofa, the red brick fireplace, the stacks of boxes next to the black baby grand piano at the back of the long room, and finally up at the crystal chandelier hanging from the middle of the vaulted ceiling. So, so quiet—like no one had been there for ages, which couldn't possibly be true. She crossed toward the outside wall and was just about to sit on the sofa when something rustled behind her.

Mikaela turned. Brown and black zigzag fabric filled her view. She looked up . . . up . . . about seven feet to the rounded, brown top of something covered in long green vines—hair?—and lowered her gaze to a pair of brown eyes peering at her from behind glasses. "Brentin?"

"The leaves gave me away, didn't they?"

"What are you?"

"I'd hoped it would be obvious. Think Tolkien."

Once more she looked up and down the length of his costume. His headpiece, hood, and shoe covers were made from the same tree-bark mottled fabric as his robe, and he wore gnarled, long-fingered brown gloves. "An Ent?"

He smiled. His white teeth shone out from his brown face. "Treebeard. Pretty cool, don't you think? I found most of the pieces at the store, and Tui let me cut leaves from the vines out front. Maybe I should have asked you instead, being the granddaughter of the owner and all. I hope you don't mind."

"I love it. I wish I were a termite." His smile froze, but something glinted so warmly behind his eyes that she winced in embarrassment. "That came out wrong. I was just—sometimes I say things before thinking about how they'll sound. Sorry."

He glossed past her excuse with a quick wave of his gloved hand and quickly squeezed then released her shoulder. "You're a great-looking Elf, but I think you should have kept your own hair. It might be shorter, but its color is much more vibrant. It would make you stand out more."

The skin on Mikaela's shoulder still felt warm where he'd touched it. "Thanks, but I'd rather blend in with the crowd."

"Me too. Working behind the scenes."

"Brentin!"

They turned as Amiria walked, almost glided, toward them from the entry. "You're such a tease. A room full of people and a tall tree. Which do you think everyone will notice?"

Mikaela stepped out from behind Brentin to get a good look at Amiria dressed as Arden. Her long, black hair draped down the length of her back; her deep-red, velvet dress, which barely brushed the floor when she walked, provided such an exotic contrast to her light-brown skin that for a moment Mikaela thought she really did have royal blood.

"Not if there are other Ents there. I counted five at the last convention I attended." Brentin clasped Amiria's hand when she reached out for him and released it just as quickly as he'd released Mikaela's shoulder moments before. "Let's go." He removed his headpiece and handed it to Amiria. "But I definitely can't drive with this on."

Mikaela smiled—he'd made it out of a wastebasket. Quite creative.

Brentin slid on a large red backpack that lay against the wall next to the entryway. He grabbed his even larger camera bag from beside it. "Amiria said you'll be taking a cab, so we'll wait for you at the entrance."

"You have a lot of filming to do," Amiria said. "I can wait for her."

"It's not a problem. Might even work out better. I'd like to get a few minutes of film of people entering the building. Besides, Ms. Sabey—" he looked at Mikaela—"she's the woman who hired me. Anyway, she said they'll waive your entrance fee tonight, just as they waived Amiria's. We just have to go in together."

Amiria smiled into his eyes and wrapped her free hand through his arm, er, branch. "I'd say Mikaela and I are two of the luckiest girls in town. I'll make sure I thank Ms. Sabey."

Brentin smiled down at her. Neither spoke, only looked at each other for a long moment.

Mikaela cleared her throat. "I hope you'll introduce Ms. Sabey to me too. I'd also like to thank her."

At last, both looked at her. Their gazes seemed slightly dazed. Had they forgotten she was there? Mikaela glanced down at her feet. Once upon a time, she and Trevor had acted just like that.

"I'll be sure to introduce you," Brentin said.

The three left the lounge. Amiria, still carrying Brentin's headpiece, opened the front door, while Mikaela, balancing the doll box under her arm, helped Brentin maneuver both himself and his gear through the door.

After Amiria closed the door behind them, Mikaela looked toward the parking area. Her taxi had arrived. "See you soon."

The driver must have been watching for her because when she cleared the bottom stair, he climbed out of the car, opened the rear door, and stood waiting for her.

"We'll watch for you," Brentin called.

* * *

Hunapo sat up in his bed and adjusted his serving table to a more comfortable position on his lap. Already, he felt weaker than a dying mongrel, and he hadn't even had his last round of chemotherapy. He growled. No matter. All he needed was enough strength to complete his work.

He moved the blue card back and forth in front of him until the words came into focus:

*Mary Ann Cotton*
*She's dead and forgotten,*
*She lies in a grave with her bones all-rotten;*
*Sing, sing, oh, what can we sing,*
*Mary Ann Cotton is tied up with string.*

The verse wasn't quite as fitting as those he'd put in the last two sympathy cards, but it was a rhyme about a woman who'd poisoned people. It would have to do. *Isn't that right, ancestors?*

He listened for their guiding voices, but all he heard were the clinking sounds coming from his kitchen. His home care nurse was cleaning the breakfast dishes. He narrowed his eyes. If his no-good sons had married and borne at least one legitimate child, any one of them could have taken on these menial chores, leaving more of his income to pay for his final revenge. His utu.

Hunapo slid the card inside the blue envelope and dipped his plastic-gloved finger into the small bowl of water that sat next to the other sympathy cards. He ran it along the envelope's seal. Had Joseph read the last card? Did he yet recognize the part it, and he, had played in Marge's death? In the deaths still to come? Probably not. Joseph wouldn't see a lion walking among the sheep if his life depended on it. Which it did. For him and his granddaughter.

He called for his nurse and handed her the card. "I need to drop this off at the post office on our way to the hospital."

"You forgot your return address. Do you want me to write it for you?"

"No. Just send it express."

She frowned, but she asked no more questions. *Good.* At least she'd learned that much from him in the months she'd waited on him.

When she left the room, Hunapo took his cell phone from the far right corner of the table and sent a quick text.

*Mary Ann Cotton. Now.*

# Chapter 8

Brentin stood in the shade beneath the curved roofline that extended beyond the convention center's main entrance. He aimed his camera lens toward the road. The autumn air had cooled after the warmth of the day, but unlike the soft, yellow leaves he'd attached to his Ent costume, the pines across the road grew straight and green—the perfect Middle Earth setting. All he needed now were cosplayers to walk in front of it long enough for him to take the footage.

Amiria, dutifully watching over his video equipment, stood next to the pillar closest to him. She'd said nothing as he'd paced over the faded, brown-brick walkway, searching the setting, the angles, the subjects for his next photo or video clip, but it wasn't long before she crossed and uncrossed her arms, tapped her foot, and frequently glanced at the glass door. *Poor girl. She loves the limelight almost as much as I hate it, yet she still sticks with me.*

"Do you want me to set up your tripod?" she asked.

"No, thanks. I'm not ready for it yet." He aimed his camera at a particularly well-dressed group of dwarves walking up the sidewalk from the parking lot. They laughed loudly and waved at him. He zoomed in for a close-up. "We shouldn't have to be out here much longer," he added.

"All right." Amiria yawned.

Three Black Riders, their capes flapping behind them, strode up the sidewalk toward the entrance. Brentin cut away from the dwarves and focused on the new group until a taxi pulled into the parking lot. Was Mikaela already there? He moved his camera toward it, followed it, waited for the passenger to open the door. Out stepped a female Hobbit with big, hairy feet. Definitely not Mikaela.

He glanced back to Amiria. Two tall, husky Orcs stood in front of her. They were both perfectly ugly, but when one spoke to her, she smiled and lowered her gaze. Were they flirting? Maybe he ought to let them know she wasn't alone. When Brentin started toward them, the two men glanced up at him, nodded to Amiria, and left.

Amiria met Brentin halfway across the walk. She set his camera bag next to his feet. "You're frowning. Is something wrong?"

"No."

"I don't believe you."

"Smart girl." She didn't smile at his quip. "I was just wondering about those Orcs you were talking to. Should I interview them? Are they interesting?"

"A mite. They said they're on the All Blacks rugby team." Pink rose from Amiria's throat to her cheeks. So that—the rugby team—was what had caught her attention. Amiria was exciting and exotic. That was what had drawn him, a lanky teenager, to her in the first place. It was only natural she'd be drawn to others with the same characteristics. But standing there, watching her hobnob with those men, he couldn't help but wonder why she'd fallen for him. Was it because he lived in America? Several of her past e-mails had mentioned the *exotic* Rocky Mountains.

"Do you want me to see if I can find them again?" Amiria's eyes lit up more than he wanted them to.

"Naw. Let me think about it a bit longer."

Her gaze shifted toward the parking lot, and her eyes widened. "That's Andrew Evans. Maybe he'd be good to interview. He's the one dressed as Boromir."

"The tall, dark-haired Boromir or the short one?"

"The tall one. He's a reporter for the *Rotorua Daily Post*." Amiria lifted onto her toes and waved her hand over her head. Andrew, seeing her, waved back.

Brentin scanned the man's costume. It was perfect in every detail—from the woven chainmail across his chest to his leather boots to the horn of Gondor strapped over his shoulder. Well built. That kind of guy would turn any girl's head. He glanced at Amiria. Had he turned hers?

"Do you want me to ask him if he'll talk to you?" Amiria's sudden grin reminded Brentin of the selfies he'd taken of the two of them standing together on the beach. He'd once shown it to the guys back home. They'd practically drooled over it, and he'd liked their jealousy. A match made in heaven, his sister had once said, and he'd believed her. Then.

"Let's wait before we ask him too," he said.

Amiria's grin drooped, and he pointed his lens toward another group of Dwarves. She was being a good sport. Shouldn't he be one too? "You know what?" he said. "I've changed my mind. Why don't you go on inside and talk with him? Let me know if he says anything interesting. I'll keep working out here. And wait for Mikaela."

Amiria glanced at Boromir—Andrew—who had just opened the glass door. "Are you sure? I don't want to leave you in a bind with all this equipment to haul around."

"I'll ask Mikaela to help me if I have any trouble. Also, could you choose a table for us in the banquet room and save three places?"

"Sure." She gave him a quick kiss on the cheek. "It might be better this way, you know."

"You're that anxious to get away from me?"

She grinned and squeezed his hand. "Not at all. Remember what I told you about Mikaela's grandfather? How he asked me to do what I can to get Mikaela to go out a bit?"

"Yeah." Brentin touched the tip of her chin with his finger. "You're doing a great job."

"Thanks, but that got me to thinking. Why don't you ask her to help you with your interviews? She seems to like this kind of stuff, and it would force her to get out of the inn more."

He glanced at the cosplayers entering the building behind her, and he shifted his weight to his other foot. It wasn't a blind date, or anything like it, but it felt like one—one set up by Amiria. "I thought you were going to help me. So we could spend more time together."

"I thought so too, but the way it is, you're always off by yourself anyway, figuring out how you want to film everything. And you should do that. But maybe it'd be better, maybe we'd actually spend more time together if, while you're working, I planned things for us to do when you're not."

He groaned inside. "Are you sure that's what you want to do?"

"I am. Have her do my job, take care of your stuff. Mum needs me to help out more with the inn right now anyway. Tell Mikaela I've left you in a bind."

"What makes you think she'd even go for it? Isn't she here to watch over the renovations?"

"Which the police have stopped. C'mon, mate. Please?" Amiria's exaggerated kiwi accent always turned his willpower to goo, and she knew it.

"All right. I'll ask her."

She squeezed his hand then pressed her palm against his costumed chest. "You're the perfect man. You know that, don't you?"

"I'm glad you noticed."

She laughed and started for the entrance. "Try not to be too long. It's getting close to six o'clock."

"We'll be in just as soon as Mikaela gets here."

She went inside. He watched her through the glass until he could no longer see her and then panned the arriving cosplayers. Another woman dressed as Arwen moved toward the entrance. She was beautiful enough, he supposed, but she didn't quite carry herself with the same regal air Amiria did. *Amiria.* Was she already talking to the reporter? An uncomfortable lump knotted in his throat like a dry jawbreaker, and he tightened his grip on his camera. She had just arranged for them not to spend so much time together. Was that actually a nice way of saying she was tired of him? If so, shouldn't he feel more—what would his sisters call it? Devastated?

He lifted his camera and again looked through the viewfinder. He panned . . . panned . . . Finally, after he'd taken several more shots and recorded eight minutes of video footage, a taxi pulled up, and Mikaela climbed out. She looked at him, smiling slightly.

Brentin caught his breath and stared. And stared. She'd looked pretty enough in that blue gown back at the inn, but now! How had he not noticed how that color brought out the warmth of her skin? How the sheer, outer layer of her dress draped softly down the length of her body? He gulped and dropped his gaze. *Wait!* Was that—? He looked closer. She wore sneakers. Had she been wearing them back at Kotuku Inn?

Mikaela walked straight toward him. Something—but not the box she'd had before—bulged beneath her cape from under her arm. "I'm glad that's out of the way," she said. "Where's Amiria?"

"Saving us a place inside." He reached down for his backpack but in doing so, tilted his head just enough that his wastebasket-headpiece slid forward.

Mikaela grabbed it. Two white ballerina slippers dropped from under her cape. Laughing, she settled the wastebasket back on his head and scooped up the slippers. "Why don't you let me carry that bag for you. Your camera too, if it'll help."

He rebalanced the wastebasket. "Thanks. Looks like someone has to help me keep my head on straight."

# one fell down

"Glad to do it."

A medieval peasant woman and a red-haired man with a full beard walked past them. Brentin aimed his camera and took the shot. It was a bit out of focus, but at least he'd gotten it. He glanced at Mikaela. Her brilliant green eyes met his. Something tugged on his heart as if it were a balloon attached to a string. Maybe having her help wouldn't be as uncomfortable as he'd thought. "I do need your help, if you don't mind."

She removed the pack from his back. "What do you need?"

"Help with the interviews. I have to create two short films which include a few of the current attendees for the opening and closing ceremonies."

"I guess. I don't have anything else planned for tonight. But I thought Amiria was helping you."

"Tui needs her back at the inn. She has a lot of extra work over the next few days." He grimaced inwardly. It was the truth, as far as it went, yet it felt like a deception.

"Oh. Okay."

"Any chance you can help me until the convention's over? Not just for tonight?"

Her lips—with light-pink gloss—moved sideways into an uncertain wince. "I don't know anything about filming. Or interviewing. Or any of that stuff."

He motioned for her to walk with him to the entrance. "Maybe not, but you're creative. Tui said you're an artist studying to be an architect. I have no worries." Oddly, that was the truth.

Mikaela's face pinked prettily, and she quickly looked away. "I suppose I can for now, but when the police say the builders can get back to work, I might have to quit."

"Whatever you can do'll be great." He reached for the front door handle, but she stepped in front of him.

"Let me do that. You need to fix your head before it falls off."

*What?* Oh. The wastebasket. He again readjusted his costume, and the two entered the convention center. They went directly to the ticket booth. Brentin pulled his pass out from his camera bag and handed it to the elderly woman behind the counter.

"Brentin."

Brentin startled upright. He focused on her face. She wore Elf ears, but her short curly white hair, bright blue eyes, and crinkled smile were just as he remembered them. "Hello, Ms. Sabey."

"I hoped I'd get a chance to see you tonight," she said. "I'm so glad you could make it. It wouldn't seem right to have the convention without you."

"I'm glad you thought of me. I've been trying for more opportunities like this."

"Not satisfied being a teacher?"

"That's not it at all. I love film. And it's a good side income, you know?"

She nodded, still smiling, and looked to Mikaela.

"This is Mikaela York," Brentin added, "the girl I told you would be coming with Amiria and me. And this, Mikaela, is Leanne Sabey. This convention wouldn't have happened without her."

"Oh, you!" Ms. Sabey reached through the opening beneath the clear barrier and patted Mikaela's hand where it rested on the counter. "Welcome, my dear. I understand you're Joseph Parker's granddaughter."

"I am."

"A fortunate man to have such a beautiful granddaughter."

"Thank you," Mikaela said.

"Mikaela will be helping me with the films," Brentin said.

"Is that so? We better get her an all-event pass, then. Stop by on your way out tonight, and I'll have it here for you."

Mikaela set her long fingers on the edge of the counter. "That's kind of you, but I don't expect I'll be here all that much. And anyway, if I come I'm sure I can pay for my own ticket."

"Nonsense. We can't make you pay to hang out with this guy. Besides that, I owe him."

Brentin coughed. "Not that again."

"I won't forget until the debt is paid," Ms. Sabey said. "Now the two of you better get on into the banquet room. They'll be serving dinner soon."

Brentin squeezed Ms. Sabey's hand and motioned for Mikaela to follow him across the foyer. A group of Dwarves stood in front of the banquet room's open doorway.

"Help me remember to interview her for the last film," he said under his breath before stepping into the hall.

"Okay." Mikaela drew her eyebrows together. "What was all that about her owing you?"

"She doesn't owe me anything. She just says that. Tui had me do odd jobs for Ms. Sabey that summer I was here, that's all. I was seventeen."

"Seventeen, huh? She probably figured you needed something constructive to do."

Brentin laughed, and without thinking he let his gaze follow the smooth outline of her profile down the length of her scar—*how did she get it?*—and across her upper neck to where her ear would be if he could see it behind her wig.

Mikaela pressed her fingertips over the scar and looked away from him. "Where's Amiria?"

"Over there." He whipped his gaze from Mikaela and motioned to Amiria on the opposite side of the room. Amiria stood tall, confidently, like the queen he'd always pictured her as, next to one of the round tables. It was empty, but several Orcs sat at the table beside it. They watched her, almost hovered over every move she made. Were they the same All Blacks team members she'd talked to earlier?

"I know we need to sit," Mikaela said as he led her across the room, weaving between the tables, "but why don't you take a moment and pan the attendees? It'll give your audience—both here and on YouTube—a good idea of just how big this event is."

He looked to Amiria—still alone, still waiting for him—and turned his wastebasket head toward Mikaela. "Good thinking. Come on. " He indicated to Amiria that they'd be another couple of minutes, and he and Mikaela walked back to the wall near the entrance. He slowly panned the room three times before returning the camera to his bag. He glanced up at Mikaela. Unlike Amiria, rather than yawning, she also scanned the room and—nodded to someone? He followed her gaze. Andrew Evans stood at a table a short distance from where Amiria sat. He stared directly at Mikaela.

"Do you know him?" Brentin asked her.

"No, but he keeps looking at me like he does. I wonder what he wants."

"Amiria says he's a reporter. Maybe he's already heard about the body at the inn and wants to talk to you. I can ask him if you want. Amiria wants me to interview him anyway."

"Don't worry about it. He can talk to me if he wants, but it won't help him any. I don't know anything."

At last they made their way across the room to Amiria. She immediately took Brentin's bag and backpack from him. "Let's put your gear over by the wall out of the way. The waitresses are starting to serve the meals."

"Very well."

She and Mikaela set his film equipment where Amiria had suggested and claimed chairs at the table. Amiria chose the one on Brentin's right side. Mikaela took the one on his left.

"By the way," Mikaela said, "what did I order?"

"The extra meals are all the same," Amiria said. "Beef, mushrooms, and taters, in honor of Samwise Gamgee."

"Love it." Mikaela shifted in her seat and looked over her shoulder toward the three servers on the other side of the room. "I hope you don't mind, Amiria," she said, "but I'd really like to change out of these sneakers and into my slippers. Do you know where the restroom is? And maybe someplace I can hide my shoes?"

Brentin laughed under his breath. He couldn't help it. Amiria, however, scowled slightly. Hadn't she noticed Mikaela's shoes before now? Or was her leaving the table so close to serving time a worse faux pas? Whatever the case, he'd likely hear about it later. Amiria put a great deal of stock in appearances.

"The restroom is around the corner from the door," Amiria said.

"I bet Ms. Sabey would let you keep your sneakers in the ticket office," Brentin whispered.

"That'd be great. Thanks." Mikaela pushed the strands of her long wig over her shoulders and headed toward the entrance. Brentin looked back to Amiria.

"Well?" Amiria said. "Did she agree to help you?"

"Yeah. Like you said, I think it's going to work out pretty well. She seems to have an instinct for what I need. For the film."

He hadn't meant to imply anything, but Amiria had obviously noticed it. She lowered her gaze to the table and nudged her fork. "I suppose it would be easy for you to talk to her since she's also from America."

He squeezed her hand. How could she be jealous? She was the one who'd asked him to ask Mikaela for her help. "All we talked about were the films, sweetheart."

"Of course." She squeezed his hand back and smiled in a way that always made his heart feel like it was a bit too big for his chest. "By the way, don't worry about interviewing Andrew unless you really want to. He's a fan but not more than anyone else around here. He wants to talk to Mikaela though. About the body."

So he'd been right.

"Are these seats taken?"

Amiria looked up toward the man's voice. He and the woman with him were dressed as Gandalf and Eowan.

"This one is." Amiria pointed to Mikaela's seat. "But you're welcome to sit there."

Gandalf nodded to her and walked around to the chair on the other side of Amiria. He pulled it out for Eowan then sat beside her.

"I think they're about to serve dinner," Amiria said. "I hope Mikaela gets back soon."

*Mikaela.* For no good reason, Brentin's pulse throbbed against his Adam's apple, and the corners of Amiria's lips drooped. They stayed that way until Mikaela returned a few minutes later with two tall and slender dark-haired cosplayers dressed as Elves.

"Good. There are still seats left." Mikaela motioned to the empty ones next to hers and turned to Amiria. "This is Jewell and Noah Cooper. I met them out in the foyer a minute ago." Suddenly she looked at Brentin with such expectant—no, respectful, no, *what the heck is it?*—trust that it took all his strength to pull his gaze away from hers. "They're really big Tolkien fans," she added.

"Aren't we all?" Eowan said.

The others laughed softly.

"I suppose that's true." Mikaela glanced between Brentin and the Coopers. "But these folks are *really* big fans. They own the Middle Earth Hotel and Spa near the lake."

Gandalf nodded at Mr. Cooper. "Near the Government Gardens, eh. I haven't had the pleasure of staying there, but I love the food in your restaurant. I took a business colleague there a couple of months ago, when you had your Hobbit theme."

Brentin focused on the four people sitting across from them. He only had to ignore Mikaela for a few more moments until whatever had come over him passed and he no longer felt heat rushing through his skin.

Jewell Cooper spread her ringed and manicured fingers on the tabletop. "My father always said if you start out with a bang, the rest of the month will fill your pockets."

Noah Cooper sat beside her. He steepled his fingertips. "We have a different Tolkien theme the first day of every month."

Mikaela leaned close to Brentin's ear. He stiffened at her nearness. "Did you get my hint?" she whispered. "I thought you might want to interview them for your film. Oh, and on the other side of the room, close to the doors, I saw a little boy decked out as Frodo. He's the youngest I've seen here so far. Maybe we can catch him and his parents tonight before they leave."

Brentin let himself look at her. "That would be perfect."

"I can hurry over before the servers get here and ask them to meet with us after dinner if you'd like?"

"Ask who?"

"Frodo's parents. For permission. You want to interview the boy, don't you?"

"Oh. Yes, of course." Brentin smiled hesitantly until the fluttery feeling in his stomach settled.

"Great. I'll be back in a minute." She pushed up from the table. Her arm bumped his. "Sorry."

*I'm not.* He shifted in his seat. He hadn't really thought that, had he? He looked at Amiria, and she looked back at him. Sadness touched her gaze. *What kind of a fool am I?*

# Chapter 9

MIKAELA FELT FOOLISH JUMPING OUT of the backseat of Brentin's car the moment he parked in Kotuku Inn's parking lot, but hanging back with him and Amiria felt even more uncomfortable. They needed to be alone to work out whatever had happened between them after she'd left the table to find young Frodo. Something had definitely happened; the longer the night wore on, the more withdrawn and sad Amiria became even though Brentin seemed more attentive to her than Mikaela had yet seen him.

A car door closed behind her. "I'll see you in the morning," Brentin said.

Mikaela focused on the porch light as if it were a lighthouse on the edge of a turbulent shoreline. "Six thirty. I know. I'll be ready." She and Brentin had scheduled an interview with the Coopers for the next morning.

Behind her, gravel scratched beneath footsteps, and another car door opened and closed. Mikaela glanced back at them. "Thanks again for inviting me, Amiria. It was fun." And it was, despite Amira and Brentin's whatever-it-was.

Mikaela, holding her slippers with one hand and in the other, the small box of candy Andrew Evans had given her with a request to talk with her tomorrow—*it's so weird that he had that with him*—stepped off the gravel onto the cobblestone walk and raced up the stairs. She bustled into the quiet entry hall and turned to close the door, but before she latched it, she couldn't help but again glance back at Brentin and Amiria. They were holding hands, walking slowly, talking. *Good.*

Stepping as lightly as she could so she wouldn't wake anyone, she hurried up the stairs to her room. But when she switched on the light and locked the door, a cool breeze brushed over her shoulders. She shivered. Slowly, slowly, she faced her room, scanning it. "Is someone here?"

No one answered, but her curtain billowed like a ghost's dress. Someone had cracked open the window. And made her bed. And set a covered metal pitcher in the middle of the small table. Steam rose from it. Had Tui been in there? Was this part of her regular housekeeping routine?

Another breeze gusted over her, and once again Mikaela checked the room, including the bathroom and closet, before at last shutting the window. It was strange how closing a window could empty noise from a quiet room.

Ignoring the shivers spanning the width of her shoulders, Mikaela slid off her sneakers, set her slippers by the wardrobe and the candy on the table, and placed her chilled hands around the outside of the metal pitcher. Hot water. Next to it was a molded white glass cup with packets of coffee and hot cocoa inside; next to that lay a thick piece of string on top of an old-fashioned picture of Old Mother Hubbard. Was Tui leaving her some kind of cryptic message? If so, the picture didn't look much like the doll. And what did string have to do with either the doll or the nursery rhyme? Besides, Mikaela had already done as Tui had asked and moved the doll out of the inn.

She frowned, removed her wig, and pulled the bobby pins one by one from her hair. She set them on the table and scratched her scalp. Again, she glanced at the picture.

Maybe she was being too hasty in her criticism. Maybe the picture didn't have anything to do with the doll. Maybe it was simply part of some kind of tradition. And the string meant . . . what? Tomorrow, she'd ask Tui, but for now, Mikaela scooped the bobby pins into her hand, carried them to the bathroom, and changed into her night robe. Amiria's elegant dress had been a fun break from her everyday clothing, but the thought of wrapping up inside something thick, loose, and fluffy seemed the perfect end to the day. That and drinking—she smiled as the local vernacular filled her mind—a *cuppa* hot cocoa.

She set her phone next to her, slid the picture and string to the center of the table, and opened the box of chocolates. Next, she poured the liquid into the cup. She mixed in the hot cocoa. Oddly, it bubbled lightly against the sides of the cup, almost like a fizz, then settled into creamy, sweet goodness. Finally, Mikaela lowered herself into the chair and picked up her phone. She checked her e-mail. Her grandfather had sent her a message.

*Dear Mikaela,*

*I wonder if that earring belonged to Caroline Evans. She's the woman who owned Kotuku Inn before we did, and she collected fishhook ornaments. Your grandmother liked the symbol too, so we never got rid of them. Now, they just seem to belong with the inn.*

Mikaela touched the edge of the cup against her mouth, but the steam burned her lip. She lowered the cup, looked at the open box of chocolates. Delicious, very likely, but so much sugar before bed? She'd be better off waiting until tomorrow to eat them. She put the lid back on the box and continued to read her grandfather's note.

*I do like your idea of putting the earring in the safe deposit box with the doll. When I ran Kotuku Inn for Caroline, she treated me like her own son. I appreciated her kindness. But now, looking back, I wish I would have done more to help her. I'm sure she's passed now, but maybe I can find her relatives, and if the earring is hers, I'll give it to them. Whatever the case, I suppose a decision can wait until I get there.*

*By the way, I asked your Aunt Maureen about the sympathy card, but like you, she had no idea where it may have come from. I finally threw it away, but I can't get those words out of my mind:* Humpty Dumpty had a great fall. *My Marge's death was an accident, wasn't it?*

A sharp, needlelike shiver shot through Mikaela's heart, and she jolted slightly, splashing hot liquid onto her hands and the sleeve of her bathrobe. What? Of course Grandma's death was an accident. To think otherwise . . .

She quickly dried her hands and robe with a couple of napkins and returned to his e-mail.

*Never mind. More than likely it's just the overactive imagination of a heartbroken old man. It's only that there are things about her death and the discovery of that old skeleton that drum up long-ago memories. I expect you know nothing more about the body than what you've told me? Like who it might have been? Your grandma once said she felt our property had a sacred feeling about it, like it was anciently a burial ground. Could she have been right after all? I wouldn't put it past her. She had a much better sense about the spirit of things than I did.*

*Thank you for all you're doing. I don't know how I could ever have managed without you. See you soon.*

*Love,*

*Grandpa*

Mikaela tapped the rim of the mostly full cup and bit the inside of her lower lip. Her grandfather hadn't said the words, but the haphazard way he'd arranged his sentences told her he was struggling with his emotions the same way she'd struggled with hers soon after Trevor had died. She'd imagined lots of crazy things then too.

She brushed her hand past the scar on her face, pushed her cuppa cocoa to the far side of the table, and hit REPLY. She typed in the only words she could think to say.

> *Grandpa,*
> *I love you.*
> *Mikaela*

*Click.* Mikaela looked up to the sound. Was someone at her door? She waited, listened, but when the noise didn't repeat itself, she got up from the table and dressed for bed. If only the hot chocolate would still be good in the morning.

# Chapter 10

AT 6:40 A.M., MIKAELA CREPT from her room to the top of the stairs. Instead of her dark-blue blouse and black slacks, she'd put on jeans, a black sweater over a white T-shirt, and sneakers. It wasn't the most professional-looking outfit, but that morning it was the only one that had felt right. Why she'd even packed those dressier clothes, she didn't know. They'd always reminded her of how Trevor had favored that look on her, of how much she'd lost. But today she didn't want to think of any of those things. Instead, she'd stuffed her dress clothes way back in the closet and had hurried down the stairs.

She stopped in front of the arched doorway to the lounge. A small wall lamp to the side of the large bowed windows lit the room enough that she could see Brentin wasn't there. She crossed to the couch and sat. The white-and-beige flowered cushions plumped around her.

She checked the time on her cell phone. *6:42.* She took a deep breath and scanned from the wall paintings to the back window and across the piano. Did anyone ever play it?

"You look cheerful this morning."

Mikaela turned to Brentin's voice, but when she saw him standing in the doorway, her mouth involuntarily dropped open. He still had the same long-on-top and short-on-the-sides haircut, but rather than his bangs occasionally falling into his face, they were smoothed back with the rest of his hair. He also had a clean-shaven chin. "Where are your glasses?" She couldn't think of anything else to say.

"Contacts. My luggage was in my room when I got back last night. Ready for the Coopers?"

"Sure. Where's your camera bag?"

"Already in the car."

She followed him into the hallway and toward the front door. "What'd you do? Leave it in the trunk last night? I didn't hear a single door open while I was waiting."

"That's probably because the walls are so thick. But then, since you're an architect, you probably already noticed that."

"I'm not an architect."

"Not yet, but I bet you already think like one." He quietly opened the door and waited.

Mikaela stepped outside. She gazed through the trees toward the quick-moving headlights racing along the highway. Darkness still edged the morning, but it didn't—she glanced to the far side of the building—hide the crime scene tape. "I wonder if the police were right. If the body was Caroline Evans."

"I expect we'll find out soon."

When they reached his small red car, which looked purple in the almost dark, she instinctively walked to the right side. He grinned from where he stood on the left side—the passenger's side—and held out the keys. "Looks like you want to drive?"

"What?! Oh, yeah, sorry. No, I definitely don't want to drive here." She hurried around to the other side.

"I keep doing that too. The last time was at the gas station. The man in the car behind me kept laughing." Brentin walked around to the driver's seat and backed out of his parking spot. He kept glancing at her and opening his mouth and closing it again—as if he wanted to say something. But it wasn't until he'd driven down the lane and turned right onto Tarawera Road that he said, "I know it's not my place to say anything, and I hope it doesn't happen, but you do realize that finding a body on the property could be bad for business, don't you?"

"Yeah, maybe, but then sometimes horrible things like that attract people. I wrote a paper on unique buildings a couple of years ago, and while I was doing research, I found information on a popular Lizzie Borden bed and breakfast in England. She was a serial killer."

"Somehow, I don't think Tui will go for a murderer-themed inn."

"Probably not."

Again, neither spoke. Normally, the quiet didn't bother Mikaela, but something about sitting next to Brentin and looking out at the tree-lined grayness of the New Zealand morning brought back her last drive with Trevor through the canyon. Perhaps if she'd released her seat belt and thrown herself in front of Trevor instead of bracing herself against the dashboard, he'd still be alive.

A raindrop splattered the glass. Brentin stopped at the traffic light. "Have I upset you?"

"No." She sniffed. "I'll be all right in a minute."

"Is it because of—Amiria said you're mourning."

*Please don't ask that. I'm barely keeping my emotions under control as it is.*

The light turned green. Brentin turned left toward town, and Mikaela looked out her side window. "My grandmother died while hiking through a canyon. Most of the trail was rather easy, but—I suppose the trees reminded me of her. It doesn't make much sense, does it?"

"Actually, it does."

She looked at him.

His eyes, though seemingly focused on the road ahead of them, narrowed into a slight squint. "My father died when I was eighteen. It was unexpected, but my mom, sisters, and I got along okay. He'd always taken care of us. But sometimes when someone says something or I see something that reminds me of him—like whenever I smell bacon, I think of my father. He used to make it for us on Saturday mornings."

"So it doesn't get any easier?"

"Not really. It just gets so you don't think about it all the time." Brentin glanced at her out of the corner of his eye. "Why do I get the feeling there's more to that question than—that question?"

"More than that I'm still mourning?"

"Yes. No. I don't know. I'm sorry. Forget I said anything."

Mikaela watched him. Was he fighting feelings or words? She couldn't tell, but something in his expression, the way he rubbed his hand over his mouth, tightened the air between them.

Brentin stopped at the next red light. He signaled right. "You look tired."

"I am tired." *Tired of being sad. Tired of everyone dying. Tired of not knowing who I am anymore.* She looked back at him.

He cleared his throat. "Why don't you tell me about your studies. What kind of architecture are you leaning toward? Commercial? Residential?"

"I'm not going to be an architect anymore."

"You changed your major? I did that a couple of times before I finally settled on secondary education. What's your plan now? Something else art related?"

"I don't know yet."

He frowned, and something inside her stomach twisted. She searched his face. Confusion and worry but mostly honesty. And friendship. The comfortable kind. She ran her palms across the top of her pant legs and took a deep breath. "Tui and Amiria don't know this, so please . . ."

His gaze didn't leave the road ahead of them. "Of course."

"The truth is I can't even look at an art book anymore."

His left eyebrow arched, but still he said nothing.

"Because . . . my grandmother isn't the only one who died recently. My fiancé, Trevor, died a year ago last December. He was the one who helped me choose to go into architecture."

Brentin said nothing, only drove another block and pulled into the parking lot outside the Middle Earth Hotel and Spa. Sunrise had lightened the horizon behind it, and the front lobby window, though dimly lit, showed a lone man walking out from behind the front desk and through another door.

"I'm sorry," Brentin said at last.

"Thanks."

He opened his door and climbed out. Mikaela opened her door too, but rather than immediately climbing out, she leaned her head against the headrest and expelled a long sigh. It had been hard to tell him, but she'd done it, and somehow she felt better. Maybe the old idiom was true: that it's sometimes easier to tell strangers, rather than friends, the tough things from our hearts.

Brentin popped the trunk, and Mikaela walked around to it. He handed her his backpack. "Last night your suggestions were spot on, so this morning if you happen to see anything I should do differently, let me know, okay? Unless it's too hard for you, you know, to be creative. Don't worry about it."

"Thanks, but as long as I don't have to draw anything, I'm good." *I think.*

\* \* \*

*Buzz.*

Hunapo took a shallow breath and slowly reached across his double bed to the pressed maple wood end table next to him. His neighbor had given him the table to replace one of his favorite Maori pieces he'd sold a few months earlier. Hunapo would never be able to repay the gesture, could never tell the man that while he did need the money to pay for his chemotherapy treatments, the only reason he continued the treatment was to give him time to complete this final act of utu. But sometime, somewhere, the tupunas would create the needed balance for that man just as they had for him.

He grabbed the phone, closed his eyes, and lowered his head back onto his pillow. The fan blades on the ceiling above him whirred. Soft pockets of air puffed over the rash that grew in patches over his skin. The sores in his mouth burned. But at last he picked up the phone and read the message.

*Tried but she didn't even taste it. Forming new plan. Will let you know more soon.*

Hunapo's jaw muscles tightened. If he were a healthy man, he wouldn't have to rely on such deficiencies. He'd complete the tasks himself. But as it was . . . His stomach turned over, and he rolled onto his side. He pressed his pillow against his mouth, but the nausea only intensified. He clutched his arm across his middle. He could handle this. He was a strong Maori man. And just as his grandfather had always told him before administering his hardboard discipline, pain turned weakness into strength.

He sent his reply.

*I don't have long to wait.*

He then settled back into his pillow and closed his eyes. He pictured his tupunas standing round Kotuku Inn, calling on the law of utu, prowling round and round Joseph and his granddaughter like wolves among blind sheep. One wolf, two wolves, three . . .

# Chapter 11

*IF ONLY THE MIDDLE EARTH Hotel and Spa was bigger,* Brentin thought. *It've been the perfect venue for the convention.* Yeah, they'd have to change up the restaurant a little and get rid of the furniture, but—he looked up, down, and from one end of the room to the other—*incredible!* The wood-paneled walls and floor almost replicated the sparsely decorated castle from the fictional city of Rohan. He expelled a long, low whistle. "This is cool."

When Mikaela didn't respond, he glanced at her out of the corner of his eye. She'd lifted her gaze to the intricately carved ceiling rafters. Did she know they were thematically Maori? He opened his mouth to ask her, but when her gaze clouded and seemingly focused on the front desk, he closed it again. Maybe he'd be better off keeping the architecture stuff to himself.

"You don't think the Coopers forgot we were coming, do you?" Mikaela asked.

"I doubt it." He searched her face—calm; questioning; deep-green eyes; soft, almost open lips. Had he been wrong in thinking she was upset? The emotion he'd seen in her eyes only a moment ago had disappeared. *Girls are so confusing.*

They walked up to the check-in desk, and he reached for the service bell. The framed sign next to it had a caricature of Frodo saying, *Ring with care. It's heavy to bear.* Brentin pointed it out to Mikaela. She smiled slightly and said, "Cute."

He tapped the bell.

Noah Cooper walked out of the door behind the front desk. Though he no longer wore his costume, the straight, thin lines of his face made him seem even more Elven than he'd looked the night before. "Mr. Williams,

Miss York. Please come this way. My wife is waiting for you in our living quarters. She's looking forward to your interview."

"You too, I hope?" Brentin said.

"Of course. But I'm sorry; we do have to take turns minding the desk. Our receptionist called in sick this morning."

"That'll be fine."

Noah led them through a long, narrow room that looked much like the teacher's lounge back at the high school where Brentin taught photography and physics. When they reached the closed door on the opposite side of the room, he motioned them inside. "I'll be just out here when you're ready for my wife and me to switch places."

When he left, Brentin scanned the room. Several chairs, a brown couch, and a vase of orange flowers in the middle of a heavy mahogany coffee table adorned the central living space. The floor and most of the walls were wood paneled. A rock fireplace, with a small fire burning inside, covered most of the opposite wall. Jewell Cooper stood in front of it. Though she had to be more than sixty years old, she was definitely not frumpy. Silver, moon-shaped earrings dangled from her ears, rings adorned her fingers, and she wore a black, slightly low-cut dress suit that would have revealed unseemly bulges on a less fit woman.

"Good morning, Brentin, Mikaela. It's good to see you again." She glanced about the room. "Where would you like me to stand?"

"This room has so many interesting features . . ." Brentin looked to Mikaela. "What do you suggest?"

She lifted her eyebrows as if surprised he'd asked her and tilted her head sideways. She pointed to a large painting of a tall, black volcano. "Since this interview's for the Tolkien convention, how about there? It's Mount Doom, isn't it?"

Jewell smiled. "That's not its real name, but yes, it is the volcano they used in the movie."

"Perfect." Brentin said.

Mikaela's cheeks reddened, and her gaze flashed away from him. What did he say to deserve that response? Did she normally blush so easily? Or maybe it wasn't an embarrassed blush. Had his word, *perfect*, maybe pricked a nerve? Reminded her of something her grandmother had said? Or her fiancé? He swallowed the dry lump that suddenly scratched at his throat like a hundred tiny pieces of cement.

Jewell moved in front of the painting. "Should I stand here?"

"Yes," Mikaela said.

Brentin watched Mikaela—not watching, just monitoring her movements, er, decisions—through the corner of his eye as he unlocked the telescoping legs of his tripod. He carefully said, "The questions are on a yellow sheet of paper inside the backpack."

"Got it. Could you step to the right a bit, Mrs. Cooper? A bit more. One more step. Good."

*Maybe she isn't upset. She certainly doesn't seem nervous.* Brentin attached the camera to the tripod.

"How's that?" Mikaela said to him.

Brentin shifted his camera and tripod a few feet away and peered at Jewell through his viewfinder. "Per—great."

Mikaela shuffled through the papers in his backpack and pulled out his list of questions.

"All right, Mrs. Cooper," Brentin said. "When I give you the signal, please tell us your name, where you're from, and a little about yourself."

"Very well." Jewell angled herself between the camera and the painting in such a way that it highlighted both her face and her full-figured profile.

Brentin stepped back. He adjusted the focus and flicked his hand.

"I'm Jewell Cooper," she began. "My father, God rest his soul, loved J. R. R. Tolkien's work so much that he and my mother started up this hotel. I was born"—she smiled—"sometime after that. You could say my entire life has revolved around the Middle Earth Hotel and Spa. It is my husband's and my home. We inherited it from my father." She glanced at the picture. "Actually, Noah proposed to me while we were climbing this volcano. It wasn't as famous then as it is now, but we've always loved it."

Brentin focused on the painting then moved his viewfinder back to Mrs. Cooper.

"It may not seem very romantic to you," Jewell went on, "but I love this area and this business. Noah knew that. Our engagement was idyllic."

Mikaela furrowed her brows at Brentin and again looked at the list. Had her gaze lingered just a little longer than necessary? *Get back to work.* "I understand you celebrate Tolkien and *The Lord of the Rings* through monthly theme parties in your hotel restaurant," he said.

"Yes. At the beginning of every month."

"Why at that time?"

Jewell stared at a point behind Brentin, and Brentin looked over his shoulder. Noah Cooper had stepped into the room.

"My husband proposed to me on the first Saturday in June," Jewell said. "The Queen's Birthday. At first, we thought a theme party would commemorate both the queen and our engagement, but eventually it evolved into a Tolkien tradition."

"What a lovely way to remember such an event." Mikaela turned to Brentin. "Do you have any more questions?"

Brentin again looked into the viewfinder. It had bumped—focused—on Mikaela's smooth-skinned throat. He moved it to Jewell and stood. "No. Thank you, Jewell. Now if you could please trade places with your husband?"

Noah stepped away from the door. He met his wife halfway across the room, briefly touched her elbow, and continued to the painting. Jewell left. Mikaela shook Noah's hand.

"We'll begin just as we did with your wife," Brentin said. "As soon as I signal, please state your name, where you're from, and a little about yourself."

"All right." Noah ran his hand over the top of his silver hair.

"Will you please stand there, on the other side of the painting?" Mikaela instructed.

Noah obeyed, and Brentin turned his camera left to where Mikaela pointed. He adjusted the focus on his viewfinder.

"What do you think?" she said.

Brentin quick-scanned the setup and looked straight at her. How did she recognize the balance and form of things so easily? "Perfect." He pressed his lips together, afraid he'd unthinkingly said the wrong word, but this time, rather than blushing, something altered behind her eyes. She turned away from him.

Brentin looked into the viewfinder. He lifted his hand to Noah. "Now."

"I'm Noah Cooper. My wife, Jewell, and I own the Middle Earth Hotel and Spa in Rotorua, New Zealand. We are huge Tolkien fans. I've read all his books dozens of times, and I've seen *The Lord of the Rings* series, *The Hobbit*, all the movies more often than I care to count." He held his smile as if he was used to being in the limelight and shifted his gaze toward Mikaela.

"Where are you from, originally?" Mikaela said.

"Taupo. It's south of here. Closer to this volcano." He gave a hesitant smile. "Jewell's father asked me once if seeing this painting was what had attracted me to this area, but the truth is I fell in love with Jewell the first time I saw her."

"Where did you two meet?"

"At a milk bar. I have to take her word on it that she was with a group of other girls. She was the only one I saw." He stared at a point on the ground in front of Mikaela.

"And the rest is history," Mikaela said.

Noah looked up to her. He lifted an eyebrow like he was surprised to see her. "Yes."

Mikaela lowered the sheet of paper. "Would you mind telling us about your proposal?"

Brentin's gaze shot over at her. That question wasn't on the list, and yet a lot of viewers, especially women, would likely find it intriguing. Mikaela was amazing.

"Your wife said you proposed on that volcano," Mikaela prompted.

"There isn't much to tell. I wanted to get her away from, well, everything when I asked her, so I took her on a hike. I expect you already know it wasn't known as Mount Doom at that time, but I did give her a gold ring." He smiled slightly and nodded to a large, framed picture on the opposite wall. "Did you get a chance to see our engagement portrait?"

Brentin aimed the camera lens to where Noah pointed. The black-and-white photograph depicted a younger Noah and Jewell, but they had the same smiles, the same way of presenting themselves as they did that morning.

"Do you have any more questions?" Noah said.

"I think we're good." Brentin gathered up his equipment and restocked his bags. "If you're able to make it, these clips will be shown before the closing charity drive. If not, the convention board will put it on YouTube sometime next month."

"We'll be at the charity drive."

As Noah led them back to the lobby, Mikaela looked at the arched ceiling rafters the way she had when they'd first entered the building. "This is a beautiful structure," she said.

Brentin smiled to himself. She might not realize it, or want to realize it, but art and architecture were still very much part of who she was. He again pulled his camera from his bag, panned the room, and looked over his shoulder at Noah. "Did the hotel look like this when you and your wife met? Or have you made changes since then?"

Jewell, who was standing beside the cash register, opened a drawer beneath the counter. "We've made quite a few changes. It's always had a restaurant, but the spa came later."

"We added rooms too," Noah said. "Jewell's father believed money was available for those who were willing to work for it, so we've tried to live by that law—to follow in his footsteps."

Jewell looked at her husband. "I didn't know you remembered that."

"I had to win you, didn't I?"

Their gazes met.

Brentin swallowed and backed against the outside glass door. "Thanks again for your help."

After Brentin and Mikaela left the hotel and crossed to the parking lot, Mikaela said, "Do you have enough footage now?"

"I still have that interview with Ms. Sabey, but it's quite a bit later, at four thirty. She was busy until then."

They reached the car. He opened the driver's side door and pushed the button that released the trunk. As he set his camera bag in the trunk, he said, "Thanks for your work in there. You did a great job."

She set the backpack beside his camera bag and tripod. "They were your questions."

"Not all of them. You had some pretty good ideas of your own."

"You didn't mind me asking them?"

"Are you kidding? I loved them." He followed her to the passenger door, opened it, and waited for her to climb inside, but when she didn't, he looked over and found her gazing toward the spa. "What is it?" he asked.

"I haven't seen a sculpture like that before. Have you?"

"That fishhook in front of the main window?"

"Yeah. There are fishhooks all around town—and at the inn. But that one's different. It feels different."

He peered closer at the white stone figure. It wasn't imposing—it only reached as high as his waist—but the top of the hook didn't end where the fisherman's line would normally connect with it. Instead, it twisted with what looked like the end of a fish tail and joined with the hook. For no good reason, his pulse quickened. "It should feel different. The twist is another Maori symbol. I haven't seen it for a while, but it represents a never-ending bond of love between two people."

"I wonder if my grandfather would want something like that on the grounds at Kotuku Inn. It was his and Grandma's first home as a couple."

"Tell him about it and find out."

"I will—only I'm not sure I can describe it to him well enough."

"Show it to him then. He'll be here in a few days." Brentin closed her door after she climbed inside.

"I could do that, I guess, after he got here," she continued when he climbed in beside her, "but Mr. Norris—the contractor Grandpa hired—told me he'd like to get going on it as soon as he can. And since the police have stopped their work, well, if he could take care of that, at least the renovations would move forward. Maybe I should just go take a picture and text it to him."

"That could work, but wouldn't it be better if you drew it and then showed it to him over Skype? That way you could also talk about it."

Her posture grew as stiff as a blank chalkboard. Her fingers clenched so tightly around the edge of the car seat he thought she might rip the fabric. "Draw it?" she echoed.

"I'm sorry. I shouldn't have butted in. It's just—never mind."

"Just what?"

"It's just like you saw right off. The best part about that sculpture is the feeling you get when you look at it. I've never been able to capture something like that in a photo, but an artist like you could." The air around him tensed. "I—I can bring you some new pencils. And a notebook, if it'll help."

"Don't worry about it," she said so softly that at first he wasn't sure he'd heard her. "I have some in my desk back at the inn."

"You'll do it?"

"It's a simple project. And I—I want to do this right for my grandfather."

Brentin started the ignition. He eased his foot off the brake, but when the car began to move, he stepped on the pedal again. The car lurched forward. Mikaela braced her hands against the dashboard. Her eyes widened, and she looked over both shoulders. "What happened?"

*My mind's on you instead of my driving.* "Nothing. Sorry."

"Are you sure?"

"I'm sure." *Think about Amiria.* He exhaled and backed out of the parking space, albeit a bit too fast. *Very well then, if not her, think about filming.*

# Chapter 12

MIKAELA CHOKED THE MOMENT THE Kotuku Inn came into view. Several white police cars with yellow-and-blue stripes across their fronts and sides had parked alongside the crime scene tape. It divided the front from the back of the property. "Uh-oh."

Brentin glanced at her but said nothing until he parked and turned off the car. "Now what's up?"

Mikaela, scanning the area from one end of the house to the other, climbed out of the car. The detective she'd spoken with yesterday, Sergeant Hoffman, walked toward them from the left side of the house. He waved his hand sharply over his head, signaling for them to wait for him. "I guess we're about to find out," she said.

When they met up with the officer in front of the porch stairs, Sergeant Hoffman pressed his lips into a tight frown and looked directly at Mikaela. "Some information has come to light that's given us a few more questions we hoped you could clear up."

"What are they?"

He pulled a small notebook from his jacket pocket. "About the earring the renovators found. Have you heard back from your grandfather? You told us you'd e-mailed him about it."

"He only said he wondered if it might have belonged to the woman who owned the property before him. Her name was Caroline Evans."

"Did he tell you why, exactly, he thought that?"

"Because it's a fishhook and she collected fishhook symbols. They're all over this place."

Sergeant Hoffman wrote something in his notebook. "I understand your grandfather lived here before he purchased the inn from her, is that correct?"

"Yes. He was a handyman of sorts, helping Mrs. Evans with some of the physical things that were difficult for her after her husband died. His work helped him pay for his room and board."

"Do you know how soon after your grandfather bought Kotuku Inn that Mrs. Evans moved from the premises?"

Mikaela wrinkled her brow. That information might have been on the papers she'd taken to the safety deposit box, but she hadn't looked at them closely enough to remember such details. "I don't know. Grandpa said they did a bit of remodeling before they moved in."

"They? You mean him and his wife?"

"No. Actually, I don't believe they'd met then. Grandpa had a business partner."

The officer poised the tip of his pen against the open notebook. "Could you give me the partner's name?"

"I don't know it, but I'll ask my grandfather about him if you'd like."

"Please do." Sergeant Hoffman again wrote in his notebook. "How did your grandfather feel about Mrs. Evans?"

"Why all the questions about Caroline Evans?" Brentin asked.

The officer's facial muscles tensed, and all at once, Mikaela suspected what he would not say. "Is it certain, then? That it is her body out there?"

"All I can tell you, officially, is the body is female."

"But unofficially?" Brentin prodded.

Sergeant Hoffman glanced between the two of them then held Mikaela's gaze. "I suppose I might as well tell you since it might already be in the news. We don't know how it was leaked, but . . . Unofficially, the body did have some belongings that indicate she might have been Caroline Evans. We're investigating that possibility while we wait for more conclusive proof. So again, Miss York, how did your grandfather feel about Mrs. Evans?"

"All he ever told me was he loved her like a mother and she cared for him like a son."

"Shouldn't you be asking her grandfather these questions?" Brentin asked.

"We will," the sergeant said without looking away from Mikaela. "Did your grandfather have anything to gain from Mrs. Evans's death?"

"No. What could there be? He already owned this property." Mikaela's stomach churned. She pinched the skin at her throat to stop her fingers from trembling, but they didn't.

"Money, perhaps? Records indicate she was a wealthy woman."

"That's ridiculous," Mikaela said.

"Why?"

"Because he has too soft a heart. We had to put our pet dog down a few years ago because she was dying of old age, and he couldn't bear to be with her when the vet gave her the shot."

Sergeant Hoffman wrote in his notebook, and all at once, Brentin wrapped his arm around Mikaela's shoulders and pulled her against his side. Mikaela jolted. She gaped at him and quickly looked away. What—why—since Trevor had died, no man, except her grandfather, had hugged her like that, like he was worried about her.

"I can't see the point in upsetting Miss York with such questions," Brentin said.

"It's all right." Mikaela didn't move, only felt heat creep into her cheeks. She should step away from Brentin. Why didn't she? He was dating Amiria.

Sergeant Hoffman's expression turned thoughtful. "I understand your discomfort, Miss York, and though we haven't officially determined the body is that of Mrs. Evans, she was reported missing from Auckland three weeks after she moved there from here. Perhaps your grandfather knew of her disappearance?"

"He's never said anything about it to me."

"Are you saying, then, you think Caroline Evans was murdered?" Brentin asked.

"If that is her body, then yes, we believe it is very likely. It is also why we need to question your grandfather, Miss York. Kotuku Inn and the surrounding grounds did belong to him at that time. I understand he'll be here in a few days?"

"Y-yes. My grandmother just died, and he had some business he needed to take care of, but he also—"

Sergeant Hoffman's lips formed a stiff, suspicious smile.

Mikaela frowned. *Too much info.* If the officer already suspected her grandfather of killing Mrs. Evans, telling him her grandmother had just died wouldn't help anything. "I came ahead to make sure the renovations began as planned. Actually, that's another reason he couldn't have anything to do with Mrs. Evans's death. He contracted for a new stairway right where the workers found the body. If he'd known it was there, he wouldn't have had them dig around it, would he?"

"That is an important point," he said.

Brentin squeezed Mikaela's arm, but Mikaela stepped away.

"Can you tell us how the woman died?" Brentin said.

"Blunt force trauma. She had a cracked skull."

Mikaela shoved her fingers inside her front jeans pockets. *The sergeant's watching for my response. Don't move.*

"We'll speak with your grandfather in person when he arrives," the sergeant continued. "For now, would you please give me his phone number?"

Mikaela complied.

"Is that all, Sergeant?" Brentin asked.

"Yes, for now. Thank you for your time." He closed his notebook, slid it inside his front shirt pocket, and, after a quick nod, headed toward the back of the inn.

"What should we do first?" Brentin asked when the officer was well out of earshot.

"The first thing I need to do is call my grandfather and find out what he wants me to do. You've been really great, sticking with me, but I'll take care of this. You've got your films to work on. And there's the convention. And I'm sure you've got plans with Amiria."

His eyes widened. "Don't worry about any of that. I'll figure them out. But this . . . I would like to help if I can."

"Really?"

"This is important."

Mikaela pressed her hand against her chest and looked out across the front property. "What you need to do is important too," she said at last. "Why don't you go ahead and work on your film. I have to get hold of my grandfather before I do anything else anyway. After that, if I need you, I'll knock on your door."

"Promise?"

"I promise."

"Okay." His expression tightened, but he didn't say anything more. She gave him a quick nod good-bye and walked along the length of the manicured bushes until she reached the opening that led onto the grassy field. She logged onto her Skype account. Her grandfather answered after the second ring.

"Hello? Mikaela?"

"Sorry to call at such a weird time, but something's come up." She quickly repeated what the officer had told her about the body, its supposed identity, and their desire to contact him. She also told him what little she'd told Sergeant Hoffman.

Silence filled the other end of the line.

"Grandpa? Are you okay?"

"I'm a bit shocked is all. You said Caroline went missing? I never heard anything about that. She moved out the day we closed on the house. That was the last I saw of her. It seems someone did contact my partner and me once, asking if we knew where she might be, but it was so long ago . . . How could she have come back to Rotorua, died, and been buried in my backyard without me knowing about it?"

Mikaela winced. She should have thought more about calling him before she'd done so. He'd just lost his wife and an almost-grandson-in-law. And he wasn't young. "I don't know. I hope I didn't say anything to the police that I shouldn't have."

"I'm sure you didn't. All there is to tell is the truth. But how could I not have known?" he repeated. "The only extended amount of time I wasn't there that first month was about a week after we took over the inn. I drove out to Hamilton to pick up a specially carved chair I'd purchased for the lounge, and I stayed overnight. I suppose something could have happened at that time, but even then my business partner should have been there. He'd have noticed something like that."

"Would he have told you about it if he had?"

"I believe he would have—yes."

"What was his name?"

"Hunapo Greig."

Mikaela converted the name to memory. "And Grandma wasn't there at that time, right? I'm just trying to make sure I have the time line right for the police."

"Hunapo and I ran Kotuku Inn until he married three years later. Actually, his wife introduced your grandmother to me."

"So you and Grandma got married in 19 . . ."

"—70."

"After that, you two and the Griegs ran the inn together?"

"Yes. Until 1980."

Mikaela thought she heard sadness creep into his voice. "What happened?"

"We argued over how to run the business. In the end, your grandmother and I bought out his shares to the inn, and we parted ways."

"Do you know where he is now?"

"I heard he left New Zealand. That's all I know."

"Maybe we ought to try to find him. He might know something you don't."

"I'd rather not, Mikaela."

"Why?"

"Things didn't end well between us. At any rate, it would be a waste of time and expense. He loved Mrs. Evans."

"Like you did?"

"More. This news would tear him apart."

Mikaela's voice rose slightly. "That may be, but if the police are going to get to the bottom of this, they need to contact everyone who might have known something." *I won't let them pin this on you.*

# Chapter 13

BRENTIN SHOULD HAVE GONE TO his room to work on his film as he'd told Mikaela he would, but as he watched her walk toward the outlying grove of trees, he realized there was no way he could concentrate on his work. Not with her troubled eyes staring at him through the back of his thoughts. First, he'd make sure Mikaela was all right, and then he'd work. No one, not even Amiria, could fault him for that.

The front door swung open behind him. Brentin, at the top of the porch staircase, looked over his shoulder just as Frank Kendrick rushed past him. He leapt down the stairs and raced across the driveway to his Nissan.

"Hey!" Brentin called. "Has something happened?"

Frank didn't respond. He only jumped in his car and skidded down the lane.

Worry stomped on Brentin's gut. Was someone hurt? Like Frank's new wife, Sara? Or Amiria? He scanned the windows and roofline—no sign of danger—and hurried to the door, but as he grabbed the handle, Sara pushed it open. Brentin jolted backward against the exterior wall.

"He left?" Sara raced to the edge of the porch and looked back at Brentin. Red rimmed her eyes, and tears stained her cheeks.

Brentin moved away from the wall. He peeked through the door into the entrance hall. No change. All quiet. Tui's office door was closed just as it usually was. His nerves settled. "Yeah," he said to Sara. "Frank raced down that road as if his life depended on it. Is everything okay? No one needs a doctor or anything, do they?"

Sara shook her head. She slumped onto the top stair and lowered her face in her hands. "Men are so dumb."

Brentin arched his eyebrow. What could he say to that?

"Why would he just run off like that?" she added.

Brentin leaned back against the railing. He hated it when girls cried. He never knew what to do. His oldest sister once told him crying was a girl's relief valve and all he needed to do was listen—not give advice, to be there if she needed him. He was willing to do that, but how did a guy know when he'd listened and *been there* enough? Especially when he barely knew the girl? "I don't know why he ran off," he said, "but I expect he'll be back."

"What makes you think so?"

"He married you, didn't he?" At last, Mikaela was on her way back. She'd just crossed through the gap in the bushes and now walked across the asphalt driveway toward them. "A man doesn't just leave the woman he loves."

Sara broke into a new wave of tears. Brentin opened his mouth to say something but closed it again and instead lifted his hand to wave to Mikaela—maybe she would know what to say. Mikaela was running her hand up the length of her arm and looking from one end of the house to the other like she was searching for something or—*wait a minute. Is she nervous?*

As if on cue, prickles tapped like thousands of cold, dry raindrops across the back of his neck. Was someone watching them? He scanned the yard, the parking area, but saw nothing but cars.

Mikaela stopped at the foot of the stairs. She looked up at Brentin. "Sergeant Hoffman's still here, isn't he?"

He gave her a quick nod and glanced again at the carport.

"I thought you were going to work on your films."

He shrugged. "Did you get hold of your grandfather?"

"I did." She held his gaze for a long moment as if there was more she wanted to say, but then she looked to Sara. "Are you all right?"

Sara lifted her head like she was startled to see Mikaela standing there. "Yes. No. I don't know. Here, let me get out of your way." She quickly stood and sidestepped toward the railing.

"You're not in my way," Mikaela said.

Just then, some sort of look passed between the two women. Brentin had no idea what it meant, but Mikaela's eyes narrowed gently, and her voice softened. "But I'm happy to listen if you'd like to talk."

Sara slumped back onto the stair. She glanced between Mikaela and Brentin but finally focused on Mikaela. "I'm not wrong in thinking Frank and I should spend our honeymoon together, right?"

Mikaela's smile froze. Her posture stiffened. It was the same defensive stance Brentin's mother had taken soon after his father had died whenever people told her how sorry they were, and a lump in Brentin's throat thudded into his core like an upside-down pot of mashed potatoes. Was Mikaela trying to stop herself from crying? Was she thinking about her deceased fiancé?

"I don't think you're wrong," Mikaela said. "Newlyweds generally spend their honeymoons together."

"What did he expect me to say?" Sara blurted. "Keeping our plans flexible is great, but there are some things I don't want to miss out on while we're in New Zealand. It wasn't like what I'd asked him to do was all that much. Just a couple of activities that Frank was excited to do too. So I scheduled them. I even wrote out an itinerary. But this morning, I reminded him we were going to the Maori village today, and he said we couldn't, that we were hiking Mount Doom."

"Can you exchange the tickets for another day?" Brentin asked.

"No. I checked their website, and they're sold out for the rest of the week."

"Did you tell him that?" Mikaela said.

"Yes, but his friends who flew down here from the US with us e-mailed him last night and said they're hiking Mount Doom today. Frank told them we'd be there too. I told him I wanted to go, and I do, but on another day."

Brentin shifted his weight and looked at his hands. Alone, Mount Doom would have been his activity of choice too, but if he were a newlywed, he'd want to be with his wife most of all, no matter what the activities were. "Apparently Frank didn't agree with you," he said.

Sara stared down the drive toward the highway. "What am I supposed to do now?"

"I think you're the only one who can answer that," Mikaela said. "We don't know him the way you do."

New tears filled Sara's brown eyes.

"But I'm sure he'll come back. Trevor always came back to me after we had a disagreement." She rested her hand on Sara's shoulder, and Sara clasped it with her left hand. Her wedding ring glinted in the sunlight. Mikaela paled.

Brentin instinctively inched toward her. If Mikaela grew too upset, would she let him comfort her? Wrap his arm around her shoulders again?

"Is Trevor your boyfriend?" Sara said to Mikaela. "Or are you married?"

Mikaela clenched and unclenched her fingers. This time, Brentin stepped beside her close enough that his left elbow pressed against her right one. She didn't move away from him, but she did turn her face toward the driveway.

"Mikaela's not married," Brentin said. "Neither am I, but I do have four older sisters who are. Every time one of them gets into an argument with her spouse, one or the other always runs back because they love each other."

Sara squinted, and her face narrowed, but in the next second, she sniffed and wiped her eyes with the back of her hand. "I'm starting to think love isn't enough."

"I agree with Brentin," Mikaela whispered. She looked back to them. Her lips quivered slightly, but at least no tear tracks streaked her cheeks.

Gravel gritted along the asphalt.

"It's Frank!" Sara leapt down the stairs and raced across the sidewalk toward the driveway. She reached Frank's car just as he pulled into a parking space. He jumped out, gathered her into his arms, and kissed her.

"I'm glad that's settled," Brentin said.

"I wish everything was that easy to fix." Mikaela drew back her shoulders, stepped off the stairs, and headed—almost marched—toward the carport.

He moved in beside her. "So what happened with your grandfather?"

"He gave me the name of his partner. I figured I better pass that information on to the sergeant."

"Want help?" he said.

"Thanks, but I can take it from here. Besides, I thought you were going to work on your films."

"I'll get it done. But like I said, this is important too." They rounded the corner of the carport. He caught her arm, stopping her. "Tell me what I can do."

"Work on your films. I'd hate it if you didn't finish them because of me. And I'm fine. I have that sculpture to draw, and I also have that meeting with Andrew Evans." She checked the time on her cell phone. "He might already be here actually."

He swallowed, but the lump in his throat only grew bigger. "All right. I'll see you later, okay?"

"Sure."

He watched her turn away, watched the ends of her blonde hair wisp across the back of her neck, watched her walk around the corner of the house. At last, he inhaled and looked up at the cloudless, midmorning sky. *When did my feelings change? And why?* No answers came to him, but one truth wrapped itself around his heart. All his thoughts, emotions, senses— everything that made him who he was now urged him toward Mikaela. Not toward Amiria. The only thing he didn't know was how he was going to tell them both. Or when.

# Chapter 14

IT HAD TAKEN MIKAELA LESS than ten minutes to give Hunapo's name to the police and to return to the inn, but the moment she stepped through the back door into the kitchen, the warm aroma of sausage, pastry, and something mixed with black pepper washed over her. She hadn't eaten since the banquet the night before, and hunger gnawed at the bottom of her stomach. Andrew Evans sat at a table and looked up when she came in.

"There you are, my dear," Tui said. "Andrew Evans says he has an appointment with you."

"He does."

"You might as well get a bit of breakfast while it's still warm. I'll get you a plate." She nodded to the empty chair next to the man dressed in a black leather jacket and jeans.

"That would be great. Thanks." Mikaela scanned the dining area next to the kitchen. Ira, the blind novelist, and his assistant, Vicky, sat at the middle table, and Brentin sat alone at the table next to the left side windows. Tui and Amiria, wearing white aprons with jade humanoid tikis printed on the fronts, worked behind the *L*-shaped kitchen counter.

Mikaela looked at Brentin and lifted her hands querulously. "Your film?" she mouthed.

He shrugged and glanced between her and Amiria, who seemed to be watching Mikaela a bit closer than she usually did. Amiria wiped her hands on the front of her apron, took a plate of food to Brentin, and lowered herself into the seat across from him.

Mikaela, in turn, sat at Andrew's table. "Well, Mr. Evans? You said you have questions you think I can help you with?"

He slid his juice glass closer to his half-eaten plate of food. "Straight to the point. I like that. And call me Andrew." He rested his elbows on the table and leaned slightly toward her. "As I told you last night, Miss York, I'm a reporter with the *Daily Post*. My editor asked me to see what I could find out about the body found in your backyard. I understand it's Caroline Evans."

He paused as if he expected Mikaela to confirm or deny his statement, but when she didn't, he continued. "At any rate, since Caroline married my grandfather's brother, my editor thought I was his best choice for a more in-depth story. You'll help me with it, won't you?"

Mikaela stiffened. Was he one of the news leaks Sergeant Hoffman had warned her about? "I really don't know what I can tell you. I didn't even know the woman."

Tui placed a plate of scrambled eggs and two sausage rolls in front of Mikaela. "I must say I'm quite surprised to see you know this man."

"Do you know him?"

Andrew flashed a quick smile. "We've met on several occasions."

"Amiria and his younger sissta used to run together," Tui said as if that explained everything. She then returned to her work behind the counter.

"In any case," Andrew continued, "it seems to me we might be able to piece out how Caroline wound up out there if we work together."

Mikaela broke off a piece of her buttered toast. "What makes you think I care anything about it?"

"Don't you?"

"All that matters to me, Andrew, is that my grandfather isn't blamed for whatever happened to her. Other than that, I'm happy to let the police figure it out."

He leaned against the back of his chair, steepled his fingers, and lifted an eyebrow. "Aren't you even a little curious? Very few people find dead bodies buried in their backyards."

Suddenly, Ira slapped his hand on his tabletop. "Why are you bothering the girl with this, mate? She's not even from around here. And she certainly hasn't been alive long enough to know anything about Caroline Evans or why anyone would want to murder her."

Andrew turned slowly toward him. "I never said anything about Mrs. Evans being murdered."

"Maybe not, but the implication was there."

"I'm not saying you're right, but even if I had said she was murdered, what does it matter if I ask her about it? I have to begin my investigation somewhere."

"Bah! Why not start with your own relatives? Most murders are committed by family members."

A sliver of pressure released from around Mikaela's heart like a miniscule leak in a hot air balloon. If only the police thought like him. Maybe then they'd focus on someone other than her grandfather.

Andrew stared at Ira for a long moment. "I did talk with them before coming here, sir, and they knew only of a rumor that Caroline and her husband had kept a treasure hidden somewhere on this property and that soon after she moved to Auckland, she went missing."

"I've never heard about a treasure," Mikaela said. *Wait! Is he talking about that doll?*

"Treasure, eh," Ira said. "Worth a lot of money, I expect."

Andrew swallowed his bite of food and shrugged.

"Greed is one of the most powerful motivators," Ira added. "Who would have inherited that treasure—if there had, indeed, been one?"

"That hardly matters since no one found it and since the property now belongs to someone else. What's more, murderers can also be friends of the victim. Like Miss York's grandfather."

"My grandfather would never kill anyone."

"How do you know?"

"He's not a violent man."

"I have to agree with Mikaela on that one." Tui spread a stack of stoneware bowls across the top of the counter. "In all the years I've known him, Joseph Parker's never even raised his voice at me. By the way, for those of you staying here at Kotuku Inn, there was a produce sale at the corner dairy this morning, so I decided to make a light salad for each of your lunches. Since some of you have food allergies, I'm taping your names to the dishes."

"That's very considerate of you," Mikaela said.

Tui flicked her hand, dismissing the compliment, and walked to the refrigerator. Ira leaned back in his chair. He pressed the back of his fork against his pursed lips. "Playing devil's advocate to you, Miss York," he said. "I've researched many crimes over the years, and one thing I've learned is quiet men can be just as guilty as loud ones."

Mikaela clenched her hands together on top of the table, and Andrew briefly placed his hand over top of them. A show of kindness?

"Not in this case," she said to Ira. "He's not guilty."

"What are you getting at, Ira?" Vicky's voice, though sharp, seemed to linger over his name. "Have you noticed something the rest of us haven't?"

"Not at all. It's only that, as a writer, I must constantly ask myself *what if*? Like, what if Caroline Evans didn't come here of her own volition after she sold the place? What if whoever killed her moved her body to this location?"

"That's a pretty wild *what if*," Brentin said. "And a bit coincidental that someone would just happen to move her to where she once lived."

Mikaela looked to Brentin. His cheeks were flushed. Was it because Amiria sat so close to him?

"Perhaps," Ira said, "but while I must avoid coincidences in my books, in real life some criminals—the interesting ones anyway—do all kinds of *wild* and *coincidental* things."

"Actually," Andrew said, "your idea might not be that far-fetched. The missing person report said Caroline's car was found intact in a rural area outside of Hamilton about a year after she disappeared."

"Of course it was." Ira slapped the table again and grinned. "What a great twist to the story. Either Caroline's body or her car or both were moved to a location separate from the crime."

"Unless they're unrelated incidents," Vicky said.

Ira nodded, and Sara and Frank, holding hands, walked into the kitchen.

"Welcome, my dears," Tui said.

"It smells so good in here we couldn't resist stopping in," Sara said.

Frank's gaze hesitated on Andrew before he led Sara to the empty table between Ira and Brentin. Mikaela glanced down at her hands so as not to watch the newlyweds so closely, but in the next second, she looked up at them again. Sara sat in a chair, and Frank kissed the top of her head. She put her hand over his, where it rested on her shoulder, and held it while he sat in the chair next to her. Tui brought them their breakfast.

"Anyone can research the case as well as the police can," Ira mused, "and this one's proving to be quite interesting. I've a good mind to investigate it myself."

"I thought you already—"

He clasped Vicky's hand, stopping her from saying whatever she was about to say, and continued with, "As it is, I expect you young people are so used to the Internet you haven't even considered the library."

Mikaela furrowed her brows. Up until the last few minutes, she hadn't even known she *was* investigating.

"I've visited the place from time to time," Andrew said. "What do you suggest we look for there?"

Ira seemed pleased. "If I were you, I'd look through the archived newspapers. Start with, say, the date your aunt sold this place."

"I hardly think my aunt selling Kotuku Inn would be big enough news to make the papers," Andrew said. "At any rate, I did that already."

"Sounds like you know more about this case than you've let on," Mikaela said.

He shrugged, but his gaze focused on Ira. "Any other ideas, Mr. Lawrence?"

"What about other stories or ads that included her? As I understand it, Caroline Evans was quite well known in the area."

"Exactly." Mikaela hadn't realized she'd spoken so loudly until everyone looked at her. "I only mean there must be lots of people who might have killed her."

"You're right about her being quite the woman around town," Tui said. "My mother used to work at Kotuku Inn. She told me Mrs. Evans always donated to one cause or another, even helped finance a new school. Mum said people always figured Mrs. Evans got her money from that treasure you mentioned. I even tried to find it a year or so after I came to work for the Parkers." She sighed, placed two bowls of salad, plastic-wrapped and labeled, in the refrigerator and slid two more bowls next to her larger bowls of ingredients. "Mr. Parker said I was silly to let myself get caught up in such an unsubstantiated tale."

"Not if it was—is—real." Ira tapped his fingertips on the table next to Vicky's hand. "As I said, every good mystery comes down to motive, and a treasure—greed—is one of the strongest. So is love. But if I were investigating this case, I wouldn't stop with either of those just yet. Dig beneath the surface. You might just find other more interesting possibilities. Like the novel Vicky and I are working on right now. From the outside, the murderer's motive looks like lust, but on the inside . . ." His sudden smile reminded Mikaela of *Alice in Wonderland*'s Cheshire cat, who always knew more than he said.

"What other motives are there, generally?" Mikaela asked.

"That, my child, is the ultimate question."

"You!" Vicky lightly swatted Ira's upper arm. "Quit teasing them."

Ira's eyebrows flitted upward, but his smug expression remained.

"I'm sorry, Miss York," Vicky said. "Ira isn't so forthcoming today. There are many motives for murder, but he and I have found that the most interest-ing and possibly the most plausible ones are found through incongruences."

Brentin, who Mikaela noticed had been closely watching the exchange even as Amiria talked to him, furrowed his brows. Andrew nodded in response to Vicky's comment, and Sara and Frank played footsies under the table.

"I don't understand what you mean," Mikaela said.

"Give them an example, Vicky."

"Very well." Vicky touched Ira's hand then glanced about the room. "Amiria, do you mind if I use you as an example?"

"No, go ahead."

"Think of this," Vicky said. "Amiria studies fashion magazines, and she dresses in the most up-to-date styles when she goes out, but she spends most of her days and almost all of her nights here at Kotuku Inn, cooking and cleaning for her mother. *Why?*"

"A girl has to support herself," Amiria said. "And anyway, I love this place."

Brentin placed his hand on Amiria's forearm. "She's also loyal."

"Ah," Ira said. "What else?"

Vicky glanced at Amiria. Amiria's cheeks had flushed deep red. "No, that's enough," Vicky said. "I think they get the idea."

"I didn't," Brentin said. "What does any of that have to do with motive?"

"Only that people have many needs, some of them opposite to each other. And those needs can drive them to do things that conflict with one another. Amiria loves her home and family but wants something else. Which of her needs will win the day?" Ira held up three fingers. "See what I mean? Incongruences lead to needs which lead to motives."

Tui wiped the counter, Frank lowered his face to Sara's, and Mikaela stared at Ira. She had never before thought of motivations in that light, but Ira and Vicky were right. In fact, Mikaela had flown across the world to New Zealand because she wanted to help her grandfather even though another part of her longed to stay home with her memories.

"So, Mikaela, what do you think?" Andrew said. "Should we go to the library?"

Mikaela glanced at the others without really seeing them. "I admit this has been quite fascinating, but I'd still rather leave the investigation to the police."

"You're willing to risk your grandfather's future on them?"

"What? No. They'll figure it out."

"Will they?" Andrew held her gaze and again patted her hand. "Come with me. Let's make sure they get it right."

Mikaela looked to Tui. She seemed to trust Andrew. And her grandfather trusted Tui, so she ought to be able to trust Andrew, shouldn't she? Besides, what if the police did get it wrong and she could have helped but chose not to? "Oh, all right. I'll go. But if we don't find anything to clear his name, I'm done with it."

"Great! I'll meet you outside Tui's office as soon as you're ready. I left both helmets in there."

"Helmets?"

"I brought my motorcycle."

"I'm jealous," Frank said. "I saw it outside. Looks like a great ride, bro."

"It is."

Sara's smile wavered. "And a bit dangerous, don't you think?"

"Only a little, sweet thing," Frank said. "That's part of the fun."

Sara stared at her husband for a long moment then brushed her thumb across his cheek. "Ready to go?"

"Yeah, babe." Hand in hand, they left the kitchen.

"I'll probably be a few minutes," Mikaela said to Andrew on her way out of the kitchen. "I have something I need to do before I leave."

"I'll text you on my way to pick you up at the library about four thirty, all right?" Brentin called. "For that interview with Leanne Sabey."

Mikaela paused. Why did Brentin's face look so pinched? "Yeah, sure. That'll be fine."

"You have my number, right?"

"I have it. But Tui, if the police finish early enough for the renovators to start up again, will you please call me? I'd like to be here, if I can."

"Of course, dear."

"I'll bring you back if they do," Andrew said. "It's no problem."

Out of the corner of her eye, she saw Brentin glower. "That'd be great," she said to Andrew. "Oh, and Tui, it doesn't look like I'll make it back for lunch."

"I'll take hers," Ira said.

Vicky rolled her eyes at Ira. "You don't even like salad."

"Only because it leaves me hungry. Two salads, on the other hand . . ."

Mikaela smiled at him. "It's yours."

* * *

Inside her room, Mikaela went to her closet and pulled open the sliding door. Her backpack lay on the floor beneath her dress clothes, and her sketchbook rested on top of it. She reached for it, brushed her fingers across the cardboard cover, and before she could talk herself out of it, pulled a black, graphite pencil out of the pack's front pocket. Yes, she'd spoken rashly when she'd told Brentin she'd sketch the sculpture for her grandfather, and yes, she didn't have much time before she needed to meet Andrew, but rash or late, she would keep that commitment or die—*cry*—trying.

She took the sketchbook and pencil to the table and opened to the first blank page. *I can do this*, she thought as tears filled her eyes. *I will do this*. Brentin was right. That pencil—her art—was an extension of her, and no matter how heartbroken she might be, she had to let creativity live inside her again. If she didn't, she'd always feel empty.

No longer thinking, she quickly outlined what she could remember of the shapes and contours of the sculpture she'd seen at the Coopers' hotel that morning and held it in front of her. It was a simple sketch, one that needed more work before it was fit to show to anyone, including her grandfather, but every time her pencil glided across the paper, she felt bits of her grief slide to a new place in her heart, a place where she could bear to carry it. *Thank you, Brentin.*

At length, Mikaela grabbed a tissue from the box on her nightstand, wiped her eyes, and determined she'd find some way to thank him before he left in a couple of days. Not doing so would be selfish. And she didn't want Brentin, if he ever thought of her in the future, to remember her as selfish.

# Chapter 15

MIKAELA FOUND ANDREW IN THE foyer outside Tui's office just where he'd told her he'd be.

"Sorry I took so long," she said.

He lifted his eyes to hers. For the first time, Mikaela noticed they were the same color as his blue jeans. His lashes were also longer than any man's lashes had a right to be, but his eyes weren't nearly as charismatic as Brentin's. She swallowed. When had she noticed Brentin's eyes?

"No problem," he said. "You said you've never ridden a motorcycle before? Well, you're in for a treat."

"I'll hold you to your word."

The two left the inn and walked down the stairs to the makeshift parking lot. They stopped in front of a red-and-silver Kawasaki motorcycle. Andrew handed her a pair of goggles and a red helmet. He put on a black one. The two climbed onto the seat. Mikaela placed the flat of her hands against the sides of his waist.

He revved the engine. "Hold on!"

The motorcycle lurched backward with such force Mikaela had to clutch at his sides. The front of her helmet bumped against the back of his.

"You better hold on tighter than that." Andrew grabbed her hands, pulled them around his middle, and shifted into forward. He drove down the driveway to the main road.

The wind whipped against her cheeks and neck. She closed her eyes and didn't fully open them again until they stopped at a red traffic light about five minutes later. Mikaela, still holding onto Andrew's waist, slid backward until there were several inches between them.

"Don't let go yet," Andrew said. "The closer we get into town, the more traffic we'll have to weave through."

The light turned green. Andrew followed the car ahead of them toward town. He smoothly moved in and out of the traffic and had almost caught the next green light when his shoulders tensed. He leaned forward, swore, and swerved into the outside lane. A green pickup entered the intersection in front of them. Andrew braked.

Mikaela jerked forward, her helmet crashing against Andrew's. The motorcycle skidded to a stop, barely missing the pickup.

Andrew slammed on his horn. "Are you trying to kill us?"

The driver—man or woman, she couldn't tell—barely looked their direction before completing the turn and continuing down the road.

Mikaela exhaled. "I'm glad you saw him in time."

"It did make life a bit exciting there for a minute. I know we gotta get to the library, but I feel like a drink. What do you say about stopping at a pub first?"

Mikaela stiffened and leaned back from him. "You can if you'd like, but drop me off at the library." *And you definitely won't drive me back to the inn.*

"You're not serious."

"I don't drink."

"Now I know you're not serious." But even so, he continued on to the library and didn't speak again until he'd pulled into a parking space and switched off the engine.

Mikaela climbed off the back of his motorcycle. She undid the helmet clasp and handed it to him. "Thanks for the ride."

His gaze dropped to her trembling fingers. "The drink would be on me."

She half smiled. "That's kind of you, but I really don't drink alcohol." When he furrowed his brows, she turned away from him. Her legs wobbled as she walked to the front entrance, but when she reached for the door handle, she stopped. On the ground just in front of it, red splotches stained the concrete. Someone must have spilled something. Something like juice. Mikaela's thoughts froze, and her breath knotted inside her like a ball of tightly wound rubber bands. Tui's warning dream about the doll, the tutu juice on the sidewalk, a coming murder. That near accident couldn't have had anything to do with Tui's superstitions, could it?

"Is everything okay?" Andrew asked from behind her.

"Yeah, uh—"

"What is it?"

She forced a laugh. "That coloring caught me off guard is all. Tui told me about a dream she had the other night, and it—it reminded me of it." Another fake laugh.

"It must have been some dream. Your hands are shaking even more than they were before."

"It's only that Tui was so certain." Mikaela quickly told him of the dream. "Tui's really superstitious."

"You'll find a lot of kiwis are, especially the older Maoris, but I expect nothing will come of the dream." He opened the glass door for her, and the two stepped into the entryway. An elaborate dollhouse display of a local historic mansion filled the far left corner. *Pumice concrete exterior, classic frame*, Mikaela thought, but rather than examining it further, she headed to the customer service desk at her right. The sooner she focused on something other than the doll, the better.

"So what did you do with the doll?" Andrew whispered. "Do you still have it?"

"I took it to another hotel for safekeeping."

A heavy-set Maori woman with a bulbous nose and dark curly hair looked up at her from behind the desk. "Can I help you?"

"I understand you have archives of Rotorua's newspapers," Mikaela said.

"That we do." The woman's eyes focused on a point above and behind Mikaela's right shoulder. "Gidday, Mr. Evans. It's good to see you again."

Mikaela turned to him. He placed his hand on her shoulder but looked at the librarian. "I assume the microfilm equipment is available today?"

"It is." The librarian motioned to the elderly white woman who stood next to a computer on the other side of the room to take her place at the customer service desk. When her replacement was in place, she led Mikaela and Andrew to the stairs at the back of the foyer.

"What should we start with?" Andrew asked when they reached the first-floor landing.

"Ira suggested we should start with your family."

Andrew's face muscles tightened, and Mikaela bit her lip. Right. Accusing family wasn't nice. "Sorry."

"Ira?" the woman said. "You aren't speaking of Ira Lawrence, are you?"

"He's the one who told us to come here," Mikaela said.

She led them up the next flight of stairs. "Ira and his assistant have spent a lot of time here the past few weeks. They were researching Caroline Evans, I believe."

"They were?" Mikaela said.

"Is that a problem?"

"No. But it'd be nice if he'd told us what he'd learned rather than sending us here like a couple of kids."

The three reached the second floor. The woman led them past another information desk, around the elevator, and on toward the long family history room. It contained two tables, a few chairs, and three microfilm readers. "What year?" she asked.

"I'd like to start with 1964," Mikaela said.

"The entire year?"

"Yes, if that's all right."

"O' course. Wait here. I'll get them for you." She entered the small archives area at the back of the room.

"What should we focus on first?" Andrew asked.

Mikaela removed her jacket, draped it around the chair beside the closest reader, and took the notebook and pen from her backpack. "Someone— other than my grandfather—who could have killed your aunt."

"Right. People she knew. And maybe causes she supported. They might include names of those she worked with." Andrew lowered himself into the chair next to the one she'd claimed. "I'll start with the days between when she moved from Rotorua to when my family reported her as missing."

"All right. I'll look through the days prior to that." She sat and opened her notebook to the first page. She wrote *Possible Motives* on the top line and added *Grandpa didn't profit from Caroline Evans's death; he earned all his money* on the next line. Then she turned the page, drew a line down the middle, dividing it into two columns, and wrote *Caroline Evans Facts* at the top of one column and *Miscellaneous Facts* on the other.

The librarian returned with four small white boxes which she placed on the desk with the microfilm reader. "Which month?"

"The earliest you have."

She lifted the glasses attached to the chain around her neck and read the labels on each of the boxes. "Will December 8, 1963, through February 14, 1964, do?"

"Sure."

She removed the microfilm from the box and loaded the reel into the reader. "Look through this viewfinder and turn this wheel."

Mikaela obeyed.

"I'll take this one." Andrew loaded it into the next machine.

"Let me know if I can help you with anything else," the librarian said.

"Actually," Mikaela said, "could you bring us 1963 and the rest of 1965 too?"

"And 1966," Andrew added.

"Of course."

When the librarian left, Mikaela asked him, "Why 1966?"

"I thought we ought to watch for someone with newfound wealth."

"That makes sense." Mikaela scrolled past several articles about racism against Maoris in sports. "Do you know how your great-aunt felt about the Maoris?"

"Same as any other white woman felt in those years, I suppose. Tui's mother worked for her, if that means anything."

Mikaela turned back to the first page in her notebook and under *Possible Motives*, she listed *Greed* and *Racism*.

A few minutes later, the librarian brought out more small boxes, and Mikaela replaced her reel with a new one.

"Now that's a classic," Andrew said. "An entire article on bikinis."

Ignoring him, Mikaela scrolled through the blank slides to the beginning of her new film. She rubbed at a tense knot on the back of her neck, hoping the movement would empty the image in her mind of Caroline Evans wearing her fishhook earrings and walking lightly, perhaps nostalgically, through her one-time backyard the night she'd died. "I'm starting to wonder if money might have been the least likely motive."

"Why so?"

"If someone killed her for money, why wasn't her car stripped and its parts sold? It wouldn't have been abandoned intact."

"Good point. But you're assuming the abandoned car and her death are related."

"True." Mikaela turned back to her notebook. Under *Caroline Evans Facts*, she wrote *wealthy, generous, elderly, proud,* and *alone.* On the *Miscellaneous Facts* side, she wrote *car found intact.*

Andrew watched but said nothing.

Mikaela opened to the next page and drew a horizontal line through the middle of it. She labeled the new section *Suspects.* Now, if she could only find some names to list under it.

A few minutes after two o'clock, she and Andrew had finally made it through all the reels. While they'd printed a few images, they'd mostly kept notes. Andrew lifted his arms over his head and stretched. "The names of the causes and people Caroline donated money to aren't a lot to go on."

"Maybe not, but they are interesting." Mikaela tapped her finger over the final name she'd jotted in her notebook.

Andrew glanced at it. "Leanne Sabey? Isn't that the woman you're interviewing later?"

"Yeah. Her name's in this article about Kotuku Inn's treasure hunt. It says she was Caroline Evans's friend."

He lifted an eyebrow. "A friend hunting for Caroline's treasure? That seems a bit incongruent."

Mikaela half-smiled. "Tui said she did it, and she worked for Caroline."

"What about the other two names?"

"Also friends who were hunting for her treasure."

They double-checked each of the microfilm boxes to make sure they'd closed them before returning to the main floor. The librarian stood behind the front desk. Mikaela showed her the list of names and asked if she'd heard of them, but like Mikaela, she knew only Leanne Sabey. They were welcome to look through the local telephone book though, which they did. The names weren't there.

"Maybe Ms. Sabey knows them," Andrew said.

"I hope so." Mikaela adjusted her jacket collar and looked at the time on her phone. Three thirty. "There's still almost an hour left until Brentin picks me up. I wish we could go and interview Ms. Sabey now."

He frowned. "Text Brentin and find out if we can."

"Of course! I already know what questions he wants to ask her, so if we get finished with our questions . . ." She pulled out her phone. "Maybe my phone recorder will be good enough."

She quickly texted Brentin, and he immediately responded, saying the phone's recorder wouldn't work. Unfortunately, the soonest he could get to Ms. Sabey's was four thirty, but he would meet them there.

Mikaela frowned.

"Let me guess," Andrew said. "We've still got time to kill, eh."

*Kill. Murder.* Frowning, Mikaela pushed away sudden images of the doll, the red stains on the concrete, and Tui's dream. "Any chance you'd like to spend that time hiking around the forest across from Kotuku Inn? I've been hoping to check it out before my grandfather gets here."

"The Redwoods? That's a great place, but we won't have enough time to enjoy it. How about—I know! There's a thermal park on the west side of town. We can walk the trails alongside the mud pots."

"A thermal park in the middle of town? That's pretty awesome. Let's do it."

"Great." He pulled out his phone. "Wait a second while I send my editor a text, and then we'll go."

\* \* \*

Hunapo's heart raced. He thrashed his arms over his head and pounded his pillow, but the familiar images trailing across the blackness behind his eyelids didn't go away. *Wake up!*

His eyes, his thoughts didn't listen. Instead, red-haloed images of his wife, Reka, sitting on their couch and reading to their sons from her book of nursery rhymes plodded in front of him like a slow-motion movie. Night after night Reka had read to them. Hunapo had ignored the book, ignored the action—figured it was one of her motherly idiosyncrasies— but the night she'd taken her last breath, after he'd returned home from the hospital with his heart aching for the sight of her smile and the sound of her footsteps, he'd lifted her *Nursery Rhyme Treasures* from the coffee table and opened to its title page. His throat had constricted as he'd read the handwritten inscription. How had Reka kept her true feelings from him all those years?

*Dear Reka,*

*I thought of you the moment I saw this book. It can't compare to your sweetness, but still I hope you will love its contents as much as I love you. Hunapo is a lucky man.*

*Joseph Parker*

Hunapo gasped and at last opened his eyes. *Breathe. Soon that evil will be compensated.*

He took another deep breath. And another. He stared at the second hand on the wall clock ticking *24-25-26*. He should have known that a woman as beautiful and delicate as his Reka could never have loved him more than she'd loved the white man she'd dated before him. The man he, Hunapo, had once called brother.

The kitchen faucet turned on. A cupboard door clunked closed. Hunapo pressed the tip of his tongue against the sores on the top of his dry mouth. It must have already been four hours since he'd taken his last dose of meds. The nurse only made those sounds before she brought them to him. If only the pills better controlled the chemotherapy's side effects— and stopped his nightmares.

He looked to the shelf on the wall across from the foot of his bed. He'd put Reka's book on it when he'd first been diagnosed, just as most men might have set up a television to distract them from their pain and loss. But distractions weren't what Hunapo needed to finish his final days. He needed greater resolve and cleverness. He needed his ancestors.

His phone vibrated.

Hunapo reached for it. When he saw the texter's ID, his pulse raced again. Was Mikaela gone? Was Joseph finally the only one standing between him and final restoration? He read the text.

*Next attempt soon.*

# Chapter 16

A FEW MINUTES BEFORE FOUR thirty, Mikaela and Andrew parked the motorcycle in front of Ms. Sabey's pale brick home at the end of the retirement facility's well-kept cul-de-sac. Mikaela removed her helmet and started up the cement driveway toward Ms. Sabey's front door. Her cell phone buzzed. It was a text from Brentin.

*In the middle of something I can't stop. Please keep Ms. Sabey busy until I get there at five.*

Mikaela sent a quick reply—*Will do*—and knocked on her door.

"Looks like we'll be on our own for a bit after all," she said to Andrew when he caught up to her.

Before he could respond, Ms. Sabey opened the door. "Hello." She glanced at Andrew then back to Mikaela. "Where's Brentin?"

"He's going to be a little late," Mikaela said. "This is Andrew Evans. Is it all right if we ask you a few unrelated questions until Brentin gets here?"

Again she glanced between them before saying, "Of course. Come in."

Unlike the exterior of Ms. Sabey's home, which looked exactly like the other pale-yellow ramblers on her street, the inside decor practically screamed *The Lord of the Rings*. Thick books with fantastical covers filled a floor-to-ceiling bookshelf; posters of Eowen, Frodo, and Bilbo hung on what little wall space remained next to the shelf; and a log-framed couch with red cushions—reminiscent of hobbit home decor—divided the living room from the dining area.

Ms. Sabey squeezed Mikaela's hand and motioned for them to sit on the couch. "I expect you'll want to make this quick? So you can get ready for the ball."

"That's kind of you to worry about it, but I'm not going," Mikaela said.

"Brentin can't be happy about that."

"I doubt it bothers him at all. He's taking Amiria. And anyway, it's not like he can't do without my help. "

"On the contrary. Brentin told me he admires your abilities and depends on your input." In this light, Ms. Sabey's white hair, clear blue eyes, and pixie-like features gave her a much more Elfin appearance than Mikaela remembered from their first meeting at the convention center, but that tight, almost smiling expression . . . *She's definitely thinking something she's not saying.*

Mikaela cleared her throat. She pulled her notebook and pen from her pocket and lowered herself onto the far end of the couch. Andrew sat next to her.

Ms. Sabey took her place in the rocking chair across from them. "What questions do the two of you have for me?"

"They're about Caroline Evans," Andrew said.

"I suppose I should have expected as much. But like I told the officers who came by here earlier, I really don't know what I can tell you that might be helpful."

"They were here?" Andrew asked. "What did you tell them?"

"There now, young man, I can see why Mikaela might be interested in what I have to say, but I've heard of you. You're a reporter, and I'd rather not be quoted in one of your stories."

"Will it help if I give you my word that I won't quote you?" Andrew asked.

Mikaela turned and gave him a half smile. That was really generous of him. *Maybe I'll ask him not to quote me either.* "He's more than a reporter," Mikaela said. "Caroline was his great-aunt."

Ms. Sabey clasped her fingers together and settled against the back of her chair. She smiled, but her expression narrowed as if she was analyzing their comments. No matter her age, Leanne Sabey had her faculties about her. "Very well. I'll trust you," she said at last. "What do you want to know?"

"We'd like to hear what you told the police," Andrew said, "along with anything else you knew about Caroline."

"I'd imagine you, as her relative, would know more about Caroline than I do."

"Unfortunately, all my mother and aunts say of her is she was extremely selfish and kept to herself a lot."

"I'm not surprised," Ms. Sabey said, "but they were wrong. Caroline was a very giving person. Quiet, to be sure, but never selfish."

"Maybe they thought that because she lived so simply after she sold Kotuku Inn and moved to Auckland."

"I wouldn't put it past them. The truth was Caroline was getting along in years and didn't want to be bothered with the upkeep of a yard."

Andrew leaned forward. "But it was quite a large jump in lifestyles, don't you agree? To go from owning and running Kotuku Inn to living in a one-bedroom apartment?"

"Not as big of a jump as you might think. Kotuku Inn was much more secluded and quiet in those days than it is now. Caroline kept a few boarders, but from what I could see, the money she took in barely kept her going."

"Then how do you—how did she explain all her charitable donations?"

"I assume now you're speaking of the treasure.

"I am."

Ms. Sabey lifted the corners of her mouth into an almost smile. "Actually, I used to be curious about where she got her money too, but I was enough younger than she was that I never thought it proper to ask her. Our relationship was purely peripheral. We had some similar interests and went on a few outings together, but we never discussed one another's personal affairs."

Andrew leaned back in his seat and lifted an eyebrow. "That's hard to believe."

"Life for us in those days wasn't as open as it is now, young man. We were simply two married women with similar interests who needed to escape our everyday lives once in a while. The last thing we wanted was to bring the real world into that escape."

The two stared at each other.

"What kind of things did you have in common?" Mikaela asked.

"We both loved the ocean. I painted it, and Caroline relished its rolling power, its *supernatural energy*, she called it. I figured that was why she loved the fishhook symbol so much. It reminded her of the ocean."

Mikaela pressed her hand against the base of her scar and quickly lowered it to her chest as if it was one of Tui's fishhook necklaces. "It wasn't because of its so-called protective properties?"

"Heavens, no! Caroline was much too down-to-earth to put stock into such superstitions."

Mikaela's eyes widened. What would Tui say about that?

"Is this what you told the police?" Andrew said.

"They didn't ask anything about Caroline as a person. It would have been a much more pleasant conversation if they had."

"What did they ask you about?" Mikaela asked.

"Who her friends and neighbors were and if I had any idea why someone would want to kill her. As if I'd know." Her eyes moistened. "People did think she was proud, but I never heard of anyone wanting to hurt her. At any rate, almost everyone she knew is gone now. The officer hinted someone might have killed her for her money. If that's true, whoever did this couldn't have known her well. Everyone in town knew they only had to ask and she would give them what she could. The fact that she let people know she donated to different causes didn't change her generosity one iota. How else could she leave any sort of legacy behind? She had no children."

Mikaela opened her notebook. Under *Suspects*, she wrote *a stranger to Rotorua* next to the *Greed* and *Racism* motives. "Do you? Have children, I mean?"

"No."

"Was childlessness one of the things that brought you together?"

When Ms. Sabey didn't answer her, Mikaela looked up, biting her lip. Maybe she shouldn't have asked that. It was, after all, quite personal.

"It was one of the reasons," Ms. Sabey said at last.

Mikaela exhaled in relief. As far as she could tell, Ms. Sabey hadn't taken offense.

"My aunt had quite a different opinion about the 'gifts,'" Andrew said. "She said Caroline gave away all her money because she didn't want any of it to go to her family after she died."

"This aunt doesn't happen to be related to Caroline's sister Ellen, does she?" Ms. Sabey asked.

Andrew's jaw jutted forward. "She's Ellen's daughter. Did you know her?"

"No, but Caroline spoke of her. I told you Caroline would give a person anything they asked for, but that wasn't entirely true. She had one possession she refused to part with no matter who asked it of her, and Ellen was one of those who asked."

"What was it?" Mikaela asked.

"A doll, a Maori replica of Old Mother Hubbard. Caroline treasured it."

Mikaela's mouth dropped open, but she quickly closed it again. Was the doll actually the mysterious treasure?

"We saw your name in an old newspaper article about a Kotuku Inn treasure hunt. Was that what everyone was looking for? The doll?" Andrew spoke slower than he had before, more succinctly.

"I don't know. Some were, perhaps. It seems odd now, but in those days the legendary treasure was part of the appeal of the place, and the hunt was something like a holiday celebration. Pretty much everyone you talked to believed there was a hidden treasure at Kotuku Inn that no one would find and Caroline would never speak of."

Mikaela rubbed the back of her neck. She'd told Sergeant Hoffman her grandfather had the doll. Was that why he seemed so interested in him? "You said the doll was important to her?"

"Yes. That much she did tell me. Her husband gave it to her shortly before his death."

Andrew nodded at Mikaela's notebook. "You should write that down under *greed*. The treasure could have been the motive."

"Oh. Yes." Mikaela clenched her pencil. She made herself write the words.

"The doll seems to interest you quite a bit, Mr. Evans," Ms. Sabey said.

"No more than any other fact does," Andrew said. "It—the treasure—is a legend in our family. No one seems to know much about it or what its value might be."

Ms. Sabey's gaze distanced. "Caroline said she kept details about the doll to herself because talking about them reminded her too much of her husband. Displaying the doll to the world, she'd said, would be too much like casting her pearls before swine."

Sweat pooled along Mikaela's hairline. Ira had said love was another common motive for murder, so she added it to her list, but that still didn't mean her grandfather had anything to do with Caroline's death. "There must have been others she loved or who cared about her. Any names you can give us?"

"I only remember a couple of ladies she worked with in the community every now and again. They live in the rest home down the road now."

"What are their names?"

"Mara Gates was one, and—"

Mikaela looked up at her. "Celia Wood?"

Andrew's head whipped around to look at her.

"Yes," Ms. Sabey said. "How did you know?"

Mikaela wrote *rest home* next to the women's names in her notebook. "They're the names I found at the library."

Ms. Sabey held her gaze. "I expect their caregivers will let you visit them, but I wouldn't count on them remembering much, if anything, about Caroline. As I understand it, they barely remember their own families anymore."

Mikaela sighed heavily. Another dead end.

"Is there anything more, anything at all you can remember about her?" Andrew said. "Or about the doll?"

*The doll.* Mikaela's grandfather had to have known what people thought about the doll when Caroline gave it to him. He had to have—*That's it!* She almost laughed in relief. She'd worked herself up over nothing. Her grandfather was a businessman, so after Caroline gave him the doll, he would have had it appraised. It probably wasn't worth anything more than his memories of the woman. It wasn't a motive for murder. *Right?*

"I can't think of anything else right now," Ms. Sabey said, "but if I remember something that seems important, I'll let you know."

* * *

After their interview with Ms. Sabey, Mikaela helped Brentin, oddly subdued despite how perfectly the interview had gone, take his recording equipment back to his car. He clenched and unclenched the trunk's latch.

"Is something wrong?" she asked him.

He frowned; glanced at Andrew, who still stood on the porch talking with Ms. Sabey; and shrugged.

Mikaela touched his forearm. He looked down at her fingers then back up at her. She lowered her hand. "You don't need to be nervous, if that's the problem," she said. "You have some really great footage there. Everyone at the ball will love it."

"That's not—" Again he glanced toward the porch. "I'm not at all worried about the films. You—we—it's even better than I'd hoped. I just wish I could stay. You've got me really curious about Caroline Evans."

"That's nice of you to say, but I'm sure you'll have a much better time dancing with Amiria than Andrew and I will have here."

Something in his gaze shifted, and for a moment Mikaela felt unwarranted heat rise up her neck, but thankfully, before it could reach her cheeks, Brentin half smiled and opened his driver's door. "Well, I guess I better hurry."

"Have fun."

He swallowed, held her gaze another moment, and then pulled out of the driveway.

She and Andrew left Ms. Sabey's home shortly afterward. They found and spoke with the women Ms. Sabey had told them about. Both women remembered Caroline Evans, her legendary treasure, and some of the same other information Ms. Sabey had, but that was it.

"What a waste of time," Mikaela said when they stopped for a late meal at a small Indian cafe. The dining area consisted of four two-person tables, but only one other couple was there.

"I disagree," Andrew said. "Three similar stories told by three different people indicate Ms. Sabey told us the truth."

"I suppose."

Andrew led Mikaela to the counter at the back of the room. A young man with black hair and dark eyes stood behind it. "What would you like?"

Mikaela scanned the menu on the wall. "I'll have a chicken kebab with hot chili sauce."

"A kebab for me too," Andrew said. "Pork with spicy sweet-n-sour sauce."

The young man wrote their orders on his notepad and handed them a number. "Take a seat. I'll let you know when your order's ready."

They sat at the table closest to the front counter, leaving an empty table between them and the other couple.

"Any idea what the doll's worth?" Andrew said.

"Sentimentally, probably priceless. Monetarily—I'm gonna guess it's not much." Mikaela didn't know what it was, but something in Andrew's expression shifted.

"Why do you think so?" he asked.

"My grandfather's a business man. If the doll had had any real monetary value, he would have brought it back to the United States years ago for safekeeping."

Andrew leaned back in his seat and folded his arms across his chest. "Not if the government considered it a historical treasure. They wouldn't have let him take it."

The waiter called their number. Mikaela slid out of her seat, but Andrew stood and placed his hand on her shoulder. "I'll get them," he said.

"Thanks."

He nodded, glanced at her out of the corner of his eye, and sauntered to the counter. He returned with their filled plates a few moments later. "I hope you're hungry. There's a lot of food there."

"This looks great." Mikaela pressed the pita-like bread filled with thin-sliced chicken and salad toppings to her lips and touched a bit of the hot sauce to the tip of her tongue. Perfect.

Andrew watched her take her first bite before he, too, ate.

# Chapter 17

SOMETHING WASN'T RIGHT. BRENTIN DIDN'T know what it was, but ever since he'd finished filming Ms. Sabey's interview and had left to get ready for the ball—ever since he'd left Mikaela with Andrew—he'd felt like someone had dropped a heavy block of lead on top of him, and no matter how much he tried, he couldn't focus solely on his filming. Part of it, however, he could have blamed on the frustration—envy—he felt every time Mikaela's attention had turned to Andrew rather than to him. And there was nothing he could do about it until he'd cleared things up with Amiria. But the other part? Why the prickles that moved like a long, rough-scaled snake across the back of his neck?

The first haunting notes of "May It Be" by Enya from *The Fellowship of the Ring*'s soundtrack filled the room. Brentin, dressed as Thorin, the Dwarf prince from *The Hobbit* movies, led Amiria, dressed as Eowan, a shield maiden, from the crowded theater in the middle of the convention center to the mezzanine. Vendors with themed knickknack booths filled the room and foyer. Yesterday they'd sold DVDs, statuettes, and other collectibles. This evening they also sold pictures, books, and costumes from the movies. All due, Brentin assumed, to the visiting celebrities who'd held speaking events and photo shoots earlier that day.

"Stay close," Brentin told Amiria. "I don't want to lose you in this crowd."

"I don't want to get lost." She slid her hand around the crook of his elbow just above his leather arm bracers, but something in her touch felt different than usual. Territorial? He glanced down at her. Her regal white costume shimmered so brilliantly she couldn't help but stand out from the other women in the room.

"I love your Dwarf costume," she went on. "Did I tell you that already? It makes you look so, I don't know, ruggedly exotic and exciting."

Despite himself, Brentin's cheeks warmed. His next oldest sister had told him something of the same thing back in Colorado when she'd first handed him his fur-and-leather coat. She'd said his costume fit over his muscles like a tight layer of skin, that no girl would be able to resist him when he wore it. He'd wanted to believe her but had convinced himself it was only sisterly flattery. But now . . . would his costume have attracted Mikaela? "Thanks."

"It's true, you know." The smile in Amiria's voice pulled his gaze back to hers. Her eyes shone with softness. Brentin looked quickly away. He had to stop this. Now. It simply wasn't fair to either of them to let her go on thinking he felt more for her than friendship. He scanned the room. But where—and how—could he tell her?

"Hello, Mr. Williams." The feminine voice with the British accent belonged to the tall, thirty-something energetic redhead who'd helped Ms. Sabey get the convention on its feet. He couldn't remember her name, but he'd heard rumors that she intended to head up another conference next year in her home country of England.

She shook his free hand. "That first film of yours was wonderful. I don't know how you managed to get the interviews you did. I hear the Coopers are vocal enough on community issues, but no one's ever heard them speak so personally. And that child! He was such a delightful Hobbit. I expected him to dash underneath his Orc father's legs at any moment."

Brentin smiled. Too bad Mikaela couldn't hear the woman's praise. Everything she'd mentioned about the film was due to Mikaela's influence. "I'm glad you liked it."

"Why aren't you showing it throughout the rest of the evening?" Amiria said.

Brentin made a noise in the base of his throat. He gave Amiria a sidelong glance. Did she have any idea how ungracious she sounded?

"It will run back-to-back with his new one tomorrow," the redhead said.

"Tomorrow's the best day for the showings." Brentin nodded. "It's the last day of the convention. Most of the celebrities will be here then. There will be a huge crowd."

The woman gave him a thin-lipped smile and moved toward a booth of gold rings.

Brentin motioned past a stand covered in Gandalf-shaped candlesticks. "Let's go that way."

When Amiria didn't answer, he turned to her and found her gazing toward a crowd surrounding a man who'd played one of the elves in the first *Hobbit* movie. "Amiria?"

"Yes?" She dragged her gaze back to his. "Sorry."

"No problem. Let's go this way."

The two made their way out of the mezzanine and into the cooler, though still crowded, foyer. Brentin steered Amiria to the ticketing booth, where he'd stored his camera.

"There are a lot of great costumes here tonight," he said. "I'd like to film some of them while we're waiting for the ball to start." He unlocked the door, took his camera bag from a lower cupboard, and unzipped the main compartment.

"I've disappointed you somehow, haven't I?" Amiria spoke softly.

"What?" Brentin looked up at her. "Not at all."

"Then what is it? Did I do something wrong?"

"Of course not." He pulled out his camera and scanned the area on the other side of the glass walls surrounding them. No one seemed to be looking their way, but that didn't mean this room was private enough for the conversation he needed to have with her. He'd have to find somewhere else. "I'm only thinking about the night ahead of us."

Her gaze wavered with what seemed like uncertainty, but still she edged closer to him. Her toes bumped his. "Me too. I've dreamt of a night like this with you at my side since Mum first took my brothers and me out to your home in Colorado."

"You're kidding." He drew back from her. "That was more than ten years ago. You were just a kid."

"I was twelve—and definitely old enough to know I liked you." She laughed lightly. "Come on. You had to know I had a crush on you. Why else would I ask you to be my pen pal?"

Brentin shrugged. Most of what he remembered about those days was that his mom had made him miss a camping trip with his friends so he could say good-bye to the Davies family. "I just thought it was cute that you'd asked me."

Her gaze dulled. He turned, pretending not to notice, and opened the door. The chatter in the foyer amplified with the growing crowd, and a new melody filled the air: "Aragorn's Coronation." Still not looking at Amiria, he shoved his empty bag under the counter and held out his camera. "They've started. Shall we go? This shouldn't take long."

"Very well."

As they moved back into the main foyer, Brentin panned from the crowded mezzanine doors to the line of people filing into the ballroom. Then, he and Amiria followed them inside. Candlelike lamps dimly lit the room, red velvet and long white silks draped the walls, and two golden thrones sat in the center of the exterior, bowed wall. Two people stood in front of the thrones. One dressed as King Aragorn, the other as Queen Arwen. Both wore costumes similar to those worn by the characters in this scene of the movie, except that this Arwen's silver Elven crown was more striking than the original, with small, glittering green stones fastened within it. Emerald-green like Mikaela's eyes.

Brentin cleared his throat. "The decorators really outdid themselves tonight." He moved to the left corner and looked through his viewfinder. He only needed one perfect wide-angle shot. Found it! *Click.* He took four more of the same setting to make sure he had a good one, returned his camera to the ticket booth, and met up again with Amiria on the dance floor. She urged him toward the far side of the room, close to where they'd sat during dinner the previous night.

"You used to say in your letters that you could tell me anything," she said.

Brentin frowned. Amiria obviously read his expressions a bit too easily. "I remember. Writing to you used to be one of my favorite activities."

"Used to be?"

"Yes, I—" He held her gaze. He couldn't tell her now, and yet . . .

"Come on. Let's dance." Amiria took his hand and led him to the middle of the floor, where a few couples already swayed to the slow song. Amiria wrapped her left arm over his right shoulder. "This is nice," she said as they danced.

"Yes. You've been a good friend to me, Amiria."

Her hand slid along his shoulder to the back of his neck. "More than a friend, I hope?"

"No."

"What?" Her step faltered. She paled slightly.

A chill—different than the uneasiness that still slithered across his skin—shot through Brentin's chest, and his hands felt like frozen clay. "We need to talk. But somewhere else."

She released him and, holding his gaze, nodded. Brentin scanned the room for an empty corner. Finding none, he led her back to the foyer and through the mezzanine to the empty theater on the other side. He motioned for her to sit; then he took the seat next to her. She folded her arms in front of her.

"So, uh, what is it?" Amiria said.

He took a deep breath. *Courage, man. And honesty.* "Amiria, you're a beautiful girl. And fun. I've been lucky to have you in my life, and I do care for you."

"I hear a *but*."

"When two people speak of marriage—" He groaned. His words sounded like a line from a movie.

"We've never spoken of marriage," Amiria said. "Not specifically anyway."

"Yes, but our mothers have." He hoped she'd smile at that, but when she didn't, he added, "Do you understand what I'm trying to say?"

"You haven't said anything."

"Right." He clenched then relaxed his fingers. This time, he didn't let himself look at her. "I'm not an authority on relationships by any means, but I've watched my sisters and their husbands. I've seen my friends marry and begin new lives. The one thing I'm certain of is that when two people marry, they need to feel deep inside that they belong together. You—you're one of the best girls I've had the privilege of knowing, yet I don't—I don't feel that way for you. I'm sorry."

Tears clouded her eyes. "I suppose I should have spoken sooner. Maybe it was because I didn't want to, that I wanted things to become what we'd— what I'd—hoped they were, because I do care a great deal for you. But soon after you arrived I felt—I worried—we didn't quite fit each other."

"You did?"

"I did." She looked away from him and stood. "So now what? Should we go back to the inn?"

"We don't have to go back now if you don't want to. We're still friends. We can finish the evening together."

She faced him again, tilted her head, and sniffed. "I'd like that," she said at last.

"You would? I mean, good." He offered her his arm.

Instead of taking it, she stepped in front of him and led him to the door. She took hold of the handle but paused.

"Is something wrong?"

"No. It's only—don't you think you ought to talk to Mikaela before it's too late?"

So much for thinking he'd masked his feelings. At all. "You really are one of the best girls I know."

"Don't you forget it."

Brentin smiled at her gentle jibe, but that inexplicable uneasiness still twisted inside him. He would tell Mikaela how he felt, and soon. Yet was she at all ready to hear him?

# Chapter 18

NIGHT BATHED THE SKY WHEN Mikaela and Andrew returned to Kotuku Inn. Andrew parked the motorcycle between Tui's and Vicky's cars but left the engine running.

Mikaela climbed off the seat behind him. She massaged the muscles at the back of her neck, but her headache didn't go away. Nor did the churning in her stomach. Had she eaten something that didn't agree with her?

"It looks like your renovators can get back to work tomorrow." Andrew motioned to where deep tire tracks in the muddy grass replaced the crime scene tape and police vehicles. "What? No smiles? I thought you'd be happy about that."

"I am happy. Just tired. It's been a long day."

"Long but productive." He adjusted his helmet strap. "You'll call me if you learn anything more about Caroline's death, won't you?"

Mikaela patted the pocket of her jeans, where she kept her phone. "I have your number."

"Good. I'll do the same for you."

She handed him his extra helmet and gloves and waited until she could no longer see his motorcycle on the lane before she started for the front steps. The porch light shone through the humid darkness like a welcoming symbol, but the closer she got to the inn—and the brighter the hall and kitchen lights shone—the slower she moved. She didn't want to go inside, only wanted to linger out in the darkness where she could think over the day's events and maybe curl up inside herself until her upset stomach and the anxiousness in her heart settled.

She turned away from the front door and walked around the carport. When she reached the sidewalk that led to the rear deck, she stared out toward the grove of trees at the back of the property. Their mix of pine-needled and leafy tops silhouetted the dimming skyline like a jagged fortress. Had her grandfather thought of them like that too? Like they were a divider between this place and the real world?

"Hello," a soft female voice said.

Mikaela looked toward the deck. Sara, wearing jeans and a brown, faux-leather jacket, sat on the middle rung of the staircase. She hunched her shoulders and crossed her arms in front of her so tightly that her already small frame seemed to have shrunk by at least a third.

"Are you all right?" Mikaela said.

She shrugged.

"Where's Frank?"

"I don't know."

Mikaela leaned against the railing at the bottom of the stairs. "What happened?"

Sara hesitated but only for a moment. "The day started out good. We spent most of it cycling the bike trails in the redwoods, but the harder trails up the mountainside are pretty steep in some places, and I got tired before he did. He brought me back here to rest then went back out. He said he wanted to get the last trail in before the end of the day. I don't know. Maybe I should have tried harder. Maybe I could have kept up."

"A person can only do the best they can do."

Silence slipped through the air like an invisible ghost, and Mikaela felt it as tangibly as if a silk cloth dropped on top of her. If only she could think of something comforting to say.

"You said you were close to someone once," Sara said at last. "Would you be able to sleep if he'd dropped you off like Frank did to me? On your honeymoon?"

Mikaela bit her lip. She and Trevor had planned a cruise to the Bahamas, and every activity they'd considered had starred the two of them together. "No, I wouldn't."

Sara's thick lower lip protruded over her top one. When tears filled her eyes, Mikaela looked, unseeing, toward the kitchen and moved closer to the deck. As an only child, she'd often wished she'd had an older sibling she could unload her thoughts on. That way, she'd believed, she wouldn't have felt so alone and misunderstood. Might Sara also be an only child?

"Before Frank and I got hitched," Sara said, "one of my married friends told me it would be like this, but I didn't believe her."

"You're both new to married life. Maybe Frank just doesn't know how to be a husband yet."

"Maybe."

Mikaela shifted her weight to her other foot. "Things will look better in the morning."

"You don't sound like you believe that."

Somewhere far away a car horn blared. "The truth is I don't know much about your husband, but I do believe that things, even bad things, usually look better in the morning."

"I don't mean he's bad. It's just—he loves me. I know he does, but sometimes he just drives me crazy."

Mikaela waited for her to continue, but all she did was look expectantly at Mikaela then glance away. Did she want advice? If so, what should it be? Mikaela had been engaged but never married. Never in this girl's situation enough to—her thoughts paused. *Is this why Grandma usually said so little when I used to talk to her? Because she didn't know what to say? Only knew that she loved me?* Mikaela sat on a stair near Sara, blinked back her sudden wave of missing her grandmother, and said, "Have you told him you want to be with him?"

"I'm sure he already knows that. Frank just loves to do active things. He hates sitting around, and I love that about him. But sometimes . . . he needs to stop sometimes, doesn't he? To leave room in his life for me?"

"Frank married you, so he must have already made room in his life for you. It's just that sometimes we have to give people space to make the changes they want to make. Ourselves too." Mikaela again scanned the tree-lined darkness at the back of the yard. She had no idea if anything she'd said made sense to Sara, but she hoped at least that Sara knew she wasn't alone in her troubles.

"I'd like to make changes," Sara whispered.

Mikaela nodded, wrapped her arms around her knees, and stared out at the shadowed stillness. Crickets chirped. A light, sulfuric breeze billowed the bushes, the grass, the tree branches.

"Have you had dinner tonight?" Mikaela asked.

"I wasn't hungry before."

"Are you now?"

She shrugged.

"Why don't we go inside. I bet Tui has something you can eat. You might even feel better after you've put something in your stomach."

Sara stood, and the two climbed to the top of the stairs. Mikaela reached for the door handle, but Sara stopped her.

"Thank you," she said. "You've been a good friend to me even though we hardly know each other."

"I hope I've helped."

"More than you know."

Mikaela followed Sara into the warm kitchen. It smelled of cinnamon and—

"Help!" Vicky screamed.

Panic shot down the back of Mikaela's neck and across the width of her shoulders. She ran through the kitchen toward the hallway. Vicky, pale and wide-eyed, stumbled out of Ira's suite at the end of the hall, leaving the door open.

"What's wrong?" Mikaela said.

"It's Ira! He's—he's—!"

"He's what?" Mikaela hurried past her into the dimly lit room. Ira lay on top of the made bed in the far corner. Gray colored his face, and saliva crusted his lips and chin. Was he dead? She grabbed his shoulders and shook him. "Ira! Can you hear me? Are you all right?"

His body moved limply with her shaking. She slid her trembling fingers along his throat. No pulse. She drew back from him and, wincing, looked over her shoulder. Sara and Vicky filled the doorway. Their eyes bulged. Vicky's lips trembled.

"Do either of you know how to call for an ambulance?" Mikaela asked.

Brentin, wearing a long, medieval coat, charged into the room between Vicky and Sara. He looked straight at Mikaela but spoke to Sara over his shoulder. "The number's 1-1-1."

*Brentin!* A relieved breath caught in her throat, and unexpected tears pooled in her eyes.

He leaned over Ira and shook him just as Mikaela had done. "What's happened?"

"I don't know," Mikaela said. "Sara and I heard Vicky scream. He was like this when we got here."

Sara moved to the desk next to the window and picked up the room's phone receiver. She lifted it to her ear and pressed some numbers. "Please help!"

Amiria, wearing a gown and tiara, stepped into the room and stared at them. Her mouth dropped open.

"What's the address here?" Sara asked her.

Amiria shook her head as if clearing it and grabbed the phone receiver from her. "This is Amiria Davies at Kotuku Inn. A man's hurt, and we need an ambulance. Actually, it looks like he's dead. Yes, we're just off of Tarawera Road, across from the redwoods."

Ambulances. Sirens. Each meant tragedy, fear. *Please, not again!* Mikaela pressed her hand over her mouth and focused away from Ira's face, away from the white cane lying on the floor near Brentin's feet, away from Vicky's pained stare.

"Let's wait for the police somewhere else," Brentin said.

Amiria, still on the phone, gave them a quick wave and faced the window.

"How could this have happened?" Vicky groaned when they reached the front hallway. "Ira had a scene in his book he couldn't quite figure out. He asked me to leave him alone for the rest of the afternoon. He hadn't been feeling well anyway. When he gets like that, he usually takes a nap. How was I supposed to know this—this—I just visited with Tui. That's all!"

"Where is Tui?" Brentin said.

"In her private quarters. She wanted to take an early bath." Vicky shuddered. "If only I'd checked on him sooner."

Mikaela folded and unfolded her arms. What could she say to the woman except the same words everyone had told her after Trevor and her grandmother had died? "It's not your fault."

Vicky sniffled. She wiped her tears from her cheeks. "I don't know why I'm crying so hard. He was only my employer."

"I think we both know why."

She stared at Mikaela for a long moment before her eyes filled again. "I should have told him. I wish I'd told him. At least he would have known how I felt before he—he—"

The manager's office door swung open, and Tui bustled into the hallway. Damp spots dotted the shoulders of her untucked, flowered blouse underneath her wet hair. "What's happened?"

"Ira's dead," Brentin said. "Amiria's in his room calling the police."

Tui gaped at each of them, but when she settled on Mikaela, her expression turned as gray and dark as a thundercloud. "I told you not to bring that doll into the house. I told you someone would be murdered."

Sara stepped closer to Mikaela, and Mikaela bit her lip. Trevor, Grandma, Caroline Evans, and now Ira. No way could their deaths have anything to do with her. Especially Caroline's; she'd died years ago. "There are no such things as curses. And anyway, the doll's no longer here," she defended herself.

Brentin put his hand on Tui's shoulder. "This isn't Mikaela's fault. And as far as murder goes, none of us knows how he died."

Sirens filled the distance.

Tui ran out the front door to the top of the porch staircase. The others followed. Moments later an ambulance and two police cars pulled into the driveway. They stopped beside the sidewalk in front of the porch. Medics took a gurney from the back of the ambulance, and several uniformed policemen hurried toward them. Sergeant Hoffman was among them.

"Where's the victim?" the tallest policeman asked the group.

Mikaela looked to Tui. In all other circumstances, the woman had behaved as a protective mother bear, but now she clung to the railing. Her stance drooped, and her eyes widened with the same vulnerability Mikaela had seen in her grandfather's face after he'd told her of her grandmother's death. Mikaela had to take charge. "Follow me."

Mikaela described what little she knew about Ira's death as she led the police to his suite, and Amiria met them at Ira's bedroom door. The medics and most of the officers hurried inside, but the oldest officer, Detective Eaton, asked Mikaela and the others to remain with him and Sergeant Hoffman in the hall.

Detective Eaton closed Ira's door, turned back to them, and scanned their faces. "Who was the first to find Mr. Lawrence?"

"I was," Vicky said. "I'm his assistant."

Sergeant Hoffman looked at his open notebook. "Where's Amiria Davies? She called dispatch."

Amiria glanced at Sara and stepped out from behind Tui. "I'm here."

"Very good." Detective Eaton opened the door and motioned for one of the other officers to join them. After closing the door behind him, he whispered something in Detective Eaton's ear. Detective Eaton lifted an eyebrow, stared at the man a moment longer, and again faced Mikaela. "We need to speak with each of you privately," he said.

"Perhaps the lounge will do?"

"Or my office," Tui said.

"Both will be fine." He again glanced at the closed door, only this time his eyes narrowed slightly.

"Would you like the rest of us to wait in the kitchen?" Mikaela said.

"Good idea. Officer Cooper, here, will wait with you."

*So we don't corroborate our stories.* Mikaela frowned. Was it a good or bad thing that she'd seen so many television detective shows?

"He was murdered, wasn't he?" Tui's voice shook.

"We don't know, ma'am, and we won't know until after the pathologist gets here. And maybe not until after he's had a chance to perform an autopsy. For now, expect the room to be sealed for at least a day or two."

Detective Eaton pointed his open hand toward the door. "This way," he said to Vicky.

# Chapter 19

After the officers finished interviewing each of them about an hour later, Mikaela left the others in the kitchen and moved to the base of the staircase. She stared, dazed, toward the first landing and took one upward step. How could so many things have changed so drastically in such a short time? When she'd wakened that morning, Ira had been alive and Kotuku Inn, though under construction, had been a pleasant bed and breakfast. Now it was a crime scene—the second in as many days. It reminded her of a line she'd once heard in a TV show: "Alive one minute, dead the next."

She clenched her hand and trailed it atop the smooth wooden banister, continuing up the stairs to her room. What could she possibly do to help this situation until her grandfather got there? Ira was beyond aid, and Vicky—she'd announced she couldn't possibly stay another night in this place and would leave as soon as possible. And what about Tui? Should Mikaela try to convince her and Amiria to stay? Tui was, after all, the inn's manager. But the image of Tui washing and rewashing an already clean stovetop with a trembling hand while holding her fishhook pendant with the other filled her mind. Tui had given Mikaela a pointed look and stated that while she didn't want to leave the place a mess, she would not stay in the same building as an active curse. Which meant Amiria would leave too.

Mikaela sighed and entered her bedroom. Her curtains were still open to the backyard. She went to the window. She couldn't see the distant grove of trees or the flower garden that lay just beyond the deck, but she knew they were there, just as she knew Caroline Evans's burial spot lay hidden at the bottom of the stairs—hidden the way darkness veiled nature and people buried truths in their hearts. Like Ira's murderer. The police wouldn't yet reveal many details, but they obviously suspected Ira had been murdered. But if so, why? And by whom? By someone staying—hiding—in the inn?

She shivered. The very thought of a stranger lurking around—or worse, one of the inn's guests being a murderer—seemed as ridiculous as Tui's assurance that Ira's death had been predicted by her ominous dream. And yet what other options were there?

Mikaela hugged her arms, kicked off her shoes, and headed for the desk. She hated waking her grandfather. It was two o'clock in the morning in Utah. But if ever she needed his advice, it was then. Besides, considering the circumstances, he would want her to call.

She connected to Kotuku Inn's wireless service and rang her grandfather's Skype account. Eventually, his face appeared on her screen. He wore a bathrobe, and dark circles rimmed beneath his eyes. Hadn't he been sleeping well?

"Mikaela? What's wrong? You look exhausted."

"So do you." He frowned, but when he didn't say anything more, Mikaela added, "Sorry to wake you, but I thought I better let you know there's been a death at the inn."

His eyes widened, and his face paled.

"Grandpa! Are you okay?"

"Was the—was the death another one from long ago, like Caroline?"

"It was one of the inn's guests. Ira Lawrence, the writer I told you about."

He ran his hand across the top of his nearly bald head. His fingers trembled. "How'd it happen? Was there an accident? Was he hurt on the property?"

"His aide found him lying on his bed. No one knows what happened, and the police have sealed off his room. Someone suggested he'd had a heart attack, but I don't think anyone believes that."

His stare glazed.

"Grandpa, are you okay?"

It was the first time Mikaela had ever heard him swear. Then he got down to business. "How are Tui and Amiria? I bet Tui's not taking this very well."

Mikaela's cheeks felt hot. *Blast those cheeks!* She leaned stiffly back in her chair and crossed her arms. "Amiria's fine, but Tui can't handle the stress of being here. They're leaving this evening. They'll stay with her son in Taupo for a while."

"What about you? How are you holding up?"

"I'm a bit freaked out by it all, but I mostly just want to know what I should do, since Tui's leaving."

"Of course." He rubbed the back of his neck. "Someone needs to be there as long as we have guests, but if it's dangerous—"

Mikaela stiffened upright. Dangerous? Why would he say that? She hadn't said anything about the possibility that Ira had been murdered.

"You have a good head on your shoulders, Mikaela. Do whatever you think is best, but keep in mind that your safety is more important than the inn."

"I don't feel unsafe exactly." *Or did she?* "Just a bit nervous. I've never run an inn before."

"Yes. Of course." He furrowed his brows, and though he stared at Mikaela, it seemed his gaze focused elsewhere. "Like I said, do whatever you think is best. I'll be there soon."

"So far, I've told the guests they're welcome to whatever food and other comforts they might find in the house until you arrive, but is there anything else you'd like me to do? What if the media comes around?" *What would Andrew write about this?*

"I doubt anyone will contact you about the writer's death at this point, Mikaela, but if they do, tell them you don't know any more than what the police have already said." He tapped his fingers on the desk, opened his mouth as if he were about to say something more, and closed it again.

"What?" Mikaela asked.

"You've got that look . . . is there anything else you want to talk to me about?"

"I talked to a woman named Leanne Sabey today. She used to be Caroline Evans's friend."

"A short woman with mousy black hair, as I remember her."

"It's white now. Anyway, she said that when you first bought Kotuku Inn, people around town thought Caroline had left a hidden treasure somewhere on the property and started hunting for it."

"I'd forgotten about that. I did give a few people permission to look around the property as long as they didn't tear anything up. I'd hoped it would stop the rumors. I thought it had, since I didn't hear anything more about it. Don't tell me someone's still looking for it."

"I don't know. That's just what Ms. Sabey said. But the treasure's not what I'm worried about."

He reached toward his computer screen like he wanted to touch her arm, stopped, and placed his hand back in his lap. "Caroline Evans was reclusive and more than a little eccentric. Dozens of people told odd stories about her, most of them unbelievable. She was like the town ghost." He paused. "Perhaps they were right. Is that what you're worried about?" Despite the seriousness of the situation, he smiled. "That now that they've found her body, she's a ghost and is haunting the place?"

"I'm not kidding. Ms. Sabey said the doll that you told me had belonged to Grandma had actually belonged to Caroline. She thought *it* might be the lost treasure."

"There was no treasure that I ever saw. And if there was, I can't imagine why she wouldn't have taken it with her. Yes, she gave the doll to me, but I gave it to your grandmother, and now I'm giving it to you. That's all there is to it."

Mikaela focused on a point on the wall behind him. How could she say this without him wondering if she doubted him? "The police are looking for Caroline's murderer, which means they're also looking for a motive. I'm sure the doll can't have anything to do with something like that, but since you have it, and everyone thinks it was valuable . . ."

"Did you tell the police we have it?"

"Yes. I'm sorry. I didn't know it was an issue."

"Mikaela, look at me."

She dragged her gaze back to the computer screen.

"You told the truth, so you have nothing to be sorry about. Caroline Evans was like a mother to me. We took care of each other. I'm sorry I didn't tell you more about the doll, but only because I didn't think it was important, not because I had done anything wrong."

"I know that. It's just—why did she give you the doll in the first place? Ms. Sabey said she cherished it so much she wouldn't even let anyone see it."

"Do you want the long or the short version?"

"How about long enough?"

He settled against the back of his chair and ran his hand over his mouth. "Caroline's husband gave the doll to her for their twentieth anniversary. She'd always loved the Maori people. She thought they were beautiful, but just like many other Kiwis—the white ones—who lived there at that time, she believed the Maoris had fallen from the grace of God because of their native traditions. She wanted to help them. Caroline's husband cared for the Maori people too, but he didn't worry as much about their salvation as she did." Her grandfather's voice sounded distant. "At any rate, the Evanses hired several Maoris to work for them. Most of them were mothers. Caroline taught their children English games and nursery rhymes."

Mikaela studied his expression. Had his gaze flinched? "It sounds like she tried to civilize them the way the early Americans believed they needed to civilize the Native Americans."

"Something like that, yes."

"And the doll?"

"Mr. Evans commissioned the apprentice of a renowned New Zealand craftswoman to make a Maori doll for him, only he wanted this one to also represent Old Mother Hubbard. Caroline loved it, but it meant even more to her after her husband drowned in a boating accident a month later. It was the last thing he'd given her."

"And she gave it to you because . . . ?"

"She said I'd saved her life." He grew quiet. "But now that they've found her body, it makes me wonder if she gave it to me because she'd had some kind of premonition about her death and wanted to make sure it fell into the right hands. She had premonitions like that sometimes."

"How did you save her life?"

He frowned. "Several of us had gone on an outing to Kuirau Park. Caroline tripped, I don't know on what, but I caught her just before she fell into a geothermal pool."

Though Mikaela cringed at the thought of being boiled alive, her nerves settled. Her grandfather had saved Caroline's life, and she'd given him the doll out of gratitude. It made complete sense. She tucked a strand of her hair behind her ear.

"No longer a monster?" he said.

"I never thought that."

"But you were worried." His smile drooped slightly.

"Sorry."

"It's all right. You're in a strange place with strange people, and you're under a lot of stress."

"Thanks for understanding."

"Anytime."

Mikaela scratched her cheek next to her scar. She should let him go back to bed, and she would soon, but right then just sitting and talking with him made her feel like she was safe at home, and she didn't want to lose that feeling just yet.

Her grandfather gave her a quick smile. "I'm tempted to have your aunt come and help me with the mail."

"The mail?" *That was out of the blue.* "Why? Has something else happened?"

"Not exactly. But it's troubling enough that I finally decided to talk to the police. I got another sympathy card today."

The hair on the back of Mikaela's neck lifted. "One with a nursery rhyme? What did it say?"

"I'll get it." He stood and walked away from the screen. Papers rustled nearby.

Mikaela crossed and uncrossed her knees.

"Here it is." He pulled a blue card from a blue envelope that looked just as the others had, and he read it aloud.

*Mary Ann Cotton*
*She's dead and forgotten,*
*She lies in a grave with her bones all-rotten;*
*Sing, sing, oh, what can we sing,*
*Mary Ann Cotton is tied up with string.*

Mikaela clenched her fingers around the edge of her chair where her grandfather couldn't see they were trembling. "That's creepy," she whispered.

"Most nursery rhymes are."

"Yeah, but at first glance they're usually kinda cute."

"Not this one." He frowned. "I'm getting tired of those cards, Mikaela."

"Me too." Mikaela swiped her hand across her forehead. The other two cards had arrived in conjunction with two deaths. "What are you thinking?"

"They might be some sort of threat. That's why I called the police. And now that Mr. Lawrence has died . . ."

"But the cards are there, and Ira's here. How could they be related?" Without waiting for him to answer, she added, "Hold on. Let me do a quick search. See if the Internet comes up with anything about that rhyme." She typed *Mary Ann Cotton* into the browser box. Links filled the page. "Whoa! The first site says Mary Ann Cotton was Britain's first serial killer. She poisoned twenty-one people."

"The other rhymes referred to deaths too. Wait a minute!" He sat taller. "Caroline Evans liked nursery rhymes. Maybe she has something to do with the cards."

"I don't see how she could. Unless she *is* a ghost." He didn't smile at her reference to his earlier joke. Neither did she. "Besides, who would do it?" she added. "She didn't have any kids." *But Andrew is related to her.*

"That's why I tried to fill that role," her grandfather said. "So she wouldn't be alone."

"Apparently you succeeded."

"Yes, well . . ." He stared down at his keyboard for a long moment, but when he looked up at her again, his face had paled even more. "I'm sorry, Mikaela. I shouldn't have said anything about that card. You already have a lot on your plate there without more to worry about. And anyway, if there's anything to those cards, the police will figure it out."

If that were true, why did her stomach roll over? "Of course you should have told me! I'm as involved in this as you are. I got the first card." Someone knocked on her door, and she glanced over. "I wonder who that is."

"Sounds like a good time to let you go," her grandfather said. "Thanks for calling, and keep me updated, all right? Until I can get there?"

"I will. Grandpa?"

"Yes?"

"Be careful, okay?"

He smiled and nodded. "You too, sweetheart."

# Chapter 20

MIKAELA DABBED A TISSUE TO her eyes, pinched her lips between her fingers to stop them from quivering, and opened her door. Brentin stood in the hallway. He scanned from her eyes to her feet and back to her eyes. "I was afraid you might have gone to bed."

"Not yet. What is it?"

"Detective Eaton wants to talk to us again. You especially."

She glanced down at her phone—her grandfather had hung up—and pushed up the cuffs of her sleeves. "All right."

He drew backward, giving her room to pass, and she stepped into the hallway. She closed her door. Maybe now that they were alone she could thank him for his help. It would be at least one concern she could cross off her mental to-do list. "Brentin, I wanted—" She turned to face him, but when his gaze locked on hers, adrenaline shocked her core. She back-stepped.

"Yes?" he prodded.

If he felt in any way like she did at that moment, this was definitely not the time to thank him, for if she did and he thought her gratitude implied more than—more than she meant, their relationship could get tricky.

"Do you know what they want to talk to us about?" It was a dumb question. If he'd known, he'd have already said so. Worse, when he tilted his head sideways, it was obvious he knew that she knew it was a dumb question. She had to say something to get him to look away from her so she could breathe again.

He clasped her upper arm. "What's bothering you?"

Her skin tingled at his touch. "It's hardly anything. I'm just being an idiot."

"I doubt that."

Heat warmed her cheeks. Again. Only this time it was because of his compliment. It had absolutely nothing to do with the way he looked at her or with the fact that his body was less than an arm's length away from hers. "It can't mean anything—"

"But you feel it might."

She let herself look up at him. Would it hurt to confide in him again? It wasn't like they'd be together for many more days. And anyway, she was probably just tired, and whatever was messing with her senses would right themselves soon enough. And she did trust him. "My grandfather just told me about a card he got in the mail."

When Brentin furrowed his eyebrows, she quickly told him about the cards and nursery rhymes and that they'd received them just before or just after someone had died, including the new one that had arrived less than a day before Ira had died.

"That's really weird," he said.

"That last rhyme was about a serial killer who poisoned people." Mikaela hugged her arms and backed against her door. "What do you think? Should I tell the Rotorua police about them? My grandfather said he told the authorities in Brigham City."

"I would, too, if I were him. Hopefully no one else there dies."

She coughed.

"Listen," he said, "if you're that frightened or even just worried, I say you should tell the police here. It's better to give them too much information than not enough."

"I know you're right, but I can't help worrying—what if they see the cards as another connection between my grandfather and Caroline's death? And now Ira's."

Brentin squeezed both her upper arms and stepped slightly closer to her. Her pulse pounded against her throat. "Your grandfather didn't get a card when Caroline died, did he?"

"No."

"Then how could they think this new card could connect your grandfather to Ira? They are quite coincidental, I'll give you that, but I'm having a hard time seeing how Ira's death—here in New Zealand—could have anything to do with some cards that have shown up all the way over in Utah."

"I suppose you're right." Mikaela stepped out of his grasp and headed toward the top of the stairs.

"But—"

She turned back to him.

"—while it's still possible the deaths had nothing to do with the sympathy cards, I can't see how the cards aren't connected to each other. And to your grandfather. And to—"

"Me?"

He moved in beside her, and they walked to the staircase. "I was going to say *to your family*. Have you asked any of your other relatives if they've received similar cards? If they have, maybe it'll help you figure out who's sending them."

"I'm starting to think I'm a bit of a worrier."

"There's nothing wrong with that."

"Thanks, and . . ."

"Yes?"

His warm brown eyes. She nudged his elbow with hers. "Just thanks."

"Anytime."

She nodded and started ahead of him down the stairs.

Detective Eaton, Sergeant Hoffmann, and most of Kotuku Inn's residents stood in the entry hall.

"Is everyone except Mr. Kendrick here now?" Detective Eaton said.

Mascara smeared Sara's cheeks, and watery redness lined her eyes. "Yes," she said.

Detective Eaton nodded crisply to Sergeant Hoffman, who stepped forward. "The pathologist's preliminary check of Mr. Lawrence's body indicates his death was likely not from natural causes."

Mikaela caught her breath. She'd feared that would be the case but hoped it wouldn't be.

"I told you he was murdered," Tui said.

"That is a possibility," Sergeant Hoffman said, "but it is also possible his death was self-inflicted."

Brentin cupped his hand around Mikaela's elbow, and she gave him a quick nod of thanks. Until then, she hadn't realized she was trembling.

"Does the pathologist know the cause of death? Or when it happened?" Brentin looked to the others. "Did anyone see someone go in his room?"

"Just Vicky," Sara said.

"He couldn't have been murdered," Vicky said. "He was alone in his room. And he wouldn't kill himself. I know he wouldn't."

"Which means no one knows anything," Mikaela said.

"We'll know more after the pathologist has run more tests and performed an autopsy," the officer said.

"Vicky said he felt sick after lunch," Mikaela said. "Could that be how he died? Because he got sick?"

"Maybe it was food poisoning," Vicky suggested. "From the salad he ate for lunch."

Mikaela's mouth went dry. *Poison . . . Mary Ann Cotton . . . food.*

Brentin wrapped his arm around her shoulders. "Are you all right?" he whispered.

"I said he could eat my salad," she whispered back. "What if he did and it was poisoned? What if I was the one who was supposed to die?"

His grip tightened. "I'm sure he ate his own salad too. If that was the problem, his salad could have been poisoned just as easily as yours."

Tui glared at Vicky. "It was definitely not food poisoning! Amiria and I made those meals, and the vegetables were fresh and clean. So were the dishes. We did nothing wrong."

"What about the dressing?" Sergeant Hoffman said.

"I purchased it that morning. It's in the refrigerator, if you'd like to check it." She scowled at Vicky. "It's more likely he accidentally took the wrong medicine. He was blind."

"That isn't possible," Vicky said. "I always measured out his medications for him."

Sergeant Hoffman lifted his hand, palm outward, silencing them. "As Detective Eaton said, we don't yet know all the details, but in light of this new information, we need to speak with each of you again."

"And perhaps we'll be able to speak with Mrs. Kendrick's husband this time?" Detective Eaton asked.

Sara looked out the window toward the parking lot. "He should be back anytime. Unless something has happened to him too."

"I doubt it's anything like that," Mikaela said gently.

"I hope you're right," Sara said.

"For now, Mrs. Kendrick," Detective Eaton said, "please join me in Mrs. Davies's office."

The two headed toward that room, and Sergeant Hoffman glanced between Mikaela and Brentin.

Two sets of car lights turned off the main road and onto the inn's driveway.

"Frank!" Sara charged forward, but Detective Eaton stopped her. "Hoffman, if that is indeed Mr. Kendrick, speak with him while I talk to his wife. He might have noticed something before he left."

"Will do." Sergeant Hoffman walked out the door, and Sara, frowning, followed the officer into Tui's office.

Quiet filled the hallway. Mikaela glanced at the others. They glanced at her. *Dear God in Heaven, please help me not say anything that might harm my grandfather.*

"I can't stay here," Vicky said flatly. She wrung her hands. "Not with Ira gone. But I can't leave either. I wasn't prepared for this expense. Ira had already paid for our stay here, and my plane to Australia doesn't leave for another two weeks."

Brentin stepped closer to Mikaela. He bumped her arm and muttered, "Maybe we ought to move too. Things are getting a bit uncomfortable here."

*We?* She slid away from him. "And go where?"

"How about that hotel where you took the doll? Under the circumstances, the owner might give us a good deal, especially since he knows your grandfather."

Mikaela grimaced. She wanted to be there to help her grandfather, yet running the inn on her own with the police milling about and uncertainty—murder?—around every corner would be a strain on her and a hardship on anyone who stayed.

Sara exited Tui's office. "You're next, Mikaela."

"Don't worry, Vicky," Mikaela said. "I'm sure my grandfather and I will work something out. He'll be here soon." She then stepped into the office.

Detective Eaton went straight to the point. "Please tell me again about the last time you saw Mr. Lawrence."

"Do you mind if I tell you something first? It might not mean anything, but it came up after I last spoke with you."

"Go ahead."

Mikaela briefly recounted how she and her grandfather had received the blue sympathy cards around Trevor's and her grandmother's deaths. She also described the newest card. The detective sympathized with her losses and the oddity of the situation, but like her and Brentin, he couldn't see how any of them could possibly relate to Ira's death—unless, of course, they considered that the only connection between the cards and the three deaths were her and her grandfather.

"We've had nothing to do with them," she said.

"In any case, I'm quite certain that if Ira was indeed murdered, he was not killed by someone in the United States. The perpetrator will be someone here in New Zealand, very likely in Rotorua." His gaze narrowed.

Was he implying she'd murdered him? She glanced over her shoulder as if someone was watching them, licked her lips, and clenched her fists. *Get hold of yourself.* He likely hadn't meant anything by that comment. Her nerves were simply on edge. But there was one thing she was finally certain of. Everyone needed to leave Kotuku Inn.

\* \* \*

Hunapo slowly pulled his wheeled suitcase through his bedroom door into the short, narrow hall. He could make it to the front door before weakness overcame him. He only had to place one foot in front of the other on the worn carpet. Step. Step. *Do not scratch the rash on your neck. The balm is working.*

He reached the walkway and turned right toward the door. If his doctor had known of his plans to travel to New Zealand, he would have been angry with Hunapo. He'd have lectured that the trip could force a sooner death. But who was the doctor to tell him how to spend what remained of his life? Hunapo had the right to live as he saw fit. And the best way to live was to complete what he'd started. To restore balance. To see that no more deaths were botched.

He positioned his suitcase next to the door, where he could easily grab it when his taxi arrived to take him to the airport in San Francisco. Once again, he checked the messages on his cell phone.

*Girl still alive.*

Hunapo had hoped Mikaela would be dead by now, but no matter. She would be soon, and it would only be he and Joseph left. A second text buzzed his phone.

*Where get gun?*

Hunapo pressed REPLY, typed *I'll get it,* and took another deep breath. He focused on the red wooden table beside the kitchen window. The table wasn't nearly as large or as ornately carved as the one his grandfather had owned, but it was a decent replica. Perhaps he should have sold it with the other antiques, but no matter how much money it could have brought him, he couldn't do it. He'd purchased it for Kotuku Inn long before Joseph had ever entered the Evanses' lives.

"It's good that I should sit at this table one last time," he said aloud.

He pressed the palm of his hand against the wall, leaned into it, and waited for his strength to build up before looking to the papers stacked neatly on the tabletop. Before his nurse had left him an hour earlier, she'd retrieved his last will and testament from his file cabinet. She'd also gathered the paper, pens, envelopes, and the blue sympathy cards he'd asked her to take from the junk drawer.

He walked to the table, brushed a piece of lint from his black suit coat, and lowered himself into the closest chair. He left his will in the center of the table and dragged the other items in front of him. How long this round of "good" health would last, he didn't know. Surely no more than a week, since that was the longest he'd ever gone between chemo treatments. But he would take advantage of whatever time he had.

Hunapo picked up the black pen and began to write.

*Joseph,*

*When I left Kotuku Inn, I told you it would be the last you'd hear from or see me, but time and circumstances have made it impossible for me to keep that promise. You have taken all that is important to me, and under the law of utu, I demand all that is important to you as recompense.*

*I do not tell you these things because I believe you have forgotten the wrongs you have committed against me, but I believe you may have turned an unseeing eye upon them as you did so many other times after we purchased Kotuku Inn together. I forgave your earlier offenses because Mrs. Evans taught me it was right to do so. But as time has gone on, the memory of your crimes against me have only increased my pain. Mrs. Evans's Christian ways do not have power to heal my soul as she claimed they did. That power remains with the old ways of my people, with what Caroline termed our "eye for an eye" law of utu.*

Hunapo reread the words he'd written. They weren't as fancy sounding as the will the lawyer had drawn up for him after he'd learned he had lung cancer, but it released some of the pent-up anger that had so long burned in his heart. He smiled slightly. Already, utu was leading him to satisfaction.

He set the tip of his pen back onto the paper and continued to write.

*You killed both my wife and my life. Perhaps not physically, but you stole Reka's heart and loyalty from me just as certainly as if you had shot the disease into her body and waited for its poison to overpower her. I knew you had once dated Reka, but when I married her, I believed your feelings for each other had disappeared. I don't know how or when you came to her after that, but I'm certain you did. Otherwise, why had she still pined for you?*

*But that was not your only offense against me. You persuaded Mrs. Evans to give the doll to you even though you knew it was rightly mine. I had become the son she never had when my mother went to work for them. I had helped her husband procure the doll for her. He named me in his will as second only to her. How you turned her feelings against me, I don't know. Perhaps you fed her lies. Whatever the cause, you stole that heritage of love and prosperity from me and my family, and now I, the only one who can set a fair recompense for those wrongs, exact them of you.*

*My price is the lives of you, your wife, and your granddaughter. Your life because you took the Evanses from me. Your wife because you stole my wife's heart from me. Your granddaughter because you robbed me of prosperity, and when you moved from New Zealand to care for her, you proved she meant more to you than your property. You took what I most valued; therefore, you must lose what you most value.*

*I tell you these things, not because you don't know them, but because this debt will hang over you and your family until it is paid. Why not pay it now and end your cowardice?*

*Hunapo Grieg*

Hunapo slid the letter inside the blue card. After that, he wrote Joseph's name and address across the envelope. He'd mail it from the airport. Whether Joseph received it before his death or not didn't matter. Someone would receive it. And someone would know that all had finally returned to its rightful order.

# Chapter 21

THE SUN HAD BEEN UP for more than an hour when Brentin lugged his camera bag and suitcases into the vacant lounge. Where was everyone? Tui and Amiria may have already left to stay with Tui's son, but the rest of them had agreed to meet before moving to the King's Hotel. He hadn't even seen the officers who'd stayed overnight at the inn as guards.

Brentin set his bags next to the piano and walked to the large windows at the back of the room. He scanned the yard from the deck tables, where he'd first seen Ira and Vicky, to the overturned ground where the renovators had found Caroline Evans's body. Mikaela's decision, along with her grandfather's approval, to move everyone to the King's Hotel had pleased him at first, but the longer he thought about Ira's death, the greater his concerns grew. Was it smart for all of them to move to the same place? Was it safe? More than likely, a stranger had slipped into the inn and killed Ira—perhaps a crazed fan. But what if it was one of the other guests?

He took a deep breath and clenched his fists. At least the other hotel kept security personnel stationed throughout the building. All would be well for Mikaela's—for all their sakes.

He scratched his neck. *Mikaela.* Now how was he supposed to act toward her? Many times it seemed she avoided him because she still hurt over her fiancé's death, but there were other times when he believed she felt something—dare he think a romantic something?—for him. Like last night when she'd stepped into the hallway and he'd caught her gaze. Or when she'd told him about those nursery rhymes. Even now, just thinking about her standing so close and looking into his eyes, his fingers ached to hold her hand, to touch her face, to pull her into his arms and keep her safe. And yet at other times—most times—she seemed distant.

He shook his head and once more turned his gaze to the window and bottom of the deck stairs, where he'd first seen Mikaela. Where he'd first felt the pull of her smile. No, more than that. He hadn't realized what it was at the time, but now he knew it was the pull of her character to his. Their sameness. They belonged together. And no matter how much he tried to ignore that fact or hide it, the truth of it remained. They. Belonged. Together.

Brentin again faced the room. He moved to the sofa but didn't sit. Why were Mikaela and the others taking so long?

Hard-soled footsteps clicked across the hallway's wood floor. Brentin looked to the doorway. Amiria stood there. She wore black heels and a black business suit, and pulled two large black suitcases, one stacked on top of the other, with her left hand. She carried a rose-colored gown over her right arm. "I guess this is another good-bye," she said.

"It looks that way."

She held the gown out to him. "I had this made especially for tonight, but since things have turned out the way they have . . . Will you ask Mikaela for me if she would like to wear it to the convention in my place? It seems a shame to let it go to waste."

"Why don't you ask her yourself?" His gaze flew to the empty staircase on the other side of the doorway. "She can't be far away."

"I would, but Mother wants to leave now. Will you? For an old friend's sake?"

"Since you've put it that way . . ."

She smiled. "Make sure you send me a wedding announcement."

"Amiria!" He glanced toward the doorway. Had anyone—Mikaela—heard her? He put the dress inside his suitcase. "There's nothing at all settled—not even mentioned—between Mikaela and me."

"I was afraid as much." She sighed. "Well, it's your life. I'll see you later, I hope."

"Wait a minute, Amiria. What's that sigh supposed to mean?"

She turned back to him. "I'm pretty sure you don't want to know."

"Yes, I do."

"Very well, then. It means you're being an idiot, and if you keep this up, Mikaela's going to get away."

"I'm handling this my own way, okay?"

"Avoiding, you mean, which isn't the same as handling. Look, Brentin, I know that's what you've been doing, because I've been doing the same thing. Vicky was right. I want more out of life than this, but I'm not doing anything about it—just staying with my mother where everything's comfortable. But now, Ira's death—and Caroline's—they've got me to thinking that I'm losing precious time by waiting for what I want to drop itself into my lap. I'm going to start going after what I want."

"Good for you."

"Don't you think you should do the same thing? You've only got what? A day? Two? Until you fly home?"

"I leave tomorrow morning."

She shook her head. "You call that handling it?"

"I know. And you're right. But Mikaela's—her head's wrapped around a lot of other things right now."

"Yes, and if you keep going at this rate, you'll both be right where you are now when you leave tomorrow. The end. Lost opportunity. What's the worst that can happen?"

An ache had been pushing against the inside of his ribs for so long he didn't know when it had cracked, sending thousands of frozen shards through his core. "She could tell me she's not interested."

"Then you'd know, and you could move on." As if on impulse, she grabbed his hand in both of hers and added, "But you might also find out Mikaela doesn't want to wait either."

Brentin stared at her. "Do you know something I don't? Has she said anything to you?"

"No. But I have eyes even if neither of you do."

Footsteps combined with the *clunk-clunk* of luggage wheels along the upstairs floor stopped at the top of the staircase.

"There she is," Amiria said. "Why don't you go and help her."

"You really are one of the best girls I know."

They briefly held each other's gaze, and then she headed for the front door. He ran up the narrow steps. "Can I help with your suitcases?" he asked Mikaela.

Worry clearly etched every contour of her face, but still she smiled, and Brentin, suddenly losing strength in his knees at the sight of her, grabbed the railing. Murder and threats were the last things to encourage love, but Amiria was right. Somehow, amid it all, he had to both protect her and tell her how he felt.

# Chapter 22

MIKAELA AND BRENTIN LEFT VICKY and the newlyweds near the King's Hotel's office and went on to Mikaela's suite. Brentin's was next to hers.

Mikaela opened the door and took her luggage from Brentin's arms. "Thanks for your help."

His face flushed. "I told Vicky I'd pick up something for us to eat since we missed breakfast this morning. I saw a Chinese place on the drive here. Or there's a good fish and chips diner nearby. Which do you prefer?"

Her stomach churned. She had to be doing the right thing in relocating herself and the others there, yet uneasiness wriggled through her like a long line of lost inchworms searching for a place to settle. Something definitely didn't feel right. "Whatever you want is fine."

"There's a supermarket about a mile back. How about if I buy a few supplies we can keep in the refrigerator?"

"Sure."

"Lock your door until I get back, okay? And don't let anyone inside before you know who it is and you're sure you can trust them."

She drew her eyebrows together. Did he sense her anxiousness, or did he have his own misgivings? "Okay."

"You're sure you'll be fine?"

"You saw the security man next to the elevators."

"Right." He hesitated and watched.

"See you in a little bit," she said.

At last he left, and Mikaela set her luggage on the floor, locked the door, and faced her apartment. A wide countertop divided the small living room, which contained a sofa and television, from a full, though compact, kitchen. A door at the back of the kitchen opened into what appeared to be the bed and bathroom area.

Mikaela pulled her luggage across the living room to that door. The bathroom was on her right, and just beyond it, the sleeping area consisted of a dresser, two bedside tables, and a queen bed. She glanced between the living room and bedroom: mottled cream carpet and various shades of gray and teal fabrics. Whoever had decorated the place had a good eye.

She put her luggage in the closet kitty-corner from the bathroom and pulled her phone from her pocket. Her grandfather answered after one ring. "What's wrong?"

She quickly told him that all but the police had left Kotuku Inn and that she and several of the other guests were now safely settled at the King's Hotel.

"I'm coming out there on the earliest flight I can get," he said. "You won't be alone much longer."

"I wouldn't exactly call it alone. Tui and"—he trusted Tui, but Brentin? He didn't even know him— "and Amiria have been with me."

"You said they left."

"Yes, but not until this morning."

Silence pulsed through the phone. "What about that young man from Colorado? Is he there with you? You texted you trusted him."

"He's here too. His name's Brentin. He's staying in the apartment next to mine."

"Keep him close. Something's definitely going on."

"I've got the same feeling, only I'm starting to wonder if it might be because the police said Ira had been poisoned."

"You're thinking of the card."

"You haven't learned anything more about who might have sent it, have you?"

"Only that it was posted out of California. Mikaela, I know you won't like this, but please keep someone with you as much as you can."

"You think the card might be connected to what's going on here." It was a statement, but she lilted her voice on the end as if it were a question. *Please, God, let it only be a question.*

"I don't know how they can be connected, and yet the way the other cards came just before a death . . . I've never been able to make myself believe your grandmother fell from the same canyon she'd hiked more times than I can count."

"*Humpty Dumpty had a great fall,*" Mikaela whispered. They were the words from the sympathy card she'd received at the funeral. And—prickles splashed across every inch of her skin, and she clasped her fingers together to stop them from trembling—Trevor had died in a car accident after she'd read, *Jack fell down and broke his crown.* The police had determined her car's brakes had failed even though she'd just had them inspected. She'd confronted the automotive repair shop about it, but they'd said the brakes had been fine. She'd figured either the police or the automotive shop had to have been wrong, but now . . .

Mikaela blinked. What if both the officers and the mechanics had been right? What if the brakes *had* failed but not because they were faulty, but because someone had intentionally sabotaged them?

"Remember. Try not to be alone if you can help it," her grandfather said.

"All right. Call me after you book your flight." Mikaela disconnected, and despite everything else, she exhaled in relief. New Zealand was her grandfather's country, and Kotuku Inn was his home. He would know how to protect both it and them better than she ever could.

She pulled her notebook from her backpack, taking it to the wide kitchen countertop and sitting on one of the two tall stools nestled on the living room side. She placed the newspaper clipping she'd printed at the library about her grandfather's treasure hunt on the counter and spread several blank sheets of paper in a line next to it. The detectives on her favorite mystery television shows created time lines to help them figure out who had the time and means to commit a crime, but the longer Mikaela stared at the papers, imagining the names and other facts she hadn't yet written on them, the more she realized a time line wouldn't work in this situation. Too much time and distance divided them. Maybe a collage would be more helpful.

She set her jaw and started again. She wrote *Caroline Evans* in the upper margin of one paper and slid it near the left corner of the counter. On the next few sheets, she listed everything she'd learned about the woman, including the names of those she knew and which of them were still living. Mikaela then wrote *Possible Motive—Greed* on another sheet and placed each paper in a circle around Caroline's name.

She quickly filled out several more sheets of paper with similar information about the other victims, including the possibly related nursery rhymes. She lined each collage along the kitchen side of the counter.

This time, the menagerie made more sense to her, but even after rehearsing aloud every detail and after drawing mental lines between each person and fact, she discovered no single person connected to all four victims. Not even her or her grandfather.

Mikaela scrubbed her hand over her face. What was she missing?

# Chapter 23

SomeOne knocked on Mikaela's door at the same time she received a text from her grandfather. She read the message.

*First flight leaves Salt Lake 5:10 p.m. our time. Will arrive in Auckland tomorrow 7:15 a.m. your time. Will be in Rotorua around 11.*

Mikaela peered through the door's peephole, exhaled in relief, and opened the door to Brentin. Sometime after he'd left her apartment he'd removed his jacket. He wore a dark-blue T-shirt. It looked even better on him than the green one did. "That was fast."

"It felt slow to me. I ended up in a long check-out line." He bustled inside with several grocery bags.

"You do realize we probably won't be staying here long enough to eat all that food, don't you? Especially since you fly out tomorrow?"

"I didn't know what you'd like, so I bought a variety. Where do you want me to put these?"

"Wherever you find room." She relocked the door.

Brentin nodded toward her menagerie of paper on the counter. "You've been busy."

"More like frazzled. I can't make sense of any of it. Is it too much to ask for these troubles to just go away?" *For me to feel safe again?*

"If you find the secret to making problems disappear, let me know. I've got a boatload of my own." He'd already placed two full grocery bags on the stove top, but when he placed a larger bag inside the empty sink, Mikaela noticed for the first time the red gown draped over his arm. "What's that?"

He set another bag on the floor near his feet. "Amiria gave it to me before she left. She had it made for the convention tonight, but with everything that's happened, she can't go and hoped you'd wear it in her place."

"That was nice of her, but I don't see how I can go either." She looked at the papers on the counter. "I've got to figure this out."

"I thought you'd say that, but—"

"But what?"

He took the groceries out of the bag he'd put in the sink. To his credit, along with cheese, crackers, chips, and cookies, he'd also bought a small bag of apples and an even smaller container of cut celery. No bread though. Had he expected them to make cracker sandwiches?

"I've missed a lot of the convention because of everything that's been going on," he said. "I don't think I better miss tonight. It's the premier performance of my last film. A lot of newscasters will be in attendance. Several celebrities too."

"Of course you shouldn't miss it."

"But I also don't like the idea of leaving you alone. Will you please reconsider and go with me?"

Mikaela put the cheese in the refrigerator. Her grandfather had asked her not to be alone if she could help it, and if Brentin left, her only other options were the distraught Vicky or playing third wheel to the newlyweds. In either case, she probably wouldn't be able to do much detecting. "Can I think about it?"

"Sure." He again motioned to the papers on the counter. "Have you made any sense of it all?"

"The only thing that makes sense at all is that those nursery rhymes are somehow related to the deaths, but I can't find any single person connecting them. The closest I get is either my grandfather or me, which is totally unhelpful. Why don't you look? Maybe you'll see something I haven't."

He walked around the counter and, standing next to Mikaela, studied the lists. "I'm a suspect in Ira's murder?"

"All of us are. We're the only ones who were staying at the inn when he died."

Brentin gave her a sidelong glance and trailed his forefinger down each of the facts. "This is a pretty daunting task. If the police don't have enough details to figure this out, I can't imagine we do."

"I still have to try."

"Yes."

Mikaela stared at him. He didn't smile like he was teasing her. In fact, he didn't look at her at all. "Why is that, do you think? That I have to try? I certainly don't know."

His eyes widened, and his mouth opened, but instead of answering her, he shook his head. This time he grinned.

"How is that funny?"

He clamped her shoulder. "It's not funny. It's only that your motivation in all this is so obvious your question took me by surprise. Here." He handed her a small box of tissues from the end table. "Let's take a short break. It's been a tough day—and in your case, a tough year."

"I can't waste time crying. I've got to take care of my grandfather."

His hand turned atop her shoulder as he moved in front of her. He placed his other hand on her other shoulder. "Look at me."

She glanced away, embarrassed. "Now you sound like a school teacher."

"That's easy to do."

She laughed.

He ducked and caught her gaze. She let him hold it.

"You're trying to figure this out because you love your grandfather and you're trying to protect him. No one ever said being good and noble was easy."

Brentin's words, his voice, even the intensity in his eyes seemed sincere, yet she couldn't help but say, "Please don't tease me about this. All I'm doing is running in circles."

A soft groan came from Brentin's throat. His grip tightened around her shoulders, and he shook his head. "I'm not teasing. And circles or not, you told your grandfather you would look after his interests, and that's what you're doing. He's lucky to have you. You are the most reliable person I know. It's what I most lo—" he swallowed "—like about you."

Warm moisture burned behind Mikaela's eyes, and her heart pounded against her chest like an incessant drum. She bit her lower lip, but still it trembled. Stupid lip. She pushed away the tissue box. *I will not cry.*

"Are you okay?"

"Brentin, I—"

Her phone rang. Who would be calling? Her grandfather texted or Skyped. She dragged her gaze away from Brentin's and pulled her phone out of her pocket. It was Andrew. "Hello?"

"Can you get to a television? I never checked if the inn had them, but if they do—"

"I'm not at the inn anymore, Andrew. We, uh, had to move. But, yeah, I can get to a TV."

Brentin clenched his jaw when she said Andrew's name.

"There's a news report about to come on about Caroline," Andrew said. "You've got to see it."

"What channel?" She took the remote from the coffee table, turned on the television, and clicked through to the channel he gave her. A male and female announcer sat behind a news desk. "Okay, I'm there."

"Just watch it."

She powered up the volume. "—with any information on the fifty-year-old murder of Caroline Evans," the male announcer said before the screen filled with a large photograph of a gold wedding ring made up of three bands. Each of the two outer bands contained a row of small diamonds, while the thicker middle one contained a row of small diamonds and a large central diamond surrounded by several smaller stones.

"This ring was found buried a few feet from the victim's remains when renovators discovered her body in Rotorua two days ago," the announcer continued. "The authorities hope that by releasing this information, someone will recognize the ring and report what they know. The Evans family has offered a one thousand dollar reward to anyone with information that ultimately leads to an arrest. If you know anything about this ring or this case, please contact your local authorities."

The female announcer took over, moving onto the weather report, and Mikaela turned off the television. "I didn't know the police found anything other than her body," she said to Andrew.

"Neither did I. Not until I saw that report."

"And now your family's offering a reward? After all this time?"

"That's my mother's doing. Surprised me too. She seems to have had a change of heart about her long-lost relative. But what do you think about that ring? It has to mean something."

He sounded so hopeful that Mikaela didn't have the heart to say the ring—since it wasn't actually *on* Caroline's body—might not have anything to do with her death. Kotuku Inn was a bed and breakfast, and hundreds, maybe thousands, of married couples could have been in that area and dropped the ring since she'd died. But then . . . the reporter did say the police had found it buried near her. Did that mean the police thought the ring might have been lost or buried around the same time as Caroline's death? "It's definitely worth looking into," she said.

"Exactly. So what should we do now?"

Mikaela glanced at her papers, her lists, at Brentin's hard stare. "The ring's interesting and all, but I really don't know what we can do besides wait and see if anyone comes forward with more information."

"Don't you think we ought to at least get together again and compare notes? How about dinner tonight?"

"Dinner's a nice idea, but I'm sorry. I can't." She again looked at Brentin. Why was he watching her so closely? "I—I'm going to the convention tonight."

"Maybe tomorrow night, then. What about you? Have you learned anything more about Caroline's death? Or the doll?"

"I haven't, but don't worry. I'll let you know if I do."

"Mikaela? Before you hang up, there is something I thought of. Would you be willing to let me take a picture of the doll for my article? I bet it would drum up a lot of local interest."

"I don't know. I'd have to ask my grandfather first, but with the way he's kept it hidden all these years, I really think he'll say no. But I'll ask him and let you know."

"I'd appreciate it."

They said their good-byes, and Mikaela hung up. Brentin, folding his arms, leaned back against the counter and grinned. "So you decided to come with me tonight after all."

She couldn't quite tell if he was laughing at her or pleased or something entirely different, but the glint in his eyes made her feel weak-kneed—no, embarassed. That had to be it. She couldn't feel anything close to weak-kneed about Brentin, no matter how good a man he was. He was leaving soon. And anyway, she was still in love with Trevor. And did she mention Brentin was leaving? Feeling anything for him would be foolish. *I will not be a fool.* "If by *decided*," she said, "you mean got pushed into it, then, yeah, I guess I did."

"Whatever it takes," he said.

Mikaela whirled from him and paced to the door. By the time she reached it and faced him again, she had her emotions and her thoughts under control. Time to get back to the issues at hand. "Did that ring seem at all familiar to you?" she asked him.

"Should it?"

"I don't know. Maybe I've just thought so much of earrings and dolls and treasures that something about it seemed familiar."

"Hmm." Pursing his lips, Brentin picked up the photocopied newspaper clipping of the treasure hunt at Kotuku Inn.

Mikaela moved in next to him. "Did you think of something?"

"You don't think that ring could have been the missing treasure, do you? And not the doll? It looks quite expensive, and it's small enough that maybe Caroline hid it out there."

"I suppose that's possible, but the ring seems a bit flashy for what I've seen of Caroline's tastes."

"Maybe that's why she hid it."

"But then again, if that ring was the treasure and stealing it was the murderer's motive for killing her, why didn't he or she take it with them?"

"Maybe someone or something startled him and he ran before he got caught."

"Maybe." Mikaela turned to a new page in her notebook and wrote his suggestion under *Theories* while Brentin slowly ran his finger across the picture.

"So that's the young Leanne Sabey," he said. "She's changed quite a bit. And that looks like—I wonder if that's Mr. Starks. He owned the theater years ago. And there—hey, look at this. Doesn't that look like Jewell Cooper? Her hair's still the same color and style."

"I think that is her." Images of Jewell standing in front of her fireplace while they interviewed her flashed through Mikaela's mind. And connected.

Brentin's phone buzzed. He pulled it from his pocket and stepped away from the counter. "Sorry. I better take this."

Mikaela held her breath and looked closer at the photograph. Jewell liked nice things. Jewell lived in Rotorua when Caroline Evans had died. And that ring . . . Was it—could it be the one Jewell was wearing in her engagement portrait?

"All right." Brentin slid his phone back into his pants pocket and, without looking at her, went to the couch and touched Amiria's gown.

"I think Jewell might be connected to Caroline Evans's death," Mikaela said.

He stared at her. "What makes you think so?"

She quickly told him about the Coopers' engagement portrait.

"It's hard for me to imagine Jewell killing Caroline Evans." Brentin looked doubtful.

"It is for me too, but from what I remember, the ring the police found with Caroline's body really did look like the one she was wearing. I was thinking about my engagement photos with Trevor when I was looking at it and comparing my ring to hers."

He frowned.

"Do you think we ought to call the police about it?" she asked.

"Not yet. What if you're wrong?"

"Yeah, but even if the ring isn't hers, investigating it might keep the police's scrutiny off my grandfather, at least for a while."

"The Coopers are important people in this community, Mikaela. We don't want to mess up their reputations on a guess."

"It's not a guess."

"It's not a fact either."

"All right. I won't call the police until I see their picture again and know I'm right."

His eyes widened. "I don't think I want to know how you plan to see it again."

"All we have to do is figure out how to get back into their apartment without them knowing why. How about if we ask to interview them again?"

"It's too late for that. The film's tonight, and anyway, they've already seen the finished one."

"Then we'll have to sneak in."

"Break in, you mean. What if we get caught?"

"Can you think of a better plan?"

"Lots of them."

"Like what?"

"Like, well"—he glanced across the room—"we could look at her hand. Her engagement and wedding rings might only look similar to the one on the news."

Mikaela's gaze instinctively dropped to her naked left hand. It had taken her nearly three months after Trevor's death before she could bring herself to remove her engagement ring. "The last time I saw Jewell, she wore a single gold wedding band."

"Maybe she moved her engagement ring to her right hand."

"Not when I looked. So you'll help me?"

He expelled a long, slow sigh. "Let's say you're right and that it is Jewell's ring. If she's innocent, won't she report it to the police when she sees that report?"

"And what if she's guilty?" Mikaela countered.

"She'll probably get rid of that portrait."

Mikaela looked at the papers spread across the counter. "It's the only lead I've got, Brentin."

He looked up at the ceiling, shook his head slightly, and scooped Amiria's dress up from the back of the couch. "It's against my better judgment, but I'll help you if you'll help me."

Mikaela looked at him, startled. She tilted her head to the side. "Help you with what?"

"That call I had just now. It was from Ms. Sabey. Mikaela, I need you to do more than attend the convention with me tonight."

"What?"

"It's for the entertainment. They're calling it Celebrity Couples Jeopardy. It's a dating game. They need three couples, and one of them backed out this morning because their agent booked them for another event. Ms. Sabey asked me to fill in with you as my date. Please, Mikaela. We need your help."

Mikaela crunched her toes so tightly against the bottom of her shoes they began to tingle. "But we aren't even dating."

"The audience doesn't have to know that."

"They'll know after we answer the first question."

"Not if we prepare." He cupped her elbow in his hand. "It's a charity event. A hundred dollars a plate plus a few wagers. Please? If you won't come, they won't have their third couple, and the event will be ruined."

Mikaela went to kick the nearby stool but at the last minute kicked her toe against the floor. Brentin had already done so much for her, how could she refuse? "All right. But I want you to note that I'm doing this under duress."

He grinned.

"And I'll only do it if you help me get in the Coopers' house first."

Brentin shook his head and, turning away, walked toward the television. When he reached it, he slowly faced her again and gave her a half smile. "Deal."

# Chapter 24

MIKAELA'S STOMACH KNOTTED TIGHTER WHEN Brentin parked in front of the Middle Earth Hotel and Spa.

"I hope this works," he said.

She opened her sketchbook and flipped to a blank page. "It has to. Don't worry. Most people would be flattered if an artist asked for permission to draw their historic fireplace."

Brentin reached into the backseat for his camera. "Let's hope you're right."

A few minutes later, they stepped inside the hotel's main lobby. Three couples sat in the restaurant to their left.

"No one's at the front desk," Mikaela said.

"There's probably someone in the back room. Do you want me to check?"

"Not yet." She moved to the small table and chairs beside the large front window. It overlooked the Maori sculpture she'd already drawn for her grandfather. "I'll sit here and draw for a while."

Brentin nodded, but his gaze remained on the sculpture. "Don't get caught," he muttered. Then louder, "I'll be outside if you need me."

He exited the front door, and Mikaela watched him through the window. He walked toward the sculpture, tilted his head, and moved from one side of it to the other.

"Can I help you with something?"

Mikaela caught her breath and slowly turned to the unfamiliar voice. The young woman wore brown slacks and a brown shirt with the words *Middle Earth Hotel and Spa* sewn above the left front pocket.

"No, thank you," Mikaela said. "This is great. I—and that man out there—we interviewed the Coopers the other morning, and when I saw that sculpture out front, I thought one like it would look really nice at Kotuku Inn. I'm Mikaela York. Is it all right if I sit here and draw it?"

"I don't think anyone will mind. If you need something, let me know. I'll be in the back."

Mikaela glanced at the door behind the desk. It led to the Coopers' private rooms. "Are the Coopers here today?"

"In and out. They're taking care of last-minute details for tonight's Celebrity Couples Jeopardy. Will you be attending?"

Mikaela forced a smile. *I wish I weren't.* "Actually, I'm one of the contestants."

"Really? Who's the celebrity? You or your boyfriend?"

"It's definitely not me." Mikaela motioned through the window toward Brentin. He held his viewfinder in front of his face and crouched in the driveway about fifteen feet from the sculpture. "That's Brentin Williams. He's the convention's videographer."

"A handsome bloke."

"He is."

Brentin lowered his camera and, seeing them watching him through the window, waved.

"It's a shame the Coopers aren't here," Mikaela said. "I'd wanted to draw their fireplace."

"Perhaps some other time."

"Perhaps." Mikaela watched the girl walk back to the desk. Now what? Was there a chance the Coopers' chambers were unlocked?

Mikaela carefully looked back and forth over her shoulders. Those in the restaurant had their backs to her. Mikaela shifted her chair to the right so she could keep one eye on the desk and the other eye on the sculpture. She drew a long, exact line across her page.

Brentin caught her gaze through the glass. When she nodded to him, he smiled and lifted his shoulders curiously.

Footsteps.

Mikaela looked toward the desk. The girl stepped out from the back room, took something from a drawer beneath the cash register, and went back through the door.

Mikaela added another line to her sketch. There had to be some way to get the girl to leave her post. Something or someone who could—*Brentin!*

She glanced at the desk, pulled her phone from her pocket, and sent him a text.

*Need girl to leave. Can you call her outside?*

She smudged shading into her drawing. Moments later, Brentin looked at his phone, took another picture, and headed for the door. He walked straight to Mikaela, put his hand on her shoulder, and stared down at her drawing.

"How's it going?" He spoke loudly.

"Pretty well. Getting some good pictures?"

He looked toward the still empty desk. "Quite a few, but I saw some shots toward the back of the building that I'd like to take. Is there someone here I can ask?"

The girl must have been listening because she left the back room. "May I help you, sir?"

"I hope so." Brentin moved toward the desk. "I wondered if you could help me outside for a moment. There are some gorgeous views around here, some I especially hope to photograph, but I don't want to take a picture of something I'm not supposed to. I understand you have some private spas?"

"We do, but they're fenced in. You shouldn't have any problems."

"Could you please check for me anyway? I'd feel better about it."

She looked at the front desk and scanned the lobby. "Very well. I can't be gone more than a moment though."

As soon as they stepped out of sight, Mikaela grabbed her notebook and pencil and ran through the door behind the desk to the Coopers' chambers. She turned the knob. It was unlocked. *Whew!* Nervous goose bumps shot over the length of her body, but she ignored them and stepped inside. Trespassing wasn't nearly as bad a crime as murder—if Jewell was, in fact, guilty of such a thing.

The Coopers' engagement portrait was just where it had been when she and Brentin had interviewed them. Mikaela hurried to it. Her gaze flashed from the couple's smiling faces to the ring on Mrs. Cooper's finger.

Mikaela groaned. The photograph only gave her a side view of the ring. Like the one she'd seen on the news, the ring consisted of three gold bands covered in diamonds and had a large central diamond, but she couldn't see enough of the size and shape of the stone's setting to clearly identify it.

Steady footsteps clicked across the lobby's wood floor. Had the girl returned, or—someone was definitely walking that way.

Mikaela dove for the empty space behind the couch. She held her breath. Had she closed the door? Maybe whoever it was wouldn't think to look. Better yet, maybe the person had only been a guest.

The door opened. "Who's there?"

*Jewell Cooper!* Mikaela's heartbeat pounded against her throat. She hunched lower.

"I know someone's in here. You left the door open, and Savannah's outside."

Mikaela squeezed her eyes closed. Why hadn't she closed the door? She slowly stood. "Hello, Mrs. Cooper."

Jewell stiffened. "What are you doing in here?"

Mikaela's fingers felt like icicles. She opened her mouth, but no words came.

"Savannah didn't let you in, did she?"

"No." Mikaela pressed her knees against the back of the couch for support and glanced at Jewel's hands. Just as she'd remembered, the woman wore a single gold wedding band.

"What then?" Jewel said.

Mikaela gave her a weak smile. "This is the stuff of nightmares—getting caught like this in someone else's house."

"It's even more unnerving to the homeowner."

"Of course." Mikaela's chest and throat constricted. What could she say that would make any sense? Should she try her drawing-the-fireplace excuse? Or what about the truth? "Did you watch the news today?"

Jewell's brows squished together, and her lips turned downward, but her gaze remained clear. Mikaela was probably the only guilty woman in the room. "For a few minutes during breakfast. Why?"

"The afternoon news mentioned Caroline Evans's death."

"And?"

"They showed a picture of a ring that was found near her body. They want to know if anyone knows anything about it."

"I can't see what that has to do with why you're in my home uninvited."

Mikaela glanced at the engagement picture and back at Jewell. "It was an engagement ring. I thought it was the one I'd seen in your photograph, and I wanted to look again to make sure."

Jewell's gaze widened into a hard stare. "You thought it was *my* engagement ring?"

"Yes."

The front desk bell chimed.

"I'll be with you in a moment," Jewell called through the doorway before turning back to Mikaela. "And is it the one you saw on the news?"

Mikaela shrugged. "There are similarities."

The desk bell chimed a second time. Jewell's cheek muscles tightened around her frown. "I told Samantha never to leave the desk unattended."

"That was my fault too," Mikaela said.

"I'm sorry to bother you, Mrs. Cooper," a woman's voice called from the desk, "but my husband and I are running late for our booking at Waitomo Caves, and—"

Jewell growled over the rest of the woman's words, but Mikaela moved past her toward the open door. "I honestly couldn't see enough of your ring in the picture to know whether or not it was the same one shown on the news. It was silly of me to sneak in here."

"Trespass, you mean."

"I'm sorry. Next time, I—"

Jewell followed close behind her. "*Next* time?"

"That's not what I mean—meant—I'm just so sorry." Without waiting for the woman to say anything more, Mikaela scurried through the workroom, past the front desk, and out the door. Brentin and Savannah stood on the left side of the building. Savannah looked toward the entrance, and Brentin gazed toward the backyard grounds.

"Miss York," Savannah said. "I expect you were able to get the drawing you wanted?"

Mikaela hoped her face wasn't as red as it felt, but it probably was. "Pretty much. Thank you for your help."

"I was happy to do it."

Savannah returned to the inn, and Mikaela glanced at Brentin. He moved so close that his arm brushed against hers before they started toward the parking lot.

"Did you see the photograph?" he asked.

"Yeah, but it only showed a side view of the ring. All I can say is it looked similar to the one we saw on the television, but it wasn't clear enough for me to be certain."

"What now? Go back to looking for connections?"

"Yes, but—" How could she put what she was thinking into words that would make sense?

Their footsteps plodded across the asphalt.

"But?"

"Jewell caught me in her living room."

He flinched. "Apparently she didn't call the police. What did you tell her?"

"The truth. The part about the ring anyway."

"That was bold." Brentin unlocked the passenger's side door. "How did she react?"

"You mean, did she look guilty?" Mikaela climbed inside the car. "I don't know what to think about her. She acted, I don't know, nervous maybe."

Brentin closed her door and walked around to the driver's side. He climbed in. "Not angry?"

"She was that too."

He started the engine. "At any rate, that's done. Now it's time for you to fulfill your side of the bargain."

"Tonight's Jeopardy isn't for a few hours."

"True, but we need to practice."

Prickles danced across the back of Mikaela's neck, and her pulse quickened with—*embarrassment. Remember, that's all it is. That's all it can be.*

\* \* \*

Mikaela set her sketchbook on the coffee table in her apartment.

"How about we eat while we quiz each other?" Brentin picked up the news clipping from the counter. "All this spy stuff has given me an appetite."

"Me too." Mikaela opened the refrigerator. The moment of cool air soothed her skin. Had Jewell called the police? Were they on their way for her this very minute? "Any suggestions?"

"Crackers and cottage cheese work for me."

She curled her upper lip. "I think I'd rather have *regular* cheese with crackers."

He held her gaze. "Noted."

She retrieved the refrigerated items, took the crackers from the cupboard above the microwave, and set them on the counter in front of him.

Brentin sat on a bar stool. "Question and answer time. The only chance we have of winning this thing is by finding out as much about each other as we can."

Mikaela rubbed the back of her neck. "Does it matter if we win?"

"The attendees will wager on which team they believe will win, like at a horse race. The charity represented by the winning team will receive the largest contribution. We owe it to our charity to do our best to win."

She took a roll of paper towels from the cupboard beneath the sink and opened the package of round crackers.

Brentin ripped the cover off the cottage cheese. "A bowl?"

"Use the container. I don't want any."

He dipped his cracker into the cottage cheese and plopped the whole thing in his mouth; then he pulled a folded sheet of paper from his back pocket. "Question one."

"You have a list?"

"Of course. Question one. What memory from your childhood always makes you smile?"

*Blowing bubbles from a bubble wand.* Heat burned at the back of her eyes.

"You thought of something, didn't you?"

"Can we skip that question? It's not a big deal, but it's something I'd rather not share with the world."

His gaze deepened, and she felt like he'd moved closer to her even though he hadn't. *Breathe!*

"How about this?" he said. "Only answer the questions you feel comfortable answering. And if there are any you're willing to share with me, just so I can get to know you better but that you don't want me to share with others, tell me that too."

Mikaela ran her finger down the scar on her cheek. The only other person she'd ever shared personal memories with had been Trevor, and he'd had to pull them out of her. He'd said she had a tough shell around her, but he would crack it because he loved her.

"Well?"

"The same for you? With the same questions?"

"Sure." Brentin opened a second package of crackers. "Here, I'll go first. This memory is personal, by the way, so please keep it to yourself."

"Okay." Mikaela opened a drawer and took out a butter knife.

"The childhood memory that most makes me smile is of mowing the lawn," he said. "I was fourteen years old, and I'd taken off my shirt because I thought it would make me look more like a man to the neighbors."

She sliced a bit of cheese. "And did you? Look like a man, I mean?"

He frowned, and his gaze distanced. "The reason it makes me smile is because I hated mowing the lawn. I had to do it every Saturday before I could do anything else. When my dad first assigned me that job, he spent an entire hour teaching me about the machine and how to cut around the bushes and trees. He was particular like that. He died before the next summer rolled around. Now mowing the lawn reminds me of him."

Mikaela's throat ached, and all at once she wanted to brush away the strand of hair that had dropped in front of his eyes.

"Now it's your turn," he said. "Do you have memories like that? Or would you rather not talk about them?"

Images flashed in front of her thoughts—Mom showing her how to clean the bathroom, Dad dancing with her at a daddy-daughter night. "The memory that always makes me smile is of my mother. I was five or six. I snuck up on her while she was taking a nap on the sofa and blew bubbles from a bubble wand onto her face. They landed on her nose and popped. She didn't even wake up until I laughed."

His eyes and lips curved upward. "Your turn to ask a question." He handed her his list.

She scanned them quickly and looked up. His gaze felt like it surrounded her. "Do you have any questions that aren't quite so personal?"

# Chapter 25

HUNDREDS OF MEN AND WOMEN dressed as Dwarves, Hobbits, Elves, and even a few Ents crowded the convention center's banquet room.

"You all right?" Brentin asked.

"I hadn't thought there'd be so many people."

"Is that a problem?"

"I hate being the center of attention."

He clamped his hands around hers. His fingers felt firm, calm. "Will you be okay?"

The fixed glint in his eyes and the slant of his pressed lips told her the question had been hard for him to ask. What if she'd said she wanted to back out? But he had asked it anyway. Something inside her expanded. "I've come this far," she said.

He nodded.

"I'll think of it as a chance to analyze Jewell's behavior a little more. I mean, the longer I think about when she caught me in her house, the more I wonder why she didn't get really angry at me. If I'd been in her shoes, I'd have been furious."

"Me too."

Ms. Sabey, who only moments before had greeted them at the door, came up behind them and caught hold of their elbows. "Let me show you to your seats. We can't have two of our contestants floundering about."

Mikaela started to turn toward her, but Brentin didn't let go of her hand.

"There are plenty of girls around here who'd snatch Brentin up in a heartbeat, my dear," Ms. Sabey said. "You better keep an eye on him."

Mikaela glanced over her shoulder. After their previous conversations, did Ms. Sabey still believe they were dating? But when Ms. Sabey gave her a brief, tight smile, Mikaela remembered the importance of that night's event. It was time for her to forget herself and go along with the game. "I will," she said.

Brentin did a double take, and Mikaela grinned. It had been a long time since she'd teased anyone, much less a man, and it felt good.

He grinned too and motioned toward the portable stage in front of the bowed wall. White draperies hung over the windows, and two long tables, butted together and covered by white tablecloths, filled the center stage. Noah and Jewell Cooper sat at the far right end.

Mikaela's neck felt hot. She looked everywhere but at the Coopers. Surely, if they'd intended to report her trespassing to the police, they'd have done so by now. "I heard the Coopers are tonight's game hosts," she said.

"That had been the plan," Ms. Sabey said, "but things changed a bit this afternoon. Jewell decided she's too busy taking donations to spend all her time hosting the game. She'll help with the introductions, but after that, Noah's on his own." Her voice lilted on the end as if she disagreed with the decision, but she said nothing more.

"Staying behind the scenes." Brentin nodded. "I wish I could have gotten away with that. Mikaela too, I expect."

Ms. Sabey led them between two more round tables. Brentin lifted his and Mikaela's clasped hands in front of them then lowered them again. His cheeks looked almost as flushed as Mikaela's felt, but all at once he stepped closer and whispered in her ear. His breath brushed against her hair. "We've got to pretend we're a couple."

"I thought we were doing that."

He looked at her out of the corner of his eye, released her hand, and wrapped his arm around her shoulders. "Now we are."

Mikaela's breath, her heartbeat, her thoughts paused as the two of them climbed onto the stage. Brentin was only playacting. There was nothing for her to get worked up over.

Ms. Sabey pointed to their name placards on the table at the end opposite from the Coopers. "I'll leave you two here to get settled while I find our other contestants. Good luck!" She walked away.

"I'll take the chair closest to the end," Brentin said.

Jewell, her expression blank, nodded an acknowledgment to Mikaela. Mikaela's stomach felt like someone had molded it into a hard ball and rolled it into a cluster of bowling pins, but she nodded back to Jewell and sat next to Brentin in the chair he'd pulled out for her. She looked out at the rows of quickly filling tables.

"Did Ms. Sabey seem weird to you?" Brentin said.

"I don't know. It's not often you see a seventy-plus-year-old Tolkien groupie."

He laughed. "Not that kind of weird. More like distracted?"

"I'd be distracted too if I was running this thing."

"You're probably right."

Both stared at the audience. Mikaela clasped her fingers together.

"So far so good," Brentin said. "You're in front of people, and nothing bad has happened."

"I hope you still say that after the first question."

"We'll be fine. We learned a lot about each other today."

"I hope it will be enough."

"Don't tell me you're starting to care whether we win this thing or not?"

"All right, I won't."

"If worse comes to worst, err on the side of entertainment."

Two more couples filed onto the stage. The front couple looked to be in their early forties.

"That's Jerold Phillips, the artist who created that new Frodo Baggins print we saw in the lobby the other night," Brentin whispered as the two shook hands with Noah and Jewell then took their seats next to Mikaela and Brentin.

The second couple seemed closer to thirty. They were from Wellington, Brentin told her, and she, Elisabeth Piersen, had helped with the last movie's special effects.

"I think we're supposed to smile," Mikaela muttered to Brentin out of the corner of her mouth.

The next forty minutes were filled with smiles, occasional conversations with the other contestants, and a meal of fish, sweet potatoes, and a pineapple pastry for dessert. At last two waiters removed their dishes and separated their tables. They slid the tables next to each other at the front of the stage and placed six audience-facing chairs at the tables. The male contestants sat on the left; the females sat on the right.

Jewell walked to the back of the room, and Noah moved to the podium in the center aisle and turned on the microphone. "Welcome to tonight's Tolkien Celebrity Couples Jeopardy for charity. Hasn't this been a great conference?"

Applause and whistles.

Jewell returned to the stage and placed several large sheets of white poster board along with black markers on the table in front of the contestants.

"I certainly hope you've enjoyed your meal and are ready to open your hearts, your humor, and especially your pocketbooks for New Zealand's less fortunate," Noah said. "I also wish you good luck with your pledges toward your choice of tonight's winning couple."

Laughter.

Jewell powered on the contestants' microphones and picked up the one in front of Brentin. "Ladies and gentlemen."

Though Jewell was an older woman, Mikaela had never heard her voice wobble until that moment. Was she nervous too?

"Before I introduce our contestants," Jewell continued, "I would like to say this conference couldn't have come off nearly as well without the help of so many people. A few of them are on the stage with me tonight, along with their significant others. More than that, my husband and I have held many such charity events, and this has proven to be the best attended. Thank you for your fine support."

Applause again, but this time when the audience hushed, Mikaela felt as if her stomach had bounced off the bowling pins and dammed up her throat. She sucked in a deep breath. *You can do this. Pretend the audience is looking somewhere else.*

Jewell finished introducing them and left the stage. She walked through the audience to her husband's side.

"The rules are simple," Noah said. "I will ask a question, after which each of you will write your answers on the poster boards my lovely wife has given you."

Jewell raised her hand in acknowledgment.

"After that you will reveal your answers to one another and to the audience. If your answer matches your partner's, you will receive ten points. If your answers are close but not exact, you'll receive five points. Of course, if they don't match at all, you'll receive zero points. Are you ready?"

The audience applauded, and Jewell made her way through the tables toward the back of the room. She stepped to the side of the door and folded her arms.

"Question number one is to the ladies," Noah said. "What did your significant other think of you the first time you met?"

Mikaela exhaled. Good. It was a question they'd prepared for. She quickly wrote the answer and turned her poster over.

"We'll begin with you, Mikaela. What did Brentin think of you the first time you met?"

Mikaela turned over her board. "That I had sad eyes."

"Hmm. Brentin?"

He turned over his poster. "Yes. Sad eyes. She was grieving. Her grandmother had just died."

Empathetic groans trickled throughout the audience.

"I'm sorry to hear that," Noah said. "But I expect you've now found reasons to smile?"

"Yes," Mikaela said. "New Zealand has had quite a romantic effect on me." Noah lifted an eyebrow like he expected her to say more, so she added, "And Brentin has changed my life."

The women in the audience awwwed, and Noah, still smiling, moved to the next contestants. Mikaela decidedly did *not* look at Brentin. If he later asked her about her response, she would simply refer to his help with her drawing and thank him. That should get rid of any misunderstandings.

"It looks like our contestants are on a roll," Noah said after the third couple had answered. "Ten points for each."

Ms. Sabey sidled in next to Jewell. The two left the banquet room.

"Let's try a harder question." Noah pulled a card from the stack in front of him. "This one is for the men. My girlfriend worries most about this part of her body."

*My scar.* Mikaela bit the insides of her cheeks. They hadn't talked about that question. More than that, she didn't want to talk about it. What could she say instead? The small mole on her upper right cheek? Her split ends? Her thick ankles? Finally, hoping she'd followed Brentin's advice and erred on the side of entertainment, she quickly wrote an answer and turned over her card.

"Let's see what our contestants have written," Noah said when all contestants had turned their posters face down on the table. "Mikaela, you worry most about your what?"

Mikaela showed her answer to the audience. "My ears. They're too pointed. That might be why I admire the Elves so much."

The audience laughed.

"I see nothing wrong with your ears," Noah said. "What about you, Brentin? What was your answer?"

Brentin gave Mikaela a tentative frown and turned over his poster. "The scar on her face."

Mikaela's hand instinctively flew to her cheek. Memories of breaking windshield glass and Trevor's arm moving protectively in front of her flashed through her emotions like a dull blade. The tears that suddenly built up in her eyes felt more like a pressure-release valve than a cement blockade. She blinked in surprise. The pain of Trevor's death had eased, and yet Brentin—how had he known how she felt about her scar? Were her feelings really that open to others? To him?

"I'm sorry," Noah said. "No points for that one."

Brentin's facial muscles looked strained. "Sorry," he mouthed.

"It's all right," she mouthed back. Or it would be all right as soon as her heart rate returned to normal and she no longer felt like everyone stared at her or her scar.

Brentin's jaw slackened, but he turned his attention back to Noah, who'd moved to the third couple. The second couple had earned five points with their answers.

Mikaela's gaze flashed back to the entrance area where she'd last seen Jewell. She finally found the woman near the kitchen. Jewell whispered to a woman and pointed toward the stage. Mikaela licked her lips. Hopefully she wasn't telling her about Mikaela's visit earlier that day.

"Let's move back to the ladies, shall we?" Noah said after the third couple also won five points. "What is your boyfriend's best memory?"

Mikaela bit her lip. Brentin's best childhood memory was mowing the lawn the way his father had taught him, but he'd asked her not to reveal that. Why hadn't they discussed what she could say instead?

She glanced at Brentin. He stared back hard like he was trying to tell her something with his eyes. Finally, he frowned and wrote on his card.

"Are each of you ready?" Noah said after Mikaela scribbled something on her card and turned it over. "Mikaela, we'll start with you. Tell us, what is Brentin's favorite memory?"

Brentin again stared at her, and she gave him a brief nod. *I didn't betray you.*

He nodded back. Had he understood?

"This better be an easy one," she said into the microphone.

"And if it's not?" Noah said.

"Brentin will hear about it later."

The audience laughed, and Mikaela took hold of her card.

Noise rustled through the audience. Heads turned.

Mikaela lowered her card. Her gaze flashed toward the entrance as Detective Eaton and Sergeant Hoffman stepped into the room.

"Your answer, please, Mikaela?"

The detectives headed for the podium. Ms. Sabey hurried toward them, but Jewell backed against the outer kitchen wall. Her eyes rounded, and her stance drooped.

*Are they coming for me?* Mikaela wondered.

"Mikaela?" Noah said. "Please show us your answer."

Mikaela glanced between him and the policemen. "I'm sorry. I suppose I'm a bit distracted."

The policemen stopped beside the podium.

Noah clenched the microphone. He looked toward Jewell, who'd covered her mouth with her hand. "Is there something we can do for you officers?" he said.

Detective Eaton's words were unmistakable in the now silent room. "Noah Cooper, you're under arrest for the murder of Caroline Evans."

Mikaela gasped. *What?* She stared from Noah to Jewell.

Noah's expression paled. "That's ridiculous. Let me finish here, and then we can talk. I'm sure we can clear this up in a few minutes."

"You're already finished here." Sergeant Hoffman pulled out his handcuffs.

"I tell you, you've made a mistake." Noah smiled out at the audience. "Surely you know I could no more kill someone than I could hurt the innocents we're trying to help with this fundraiser."

Detective Eaton took a photograph out of his pocket and showed it to him. "Is this your wife's engagement ring? The one you bought for her? It was found near Caroline Evans's body."

Noah's eyes widened.

"You killed her, and while you were doing it, you lost the ring. You confessed the whole thing to your wife this afternoon."

"Jewell?" Noah whirled toward his wife. She folded her arms tightly across her waist. Tears streamed down her cheeks, but she neither nodded nor shook her head.

"Put your hands behind your back," Sergeant Hoffman said.

Noah's arms and hands trembled. His gaze darted across the room. "How dare you stoop so low as to implicate my wife? She would never tell such a lie."

"She wasn't the one who turned you in." Detective Eaton cuffed Noah's wrists and less than a minute later tugged him from the banquet room. Sergeant Hoffman stepped up to Jewell. She nodded, stood taller, and, looking neither right nor left, followed him.

# Chapter 26

SEVERAL LONG MOMENTS PASSED BEFORE anyone spoke or moved. When they did, it seemed to Brentin that confusion had taken over. Men and women spoke loudly, walked from one table to the next, and even moved chairs from one section of the room to another in what seemed to be an attempt to keep busy. But Mikaela, her posture rigid and her expression blank, didn't even move. Was she in shock? Brentin moved his chair next to hers and placed his left hand on top of hers. He enjoyed the feel of her skin beneath his palm. "Are you all right?"

"Noah Cooper. Not Jewell. We almost had it right."

"Yes."

She didn't smile as he expected her to. If anything, she paled more. "I wonder who turned him in. Don't get me wrong. I'm glad it's over. I'm glad Jewell didn't do it, but he is her husband."

Brentin felt the same warmth rush through him as when, a few minutes earlier, Mikaela had indicated she'd kept his confidence about his childhood memory even though it had likely cost them the game. "At school, when one student turns in another, there can be a lot of bad blood passed around. Hatred. Bullying. But the truth is, sometimes the strongest, most right thing to do is to break a confidence."

"You think it would have been better if she had turned him in? Did you see her when she left? She was a mess."

"I'd be more surprised if she wasn't. It would be pretty hard to find out that kind of thing about the person you've loved and lived with for so many years."

"That poor woman."

Brentin squeezed Mikaela's hand. "At least now your grandfather's no longer a suspect."

"I'm definitely glad for that." She furrowed her brows. "Now the only mystery left is how did Ira die? Oh, and who sent those nursery rhymes."

"Probably some jerk," Brentin said.

"Probably."

Brentin stared at his hand still on top of Mikaela's. She hadn't pulled away from him, and despite her concerns she had to be feeling some relief. Perhaps now was the best time he'd have to tell her how he truly felt before he left. "Whatever the case may be, at least one piece of the puzzle is now solved."

When she shrugged but still didn't pull away, he settled his free arm around her shoulders.

"Thanks," she said. "How'd you know I was freezing?"

He pressed his lips together. Her voice was much too sisterly. She wasn't getting the hint. "I guessed," he said.

Ms. Sabey bustled onto the stage. "You two look good together."

Brentin rolled his eyes. If Ms. Sabey kept up that kind of talk, Mikaela might run. "Were you as surprised as we were to find out Noah was the one who killed Caroline Evans?"

"Later," Ms. Sabey muttered. She glanced between them, straightened, and whisked her hand in front of her, motioning to the other contestants. "I'm here to find out what the six of you wrote on your cards. The event may be over, but we're still holding a fundraiser. We need a winner."

"Start with us," the woman from the younger couple said. "We'd like to get out on the road before it gets much later. We're due back in Wellington tomorrow."

"Very well," Ms. Sabey said.

A dozen or more of the audience members drew close to the stage.

"You're currently tied with couple number three with fifteen points," Ms. Sabey said. "Your boyfriend's best memory is . . . ?"

Mikaela slid into her chair. "I didn't know what to put," she whispered to Brentin. "I'm sure we lost."

Brentin tightened his arm around her shoulders. She leaned slightly into him. It felt good. "Don't worry about it."

The first couple lifted their cards. He'd written his best memory was his sixteenth birthday when his father gave him his first car. She said it was the day he learned to swim. No points. Those few in the audience who were close enough to hear him groaned.

"Your total will stay at fifteen." Ms. Sabey looked to the next couple. "You currently have fifteen points. If you win this match, you will be tonight's winners. Your answers, please?"

The two lifted their cards. Both said *bungee jumping*. They matched.

"That brings your total to twenty-five points," Ms. Sabey said. "Your chosen charity has won the grand prize of ten thousand dollars."

Light applause.

"Now it's your turn, Mikaela," Ms. Sabey said. "Yours and Brentin's total is currently at ten. If your answers match, you will win second place. Mikaela, what is Brentin's best memory?"

Mikaela glanced at Brentin, took a deep breath, and turned over her card.

*The day we met.*

Adrenaline shot down the back of Brentin's spine, and his thoughts blurred.

Ms. Sabey grinned. "All right, Brentin. It's your turn."

"How did you guess?" He turned over his card. He'd written the same thing.

"I knew it," Ms. Sabey said.

Mikaela blushed. "You knew we'd come in second?"

Ms. Sabey didn't answer, only turned back to the audience close to the stage. "Tonight's proceedings will go to these charities in this order. The Child Cancer Foundation will receive $10,000 plus the pledges made by those who chose couple number two. Save the Children will receive $5,000 plus the pledges made by those who chose couple number one. And Childfund New Zealand will receive $2,000 plus the pledges from those who chose couple number three."

Applause, nods, and farewell handshakes followed Ms. Sabey's announcement, and it wasn't long before most of the guests and the other contestants had left.

Ms. Sabey pulled a chair up to their table and sat across from Brentin and Mikaela. She lowered her voice. "Jewell told me about Noah this afternoon. We'd come early to set up for tonight. She was distracted, which is not at all like her, and she looked so upset. I finally asked her what was wrong. The words sort of fell out of her. She said she hadn't known anything of his involvement until she caught you in her house today and you told her about the ring."

Mikaela shook her head. "She showed no signs that she knew anything."

"She's got a pretty good poker face," Ms. Sabey said. "It's helped her through many business deals. At any rate, Jewell looked up the report you'd mentioned, recognized the ring as the one Noah had told her he'd lost all those years ago, and confronted him with the evidence. He confessed the whole thing but made her promise she wouldn't tell anyone."

"But she told you," Brentin said.

"We've been friends for years," she said as if that absolved everything.

"Did you report it?" Mikaela said.

"No, and I have no idea who did. Maybe someone overheard us. Or maybe Jewell confided in someone else too. I must say I'm glad someone did. It's been weighing on my mind since she told me, and I hadn't decided yet what I should do about it."

"Did he tell her why he did it?" Mikaela said. "What his motive was?"

Brentin nodded slightly. Mikaela's mind was so wrapped around death and those nursery rhymes that he'd guess her next questions would be about the how.

"Jewell said Caroline caught him in the house when your grandfather and his Maori partner were gone," Ms. Sabey said. "Noah had run out of money and was deeply in debt for Jewell's ring. He'd helped your grandfather load Caroline's moving truck and hadn't seen anything of the famous treasure. Like so many others in town, he'd figured it must still be on the property. He was looking for it when Caroline knocked on the front door. He didn't answer it, but she still had a house key and let herself in. She confronted him. He panicked and hit her over the head with a statue."

"Not premeditated."

Ms. Sabey grimaced. "The first blow knocked Caroline out, but it didn't kill her. Noah ran out of the house, but when he realized he'd lose everything, including Jewell, if Caroline revealed what he'd done, he killed her and buried her body in the backyard under the bushes, where he hoped no one would notice that the earth had been moved."

"Then he abandoned her car in Hamilton." Brentin squeezed Mikaela's arm. "Nothing about nursery rhymes or Mikaela's grandfather."

"No."

"My grandfather said he was out of town at that time," Mikaela said, "but I wonder how his partner didn't know anything of it either. You'd think someone would have noticed something wasn't right when he returned. I mean, wouldn't we all notice if someone had been killed in our houses while we were gone?"

Brentin shrugged. There were too many what ifs surrounding her question and too many thoughts racing through his mind to give a definitive answer. The game had ended. People were leaving. And too soon, he'd have to say good-bye to Mikaela.

"Apparently he didn't," Ms. Sabey said. "And if nothing was broken and there wasn't any blood or if Noah cleaned things up, I'm not sure I'd have noticed either."

"I suppose that's true," Mikaela conceded.

A metal platter clattered to the floor outside the kitchen door. Mikaela looked over. The only people left in the ballroom were waiters and waitresses. "I guess it's time for us to go."

Ms. Sabey looked at Brentin. "Don't be an idiot." Her ensuing glances between him and Mikaela were so pronounced he could not mistake their meanings, but he furrowed his brows anyway. "I try not to be."

She pressed her lips into a tight frown and watched him for a long moment. "When does your grandfather arrive?" she asked Mikaela.

"Tomorrow morning."

She looked to Brentin. "And you're leaving soon too?"

"Also in the morning."

"Will you have a chance to meet her grandfather or will you two miss each other?"

Brentin looked at Mikaela.

"His flight gets in at seven," she said. "He should be here by eleven."

"My flight's at three," Brentin said, "so I need to leave here no later than ten to get there in time."

"Oh," Mikaela said.

Brentin frowned. Ms. Sabey was right. He had to tell Mikaela how he felt. Now. Before it was too late.

Ms. Sabey glanced between them. "I think that's my cue."

"Not at all," Mikaela said, standing.

Ms. Sabey held her hand out to Brentin. "It's been so good working with you and even better seeing you again. Have a safe trip back to America."

He clasped her hand. "Thank you for this opportunity. For everything, in fact. Keep in touch. Maybe I'll see you at the next convention."

"If you really don't have to go, maybe we can stay and talk," Mikaela said to her. She glanced toward the exit. "It's been an eventful day, and I need to wind down."

"That's just what I plan to do back at my house," Ms. Sabey said. "A hot bath, a cuppa coffee, and *The Hobbit* to keep me company. Good night." She squeezed both their hands, nodded once more to Brentin, and walked away.

Emptiness dropped from Brentin's heart down to his stomach. That woman had blessed his life in many ways. Would he really ever see her again?

"We might as well help clean up." Mikaela turned from him, reached for the poster boards she'd used in the game, and stepped—

Brentin caught her arm. "Wait."

She looked up at him with eyes so green that warmth flooded through him. His heartbeat pounded against his chest. *Speak now.* "My best day *was* the day we met."

"What?"

"I'm serious."

She looked down at her clasped hands. "That's the wonder of it. Thank you, Brentin."

He lowered his face to hers until she glanced up at him. "Thank you for what?"

"For being so—perfect."

His stare dazed. What did she mean by that? Was she teasing him? Trying to stop him from saying what he felt? If so, she would fail. He stepped closer to her. "Looks like I've got you fooled."

"Sorry. I'm not buying your attempt at humility," she responded.

"I'm pretty sure no one who knows me will agree with you."

"I don't need them to agree with me. I've seen it for myself."

"All right. Tell me how I'm perfect." He grinned, but she didn't crack a smile. She only folded her arms in front of her and looked straight up at him. A strand of her blonde hair fell into her eyes, and though she looked directly at him, a distance in her gaze nudged him away from her. He chose not to obey it and inched closer.

"I've wanted to tell you for some time," she said, "but now, since this is as close to a good-bye as we'll likely have, well . . ."

He placed both hands on her upper arms. "Just tell me."

She swallowed. He watched the movement.

"Thank you for being my friend," she finally said. "You've helped me get beyond myself and my losses enough to see that I have a future, that I can hope again. I doubt you have any idea how your friendship has affected me, but I want you to know I will always be grateful to you for those things."

Something shifted near Brentin's heart, and when he spoke, his voice scraped against his throat. "You've been a friend to me too, Mikaela. More than a friend."

"I have?"

His gaze wavered as he searched her eyes. "You really don't know?"

"Know what?"

He leaned toward her. Her smile, her touch, her strength of spirit—how could he explain that, of all the women in his life, she alone made him feel complete? "Thank you for your help too."

"With your films? That was fun, wasn't it?"

His breath tensed. She still didn't understand. "It was."

"Well, thanks for everything." She lifted onto her tiptoes, gave him a quick peck on the cheek, and nodded toward the exit. "Why don't we get out of here?"

Brentin's mouth went dry. The moment was fading. Tomorrow he'd leave. He had to tell her he wanted more than friendship. *Now.*

"Is there something else?" She tried to step backward.

He held her tighter. "Mikaela, I—" Not thinking, only feeling, he pulled her to him and kissed her hard on the mouth. For one heart-stopping, breathless moment, her lips responded to his. She closed her eyes. *Please let that mean she feels the same way about me.*

Mikaela lifted her hands to his chest and gently pushed him away. "What are you doing?"

He exhaled. "Telling you how I feel."

"By kissing me like that? Here?"

"You weren't leaving me many options."

"What does that mean? No. Don't tell me." She turned away from him and hurried down the stage stairs.

He ran after her, catching her arm. "I like you, Mikaela, more than just as an everyday friend. I want us to have the chance to get to know each other better."

She tensed, lifted her face to the ceiling, and slowly faced him. "I'm not sure I'm ready for that."

"But you will be sometime, and I want to be there when that happens. Okay?"

"I live in Utah, and you live in Colorado. That's quite a bit of distance."

"Only in miles. Not inside." He tapped his chest. "Where it counts."

She bit the corner of her lower lip, glanced away from him, and rubbed her hand across the base of her throat.

"Are you willing to try?" Brentin held his breath.

"Maybe," she said at last.

He exhaled. *Yes!*

"Can I think about it?" she added.

His breath stopped again. "You'll answer me before I leave?"

"I will."

# Chapter 27

MIKAELA FLOPPED ON THE BED onto her stomach and pounded her pillow. Tonight of all nights since she'd arrived she should be able to sleep. Her grandfather had been cleared from suspicion in Caroline Evans's murder, they were staying in a secured hotel, and she'd finally thanked Brentin. And yet . . . She pressed her fingertips against her lips as if she could still feel the pressure of his lips.

. . . And yet, he'd kissed her and she'd felt something and now she didn't know what to do about it. How was it possible that she could have romantic feelings for Brentin when her heart still ached for Trevor?

Mikaela rolled onto her side and kicked her legs outside her covers. But even if it was possible and even if she did agree to try a long-distance relationship with him, could her heart handle more hurt piled on top of it if it didn't work out? At the same time, if she let Brentin leave and never saw him again without finding out if it could have worked, if he was a man she could give all of herself to for the rest of eternity, could her heart handle that loss any better?

The red numbers on the alarm clock changed from *6:49* to *6:50 a.m.*

No. To both questions. She needed to fully get over Trevor before she could fully open her heart to someone else. How long would that take? Was it fair to ask Brentin to wait indefinitely?

No, again. Mikaela sat up and scratched the back of her neck. "What do I do?" she whispered.

"Face it head on." That's what her grandfather would say. But wasn't she doing that?

Her heart felt blank. Her head ached. She had to get out of there, had to find a place where she could clear her head and calm her emotions before she faced Brentin again and told him . . . something.

But where? Ira's murder hadn't been solved, and if she'd been in danger then, she still was now. She growled in frustration and flopped back on her bed. *Where can I go where I can be alone but not alone?*

The Redwoods in the Whakarewarewa Forest. Mikaela didn't know where that thought came from, but Tui had used almost those exact words when she'd described the Redwoods. Mikaela crossed the carpet to the window and peeked between the curtains at the streetcars below. Why not go to the forest? No way the bustle and noise of the town could soothe her nerves, and one of the first things the girl behind the desk told her and the other Kotuku Inn guests when they'd checked in was that they offered a complimentary shuttle to the forest every few hours. The first one left at seven fifteen in the morning and returned the occupants to the hotel at nine o'clock a.m. If she hurried, she could catch it and be back in plenty of time to talk to Brentin before he left at ten. Surely, she'd figure out what to tell him by then.

She quickly dressed, put on her warm fleece hoodie, and scrawled a quick note.

> *Brentin,*
> *I went with the tour van to Whakarewarewa Forest for a quick walk. We'll talk when I get back.*
> *Mikaela*

Mikaela slid the note under Brentin's door and hurried down to the office. Shortly after she arrived, Sara, Frank, and three other hotel guests showed up, and Mikaela sighed in relief. Despite what she'd told herself about how she wouldn't be alone, seeing them made her believe it. She'd be safe.

The tour van pulled into the driveway. Mikaela looked at her cell phone. *7:14.* She'd have nearly two hours to be alone with her thoughts, to pray, to figure out what to say to Brentin. *Please let it be enough.*

She climbed into the seat next to the driver. The others filled the seats behind them.

About ten minutes later, the driver turned left off Long Mile Road into a parking lot that butted up against a small, steep-roofed visitor center.

"It still looks pretty dark in the forest," Mikaela commented.

"It'll be light soon." The driver motioned past three—no, five—other parked cars to the visitor center's doors. "There are trail maps on the wall there and colored markers along the pathways. No need to worry about getting lost."

*Lost?* After all the hikes she'd gone on back home with her grandmother and in spite of all her grandfather's reminding her to always be prepared, Mikaela had totally spaced the possibility of getting lost. But she had her cell phone, and there were water fountains and restrooms outside the visitor center. She would be fine. "What do you know about the trails?"

He pressed a button. The van's large sliding door opened. "The shortest is labeled as a half-hour track. There are others with different times."

"Sounds perfect." Mikaela climbed out of the van and took a deep breath. The cool, pine-scented air buoyed her senses.

"Amazing how the forest makes you feel so separate from everything back in Rotorua, isn't it?" came a voice from the backseat.

Mikaela looked over her shoulder. It was Sara.

"I didn't know you were coming out here this morning," she added. "Do you want to walk with Frank and me? I haven't chatted with you in a while."

"It's nice of you to ask, but I wouldn't be good company. I've got a lot on my mind."

Sara gave Mikaela a pleading look. "You can leave us whenever you want. All the paths loop back to the visitor center."

Mikaela glanced away. So what if Sara looked worried about something. Mikaela didn't always have to be the one to help her, did she? Besides, Frank was with her. Or was Frank the problem?

Frank kissed Sara on the forehead and tightened his daypack strap around his shoulder. "You're welcome to join us. I have extra water bottles I'd rather not carry the entire trip."

"Please?" Sara practically begged.

Mikaela exhaled. Two of the other hotel guests headed to the visitor center. The other two veered toward a path just beyond the restrooms. "All right, but only for a few minutes."

"Whatever you want." Frank shrugged.

Sara motioned toward the wide path blanketed by wood chips beyond the back side of the parking lot. "Let's start there this morning."

* * *

Hunapo opened his eyes the moment the airplane's air pressure changed. Before he'd been diagnosed with cancer, he'd never been able to sleep sitting up, but on this trip, the fatigue had such a powerful hold on him that he'd slept most of the way. Even during meals. That was best anyway.

While he slept he didn't have to listen to the never-ending whines of that kid behind him.

*His father must be weak.* Hunapo rolled the kinks out of his shoulders. If that boy had been Hunapo's kid, he'd have learned long ago that such behavior was not worth the price he'd pay later.

The landing gear lowered. Hunapo pressed his aching back against his chair. Blood had pooled behind his knees and around his ankles. *Ancestors, help me complete this task.*

The airplane landed on the runway and taxied toward the terminal. Hunapo looked out his side window. It was seven in the morning and still dark. Though he hadn't been in New Zealand for more than thirty years, he knew the sun would rise soon. Some truths never left him.

The airplane jerked to a stop. Those who'd sat in the aisle seats, including the woman next to him, stood, and the pilot's quiet voice came over the loudspeaker. Hunapo strained to hear the announcement, but the other passengers were so loud he couldn't understand any of it. An electronic bell chimed a few moments later.

"What did the pilot say?" he asked the woman beside him.

She sat again. "We can't get off yet. We're early, and another plane is at our gate. The pilot said it would only be a few minutes."

Hunapo scowled. A few minutes he didn't have. He yanked out the pen and blue sympathy card he'd tucked into the pocket on the back of the seat ahead of him. He'd forgotten his rubber gloves, but what did it matter? It was the last card he would send. Ever.

He pulled out his table and placed the card on top of it. He hadn't known his wife had loved this rhyme as much as she had until his grandchild had told him she used to repeat it as she prepared food or worked around the house.

*Mikaela York:*
*Little Miss Muffet*

Hunapo wrote out the rhyme and lowered his gaze to the space beneath it. Should he sign this card as he had his last note to Joseph? It would make certain all knew that he, Hunapo Grieg, had been the one that had fulfilled the demands of utu.

The airplane moved forward. The boy behind him cried again. Hunapo looked over his shoulder. "Face it like a man!"

The mother glared at him.

Hunapo glared back and again looked to the card. He quickly scrawled his name at the bottom and sealed it in the envelope. Now he only had to hire a courier to deliver it to the King's Hotel before his grandchild had time to act. It would be a pity for Mikaela not to read the rhyme before her death.

After the courier, he'd pick up a gun from his old gang.

* * *

Mikaela's and the Kendricks' footsteps pattered the soft earth. Sometimes it was a narrow, dirt path that wound between tall grass, tangled ferns, palmettos, and tall redwoods. Other times it was a wide boardwalk that spanned a stream or otherwise uncrossable section, but mostly it seemed a calming, secluded trail someone had made only for her. Even the occasional glimpses of other walkers, joggers, and cyclists didn't take away that feeling.

She glanced up through the mix of redwoods and palm trees at the dawn-blue sky. Had Brentin wakened? Read her note? Packed for his flight? Or was he still in bed, procrastinating his departure and—thinking of her?

Once more, Mikaela forced herself not to remember the feel of Brentin's lips on hers, his arms around her shoulders . . . her waist. She closed her eyes. She couldn't let herself dwell on such things when she needed to make a rational decision. *What should I tell him?*

*Think.* She wasn't sure she'd heard the word, but the impression settled through her as if it had. What should she think about? *Brentin.*

"How do you like it out here, Mikaela?" Frank broke the silence.

Mikaela sniffled. She wasn't cold, but something in the air must have stirred her allergies. If only she'd brought some tissues. "It's even prettier than it looks from the road."

Frank and Sara chatted easily as the three rounded several easy bends and walked up two gentle inclines; Mikaela turned her thoughts into herself. The woodchipped path through the forest was soft, muffling their footsteps into light scrapes, and the forest was dense with trees of so many varieties, especially redwoods that were wider around than Mikaela could reach. Though she knew at least a dozen people, likely more, were traversing the trails, she couldn't hear or see them. Tui was right. This was a place where she could be alone but not alone. She sighed. *Grandma must have loved it here.*

"This is a pretty easy trail," Frank said. "Up for something more challenging?"

"Sure." Mikaela glanced at her cell phone. *7:45.* "But just for a few minutes."

Sara looked at Frank. "Turn at the next trailhead?"

"Yeah."

The path narrowed, and Sara took the lead. Mikaela followed her. Frank brought up the rear. They reached a track post about two minutes later. It pointed up a steep stairway and an even narrower path. Mossy logs lined the trail, and several boulders jetted out from the ground like a natural staircase. A man, sweating hard, ran down it toward them.

Mikaela and the Kendricks waited until he'd run past before they started up the incline. The trail leveled out about a hundred feet later. *Would Brentin like it here? Does he enjoy hiking?* She pictured him in his Ent costume, and she smiled. He had dressed up as a tree, but did that mean he liked being in nature? *Other than what we talked about in preparation for the game, what do I actually know about him?*

"Let's take a short break." Frank wiped the sweat from his face with his handkerchief and pulled off his backpack. He unzipped the main compartment, set the bag on one of the larger rocks near the trail, and pulled out three water bottles. He kept one for himself and handed the other two to Mikaela and Sara.

Mikaela drank half her water and smiled at Sara. It was good seeing her getting along so well with her husband. Perhaps she'd been mistaken in thinking Sara hadn't wanted to be alone with him.

"Thanks for taking care of us," Sara said to Frank. She likewise downed several gulps of water then gave him a quick peck on the cheek. "That's one of the reasons I love him," she said to Mikaela.

Mikaela nodded. She hadn't thought of it in those terms, but Brentin had given up much of his limited working-on-his-film time to help her with her investigation. He'd said it was important, and when he'd said it, she'd felt like *she* was important. He had been taking care of her.

Frank pulled together his pack's zippers. Before they connected, the opening bunched outward. A green flat lid on top of a glass jar flashed in the morning sunlight.

"A pickle jar?" Mikaela asked.

Frank lifted his eyes to hers and glared.

Goosebumps shot down the back of Mikaela's neck, and she took a quick backward step. Had she offended him somehow? Maybe he had a quick temper. Was that why he and Sara had so many arguments?

She glanced up at Sara and back to Frank. Whatever she'd seen in his eyes a moment before had disappeared. Had she imagined it? "Um, well, I think I better head back now." She tucked her water bottle inside her large hoodie pocket and started downward.

"Can you wait just a few more minutes?" Sara sounded hopeful. "Yesterday, we found a pretty stream up here that I'd really like you to see."

Mikaela looked at Frank. He half smiled and shrugged. "Sara likes water. But it's up to you."

*I like water too.*

"Please?" Sara said.

"All right."

The three again started up the trail. After climbing for what had to be more than ten minutes, Sara stepped off the main path into the tall grasses. "It's over here a few feet."

Mikaela, following her, listened. If the stream were close, shouldn't she hear it? "How did you find it in all this underbrush?"

Sara shrugged. "My grandfather says I have a sense for such things."

They walked. Mikaela checked the time. *8:18.* Stream or no, she had to head back to the visitor center, even if it did hurt Sara's feelings. The tour van would be there at eight fifty, and she still hadn't figured out what she should say to Brentin.

She looked back toward where she thought the main trail would be but saw only tall trees and dense foliage. The hair on the back of her neck straightened to attention. "I hate to say this, but I really need to go back now." She looked over her shoulder at Frank. "Could you show me how to get back to the trail?"

The glare he'd given her before returned. "Not yet."

If she even had an inkling of which way to go, she'd have left anyway, but she didn't. "Soon then, please?"

He grunted, and they continued on. Mikaela involuntarily shivered. What was going on here? Sara and Frank had said she could leave whenever she wanted, and yet Frank's refusal to tell her how to get back to the path made her feel like a hostage. Had she made him angry? Whatever the case, she had to get back to the main trail.

*8:23.* Mikaela gave Frank a tentative smile. Sara had gone so far ahead that Mikaela couldn't see her anymore. "Sorry. I've got to tie my shoe."

Frank rolled his eyes. "Hold up a minute, Sara!"

Mikaela crouched down and grabbed her laces. If anything was wrong, or even if her intuition had shot into overdrive for no reason, she'd feel better knowing she'd marked at least some portion of her path in case she had to find her way back on her own. *Heavenly Father, please help me know what I should do.*

She slowly untied the laces of one of her shoes and pulled them tight again. What could she leave behind? The water bottle? Maybe. But it was big enough that if she left it, Frank might see it and remind her to pick it up. Or someone else might come along and, thinking it was garbage, clean it up. But then, would anyone else stray out here off the main path?

Mikaela folded one shoelace under the other, tightened them, and froze. What about her shoelace?

She made herself not look back at Frank and quickly thought over each step of the process of removing her lace from her shoe. It could work if she had time. And if her shoe didn't fall off while she walked and give her away. She frowned. She needed another option.

She started to double tie her laces when the drawstring from the hood of her hoodie dropped down in front of her. Would it work? She clenched her teeth, finishing the double tie and forcing herself to breathe normally. Then, she quickly yanked the hoodie string out of its casing and dropped it on top of a large fern. She leisurely stood and turned back to Frank. Anyone could see the string if they looked. *Please don't look.*

"Ready?" Frank glanced from her face to her feet.

Mikaela pressed her lips together. Good thing she hadn't taken out her shoelace. "Sure, but after this, I've really got to get back. The bus will be back soon."

"No problem."

Mikaela angled herself in front of the fern where she'd dropped the lace and lifted her gaze to where Sara had just waved to them from behind a dense thicket of pine trees. "Over there, I take it?" It was a dumb question, but it was all she could think of to say to keep him from looking toward her drawstring.

"You got it."

Mikaela and Frank moved farther into the grassy underbrush. Moments later they reached the dense thicket.

"Keep coming." Sara was close enough that Mikaela could hear a smile in her voice. She was happy at least. "It's nice in here," Sara added. "Shady and spacious. It would be a great picnic spot if we'd brought a lunch."

Mikaela pushed through the thicket of ferns into the small grove. The branches above and around them were so dense they blocked most of the sunlight. Sara sat on the fat edge of a mossy fallen log about four feet in front of her.

"This is as good a place as any," Sara said.

"For what? Where's the stream?"

Sara leapt to her feet. Frank yanked Mikaela's arms behind her back and stuffed the handkerchief he'd used to wipe his face into Mikaela's mouth.

Mikaela gaped at them. She tried to scream, but all that came out was a tight squeal.

Frank shoved another rag into her mouth. "This'll be a lot harder on you if you fight."

Mikaela squirmed against Frank's grasp, but he held her arms so tightly that each movement felt like it would pull Mikaela's shoulders from the sockets.

"Too bad you didn't die in that car accident instead of your boyfriend," Sara said.

Dizzying black spots flashed in front of Mikaela's eyes. What did the car accident have to do with anything?

Sara stomped on Mikaela's left foot and punched her in the gut. "You don't even know what we're talking about, do you?"

Mikaela doubled over, but she found the strength to kick backward at Frank's shin. He leapt out of the way before her foot could find its mark.

"Hold her arms while I tie her up," Sara said.

Frank pulled Mikaela's arms in front of her. Sara took a rope from his backpack lying on the ground near his feet and wrapped it around Mikaela's wrists. The rope scratched and burned into her skin.

"Jack and Jill went up the hill," Sara said. "Hello, Jill."

Mikaela gasped. Her eyes bulged. The nursery rhymes, the car accident, her grandmother. Frank and Sara? Had they killed them? *Help me, Father in Heaven!*

"Let's go farther up the mountain," Frank said. "Where no one will ever find her."

Mikaela jerked sideways.

Frank caught her around the waist.

"How's our friend?" Sara asked Frank.

"Just fine." Frank nodded to his pack. "Go ahead. I've got her."

Mikaela scanned the small cove. How could she get away?

Sara picked up the pack and stepped through the wall of foliage opposite of where they'd entered the tiny clearing. Frank yanked Mikaela behind him and up the densely covered mountainside.

Mikaela clenched her teeth. She dug her heels into the soft earth. If her foot caught a large enough bramble, could she pry herself away from Frank?

# Chapter 28

BRENTIN PACED ACROSS THE STONE floor from the check-in desk, where he'd left his luggage, to the front door. He stared through the glass at the quiet parking lot and walked back to the desk. It was nearly nine thirty. Mikaela's note said she'd return with the tour van, but it had come and gone without her on it. The driver said she'd left with the Kendricks, and the three of them weren't in the parking lot when he'd returned. Frank had told the driver that he and his wife would likely take a taxi back. He'd assumed Mikaela had decided to take it with them. But that was more than fifteen minutes ago, and Mikaela had said she'd talk with Brentin before he left. Where was she?

"You'll be checking out this morning, won't you?" Chloe, the girl behind the front desk, said. When he'd first arrived in the lobby a half hour earlier, another girl had been there, and she'd asked him the same thing.

"I already did. It's all right if I wait here a little longer, isn't it?"

"Of course, sir."

He pressed Mikaela's number into his phone yet again and listened to it ring. It went to her voice mail. She wasn't intentionally ignoring him, was she? He'd taken a pretty big risk when he'd kissed her last night, but she seemed to have handled it well enough. Besides, she'd promised him she'd talk with him before he left. Surely she wouldn't stand him up.

Now it was nine thirty-five. Brentin scanned Mikaela's quickly scrawled note and paced to the front door again.

"Is something wrong, Mr. Williams?" Chloe asked. "I can check your flight if you're worried about it."

"You don't have a secret potion that would turn back time, do you?"

"Excuse me?"

"Never mind." His words were more a grunt than speech, but it was the best he could do. All he could think about was Mikaela: how she'd felt in his arms when he'd kissed her, how her lips had trembled and steadied beneath his, and how she'd ultimately promised she'd tell him whether or not she'd like to pursue a relationship. Was she all right?

Brentin's stomach churned. He paced to the desk again and back to the window. *9:40.*

"Are you waiting for someone?" Chloe asked. "Miss York, perhaps?"

He whirled. "Why?"

"Sorry. I didn't mean anything by it. It's only that the last time I saw you, the two of you were together."

"Yes, I'm waiting for her. She went on an early morning walk to the Redwoods with your tour bus, but she didn't return with them as she said she would."

"I'm sure she's fine. The Kendricks haven't returned either."

"But I have to leave soon, and I—we were supposed to meet before I left. Actually, do you have the number for the forest's visitor center? Maybe they'll know something about where she is."

Chloe pursed her lips, pulled a phone directory out from under the desk, and thumbed through the pages. "Here's the number. Would you like me to call for you?"

"I'll do it."

A woman answered the phone. She hadn't seen anyone who looked like Mikaela. He shouldn't worry though. There were enough people out on the trails that if Mikaela had fallen or something, it would have been reported.

*9:45.*

"I can tell you how to get to the forest if that will help," Chloe said.

"Thanks, but if I'm not on the road back to Auckland by ten, I'll miss my flight. Besides, I might pass Mikaela on her way back here."

The lines around her eyes softened. "Maybe you should write her a note? I can give it to her if you have to leave before she returns."

No new cars had pulled into the parking lot. "Maybe you're right." Brentin blew out a long, pent-up sigh and opened the front pocket of his backpack. Had Mikaela ultimately decided not to pursue their relationship and thought avoiding him was the easiest way to let him know? It didn't seem like something she'd do. And she had left him a note saying she'd be back. But maybe?

He fished inside the pack and pulled out a pen. He had a notebook in there somewhere.

"We have a note pad," Chloe said. "You're welcome to use it if you'd like."

*9:51.* Brentin's jaw muscles felt so tight, he could hardly move his mouth, but somehow he managed to say, "All right." He walked back to the counter.

She opened the drawer beneath the cash register. "That's weird."

"What is?"

"There's already a card here for Miss York. It must have arrived after she left." She set a blue envelope on the counter.

Brentin stared at it. As far as he knew, the only people Mikaela knew here in New Zealand were associated with Kotuku Inn, and this wasn't even postmarked. Had it been hand delivered? There was no name on the return address.

He rubbed his chin. Who could she possibly know that would bring her a—his shoulders, stomach, hands. Every part of his body tensed. Mikaela had told him the odd nursery rhymes had been written on *blue* sympathy cards.

He grabbed it.

"Hey!" Chloe said. "That doesn't belong to you."

Brentin tore it open and scanned the contents. When his gaze latched onto the word *spider*, his breath stopped. Another odd card. Another accident? He ran for the door.

"What's wrong?" Chloe said.

He flicked the card across the room to her. "Mr. Parker should be here soon. If I—or Mikaela—don't return by then, show him the card. Tell him I went to the forest looking for her."

* * *

It felt like hours passed as Frank and Sara dragged Mikaela in a zigzagged fashion up the mountain from one dark thicket to another, going so far up, so far into the forest that the only direction Mikaela could still be sure of was down. But down to where? More forest? Still she'd noted as many landmarks as she could along the way for if—*when!*—she escaped, but only three things stood out: a large tree that grew sideways straight out of the mountainside, a brook of such clear water she could see at the bottom several rocks as red as her rope-burned skin, and a pine tree whose trunk formed a sharp *V*. The

*V*-tree was closest to the thicket where Frank and Sara had captured her. If she could get back to it, she might be able to find her hoodie string—and her way back to safety. *Please help me, Heavenly Father.*

Mikaela's cell phone vibrated in her pocket for at least the dozenth time. She wanted to take it out, to call for help, but she barely had use of her arms. Besides, if her captors saw it or remembered she had it, they'd take it from her, and she didn't want that to happen. Having her phone gave her hope.

She gritted her teeth against the pain in her stomach where Sara had hit her, and she tried to yank her arm away from Frank's grasp. He held tight.

Sara shook her head. "You're not getting away from death this time, Mikaela. Your grandfather did great harm to my grandfather and to our family—to me—and according to our people's ancient law of recompense, of utu, those wrongs must be satisfied or the world's proper balance will not be restored." She pulled her own cell phone from her jacket pocket, sent a short text, and forced Mikaela down into a sitting position on top of a mossy stump.

*You're crazy!* Mikaela twisted her wrists back and forth against the rope. The burning wetness between them had to be blood.

"Hold on to her," Frank said.

Sara took Frank's place, and Frank stepped a few feet to the side. When he pulled his pack off his shoulders, his jacket lifted, revealing an approximately foot-long knife strapped in a sheath on his belt.

"Ironic, don't you think?" Sara said close to Mikaela's ear. "If your grandfather hadn't cheated mine all those years ago, we might have been friends. We'd have had the same backgrounds, the same privileges, the same happiness. My grandfather said he would have loved me as your grandfather loved you if he'd had the time and the prosperity your grandfather took from him." Sara's stare blanked, the edges of her eyes turned downward, and for a moment Mikaela's heart reached out to her. But only for a moment. Sara had obviously been abused by that man, but that didn't excuse her own cruelty.

Sara's grip tightened around Mikaela's arm. "It's time," she said to Frank. "And you better not fail this time."

"It's not my fault her fiancé died instead of her."

"I'm not talking about him. Ira! She was supposed to eat that salad. Not Ira."

"I only did what you told me to."

Mikaela winced. *I'm so sorry, Ira.*

"I expect you know how the next nursery rhyme ends." Sara reached in the pack and pulled out the pickle jar. She dangled it in front of Mikaela. "Along came a—you know what this is, don't you, Mikaela?"

Mikaela gaped at the eight-legged creature, and the blood drained from the top of her head to the tip of her toes. It looked much like a black widow, only it had a distinctive yellow stripe on its pea-sized body. Mikaela knew that a widow's bite rarely killed an otherwise healthy victim. Was it the same with this spider? But if so, would Sara and Frank have chosen it as their weapon?

"The katipo spider," Frank said. "The night stinger."

Mikaela's stomach clenched. Her eyes squeezed closed, but the spider's image filled the blackness behind her eyelids.

"Closing your eyes won't help," Sara taunted. "And unlike Miss Muffet, you won't be able to run away."

"I had a terrible time finding this little beauty the other day—" Frank said.

"—when he left me at the inn," Sara cut in.

"But I found her on the coastline, just as Sara's grandfather said I would. Where his tupunas told him to look."

Mikaela looked left, right, left again. *I have to get away.*

Frank removed the lid. The spider climbed from the middle of the jar to the inside of the upper lip. "Should I dump it on her head? Maybe down the neck of her shirt?"

Mikaela fought against Sara's too-tight grasp. She wasn't ready to die. There were still too many things she wanted to do. College. Marriage. Family. To have a daughter she could raise the way her mother would have raised her if she'd lived.

Frank carried the jar toward Mikaela. Mikaela glanced at the knife at his side.

"Wait," Sara said. "We've got to do something first. Hold her arms."

Frank grabbed Mikaela's left arm, and Sara reached inside Mikaela's pants pocket. She pulled out Mikaela's phone. "We've got to text her grandfather. He won't want to miss this."

Mikaela squirmed. She yelled against the gag. *No!*

Sara worked her way through Mikaela's phone, spoke in a message—"Trap set"—and pushed SEND. She tossed the phone on the ground about ten feet in front of Mikaela.

"You should have thrown it," Frank said.

"This is better. Close enough for her to see, too far away to help. Grandfather's happiness and mine were always just out of reach because of her grandfather."

Frank tipped the jar toward Mikaela.

Mikaela leaned back from it . . . leaned . . . leaned.

Sara flinched from the bottle. "Don't drop it on *me*, you idiot!" Her grip slackened.

*Now's your chance!* Mikaela spun free from Sara's grasp and kicked Frank hard in the groin. Frank yelled. He lost his grip on the jar and doubled over.

The spider fell on Sara's arm, and she screamed. "Where is it? Get it off me!" She brushed at her arms, her legs, her neck.

Mikaela, her hands still tied in front of her, grabbed the knife out of Frank's sheath, scooped her phone from the ground, and charged out of the thicket.

* * *

Brentin finished his phone call to Detective Eaton just before he rounded the corner onto Long Mile Road. At first, the detective asked Brentin if he was working himself up over what might turn out to be nothing. But after Brentin reminded him of the other sympathy cards and told them the name that had been written at the bottom of this one, they'd agreed his concerns were worth looking into and would meet him at the forest.

Brentin shifted his car into its highest gear, pressed the gas pedal to the floor, and scanned both sides of the tree-lined road. Mikaela had to be out there somewhere. She and the Kendricks . . . An uneasy feeling niggled at the back of his thoughts. *Please be all right.*

He reached the visitor center, grabbed his digital camera, and pressed the power button. He set it to the one photo he had of Mikaela. She wore the costume she'd worn the first night, but she still looked enough like herself for the photo to be effective.

"Help!" He waved his camera over his head at the dozen or so people walking in front of the restrooms.

They looked his direction. A few ran to him. Some were Asian tourists, and three were bicyclists, but most seemed to be locals who'd come to the forest for their morning exercise.

"This girl's life is in danger," Brentin said. "Have any of you seen her? She should be somewhere in these woods."

"Alone?" a woman said.

"I don't know. She might be with a young man and woman."

They took turns looking at the picture and shook their heads.

"This is a big forest. Trails everywhere," one of the men said from behind him, "but I'm familiar with the area. I'll help you look for her."

"How do you know she's in danger?" the female biker said.

"I believe a murderer is after her."

The girl's eyes rounded. "Up there? Why?"

"I wish I knew."

A woman looked away from him and into the trees. "Maybe we'd be wiser staying here and stopping others from going up."

Brentin's chest tightened. They were strangers. Of course he couldn't ask them to risk their safety to hunt for Mikaela. "The police are on their way, but I appreciate anything you can do."

Several big men and one woman, all wearing jogging shorts, glanced at each other. "Show us her picture again," one said. "We'll head up our regular paths. There's usually good phone service along there."

"We'll try checking the grove behind the visitor center," two couples said. "If you give us your phone number, we'll let you know if we find anything."

As he gave out his phone number, Detective Eaton and Sergeant Hoffman pulled into the parking lot.

* * *

Mikaela's lungs burned, her legs felt like jelly, and her arms ached from being tied up, but she didn't stop running until she ducked behind a fallen cedar tree. Its width was tall enough for her to hide behind, and it lay across a row of ferns, which would provide even more cover.

Time to cut off the ropes. She closed her eyes and listened. Hearing nothing but the chirp of birds and the buzz of insects, she pulled the gag from her mouth then carefully maneuvered the blade until it pressed against the rope that bound her hands together. She sawed. Up. Down. Up. *Don't slip.* Down. Up. *Don't cut my arm.* Down.

At last the rope snapped apart. The blade nicked her left wrist. Blood dripped down her arm. She wiped it on her hoodie. She was free but not safe. She peeked over the top edge of the tree trunk. She saw no sign of Sara or Frank, but she likewise saw none of the landmarks she'd noted earlier. She looked at her phone. No signal.

Staying low, she crept along the length of the dead tree toward its torn-from-the-ground roots. She stopped. About a hundred feet down the mountain below her, the trees opened into a wide clearing. If she entered it, which she'd have to do if she continued straight downward, Sara and Frank would easily see her if they were anywhere nearby.

Mikaela wrapped her trembling fingers around one of the protruding roots. Maybe her final moments had come and she would die out there, but it wouldn't be because she'd given up. She would not give up.

She moved closer to the edge of her cover and looked at her phone. A faint signal. She quickly pushed 1-1-1, the local emergency number. It rang—the call dropped. "No!"

She tried the number again. This time it didn't ring at all. She'd have to step out from under the cover of the trees if she wanted any chance of getting a stronger signal. But stepping into the clearing could mean death. Was this really the end? Had she fought and run and hid for nothing?

No thoughts. No feelings. No sounds answered her; she had to make a choice. She took a deep breath, gritted her teeth, and dashed several yards into the clearing. She had a signal. She pressed 1-1—but before she'd pressed the last number, her phone buzzed. It was her grandfather.

"Mikaela?"

# Chapter 29

AT TEN FIFTY, SEVERAL MORE police cars pulled into the parking lot. Brentin repeated what he'd told the dispatcher on the phone, and while they took control of the search, he called the hotel. Chloe answered.

"This is Brentin Williams. Has Mr. Parker arrived yet?"

"No. He hasn't called either. Perhaps he stopped somewhere along the way. Tourists often do that." The lilt in her voice told him she tried to sound hopeful. "Have you found Miss York?"

"No." Brentin gave her his phone number. "Please tell him to call me the moment he arrives."

He said good-bye, shoved his phone into his pocket, and headed toward the wide path on the other side of the parking lot. Before he reached it, a black sedan pulled into the parking spot directly in front of him. The aged driver stepped out of the car. He motioned at the crowd, including the police standing on the sidewalk. "Is all this for Mikaela York, I hope?"

"Yes." Brentin quick-scanned the length of him. Could he be Hunapo? "Do you know her?"

The man hurried past him toward the crowd. "I'm her grandfather. I just talked to her."

"What?" Brentin rushed next to him. "Where is she? Is she all right?"

"Are you Brentin?" Mr. Parker clenched his phone in front of him. "She escaped. She said the names Sara and Frank, and she tried to tell me where she was hiding when our connection broke."

Brentin grabbed Mr. Parker's phone. It obviously received a better signal than his did. "I have to talk to her." Brentin realized what he'd done and sheepishly handed back the phone. "Sorry."

Mr. Parker held his gaze. "I'll try again." He pressed one of the keys.

Brentin dragged his attention away from the man's fingers and looked up the mountainside. Where was she? Voices called her name through the trees.

"Mikaela!" Mr. Parker said.

Brentin whirled. "You got through?"

Mr. Parker put the call on speaker. "Quick. What do you see around you?"

Brentin's heart clenched as Mikaela's whisper crackled over the speaker. "Frank's nearby, but I don't think he's seen me yet."

Brentin swept his hand across his forehead. "Do you have any idea where you are?" He scanned every direction. The police should hear this, but if he left, the call might drop again, and he wanted—*needed*—to hear her voice.

"Brentin?" Mikaela said.

The back of his throat burned when he heard the tears in her voice. "Are you hurt?"

"I'm so sorry. For everything."

Brentin closed his eyes. She'd ignored his question. Did that mean she was hurt and didn't want to upset them? "There's nothing for you to feel sorry about. Just help us find you."

"They're going to kill me."

"No, they're not," Mr. Parker said. "Get hold of yourself, Mikaela. What do you see?"

"Trees. So many trees—" She gasped.

"What is it?" Brentin said.

Panting. A crackling sound.

Brentin clenched his fists. He waved at a policeman to come over, but the man didn't see him.

"Maybe we should go to him." Mr. Parker said.

"You might lose her signal."

The phone crackled. "I see Frank!" Mikaela whispered softer than before. "He's walking this direction!"

Brentin's breath stopped. His chest clenched.

"Don't hang up!" Mr. Parker yelled.

"Run!" Brentin yelled at the same time.

"I. Love. You," Mikaela panted.

Her words were barely loud enough to touch the air, but they sunk into Brentin's heart like a splintered blade. They had to have been meant for her grandfather, but he *really* wanted them to belong to him too.

Silence again.

Brentin again waved at the policeman. *Why won't he look over here?*

Wheels screeched on pavement. An engine revved. *Crash!*

A dark green car plowed into the back of Mr. Parker's sedan. The open driver's door hit Mr. Parker in the back. He fell face down on the ground, his arms sprawled. His phone lay on the asphalt several feet from him.

"What's going on?" Mikaela's voice said over the phone.

Brentin lunged to Mikaela's grandfather. A gunshot filled the air. Brentin looked at the green car. The elderly Maori driver pointed a gun out his window at Mr. Parker. "It's over, Joseph. As soon as the girl's dead, it's your turn."

Mr. Parker lifted his scraped and bleeding face to Brentin's. "Get the phone. Mikaela."

Brentin looked toward the policeman, who now crouched behind the police car two spaces away. The policeman nodded to him and pointed his gun at the Maori man. "Drop your weapon," he yelled.

"I'm not dropping it till it's finished," the Maori man called back. "Mr. Joseph Parker owes me utu."

Mr. Parker pushed up to his knees. He indicated to the officer to wait. "What are you talking about, Hunapo? I haven't seen or heard from you since you left me with the full burden of Kotuku Inn. Seems to me you owe *me* utu."

"Nice story, mate!" Hunapo said. "You tricked me into selling you my share of the business. You knew I could get the money we needed, given some time."

"We didn't have time. And while I knew you *could* get the money, you wouldn't. You were angry. You begged me to buy your share of the inn. Marge and I did it because we believed in the place, but it almost bankrupt us. You and your pride left us to suffer."

"We can sort this out later," the policeman said. "Put your gun down before things get worse."

Hunapo glared at Mr. Parker. "I'm going to see this through. Kotuku Inn was my home, and Reka was my wife. You took all I ever loved, ever had."

Brentin's body tensed at the tremor he heard in the man's voice. Hunapo had apparently lost control long ago. If he wasn't stopped soon, someone would get hurt. Or killed.

"That's a lie!" Mr. Parker said. "I never looked at your wife after you two started dating."

Hunapo's lips curled into a sneer. "That nursery rhyme book you gave her tells a different story. She read it every night."

"So?"

"I saw the inscription—but not until after her funeral." He stared at Mr. Parker like his words were supposed to mean something, but Mr. Parker just furrowed his brows. "Reka knew how important nursery rhymes were to Caroline and therefore to you, but she only knew a few. Reka thought learning more of them would please you."

Brentin inched toward the rear of Hunapo's car.

"You wrote you loved her," Hunapo said.

"She was going to be your wife, man! I would never—you and I were like brothers."

"You owe me."

Mr. Parker's stance stiffened, but his mouth slackened. "You just couldn't get utu out of your heart, could you?"

"I deserve the restoration of love and prosperity for me and my family. You took them from me, and they can only be returned when I've taken them from you."

"I'm quite certain Caroline Evans wouldn't agree."

"Leave her out of it!"

"What was it she used to say? *The only honorable utu is the one which reciprocates good deeds for all deeds, both good and bad.*"

Brentin stared at Hunapo, at his finger quivering over the trigger.

"She gave you the doll," Hunapo said.

"Yes, and she gave you, free and clear, your initial share of Kotuku Inn. You were the one she considered her son. I knew that, and somewhere inside, you know that too. But instead of accepting responsibility for the life you chose and for your own mistakes, you turned a blind eye to them and blamed me. Where is my granddaughter?"

"Dead. Or soon will be."

\* \* \*

"Grandpa!" Mikaela yelled. She clamped her hand over her mouth. *Stupid.*

Frank whirled, saw her, and charged straight toward her.

Mikaela clenched the knife in one hand and her phone in the other. She ran toward the cover of the trees.

"Mikaela?"

Mikaela's throat tightened as Brentin's voice crackled over the phone. Where was her grandfather? She ran, dove behind trees so thick she no longer saw Frank, and lifted her phone to her ear. "Shhh."

Frank's footsteps pounded over the gravel behind her. Closer, closer . . .

"Mikaela."

*Please be quiet.* She wanted to yell the words, but if she did, her voice would surely give her location away.

"Mikaela."

She began running again. Breathing hard. *Wait a second!* Her thoughts outran her legs. That wasn't Brentin's voice. Was it Frank's?

Her name floated over the air. Not Frank's voice either. It belonged to a woman. She stepped backward. Sara?

"Mi-kae-la."

Mikaela ran again. She leapt between the tall ferns. Frank's footsteps pounded behind her.

"Mikaela." Mikaela looked up toward the voice. A man and a woman stood with their bikes atop a steep path about fifty yards away. The woman held her hands to her mouth and called out, but this time Mikaela didn't hear her words. Her grandfather's voice filled the phone.

"Leave her alone," her grandfather yelled. "I'm the one he wants."

Mikaela's heartbeat pounded against her ears. Who was he talking to?

"Mikaela first." Sara's voice. Had she heard Mikaela's grandfather calling through her phone?

Mikaela whirled, but she should have jumped away, should have run. Frank grabbed her, pinning her arms to her sides. *Say something. Anything. Stop them.*

"I don't know what makes you think this is obeying some kind of law," she yelled at Sara, "but to the rest of the world, you're breaking the law. You're a criminal."

Sara stepped in front of her and shook her head. "You should thank us. Your death, along with your grandparents' deaths, are the only way anyone can restore honor to your family. As to the rest, my ancestors will protect me." She yanked the knife from Mikaela's hand.

"I thought you wanted to change," Mikaela said.

Sara's eyes wavered, and for a second Mikaela thought she'd won, that Sara wouldn't hurt her, that she would stay as alive as the forest around her—*Turn!*

She obeyed the impression just as Sara plunged the knife into Mikaela's side. Sara stepped backward and ran, followed closely by Frank.

Mikaela gaped. She dropped to her knees as pain ripped through her body. She screamed. She opened her mouth to scream again, but this time no voice came. She toppled onto her injured side. Her vision blurred. *So this is what death feels like.* Would she see her parents? Would they come for her? Trevor's face formed in front of her, but it was immediately overshadowed by other memories. Her grandmother holding her and crying with her after they'd closed her parents' caskets, her grandfather teaching her how to drive and not getting angry when she accidentally drove into the garage door, Brentin—his touch, his kiss, his kindness. *Brentin.*

Pressure on her arms. Hands rolled Mikaela onto her back. She couldn't breathe.

* * *

Brentin's breath left him. Was that Mikaela's scream?

"Your ancestors won't support the killing of innocents," Mr. Parker said.

"Mikaela has your blood. She is not innocent."

Brentin clenched his fingers around his own phone. *Please be safe, Mikaela.*

"What about Mikaela's fiancé?" Mr. Parker said. "And the writer?"

"They have nothing to do with this. They were my idiot granddaughter's mistakes. She and her husband will have to answer for those deaths, not me."

"Still passing blame."

"The time for talking is over." He glanced down at his lap then tightened his grip on the gun. He placed his finger on the trigger. "She's dead. Now it's your turn." He pulled—

*She. Can't. Be. Dead.* Brentin threw his phone at the man.

A gunshot. Another.

Mr. Parker fell backward. Hunapo dropped forward onto his steering wheel. The horn blared.

"Mikaela!" Brentin yelled into her grandfather's phone. "Answer me!"

The policeman who'd shot Hunapo slid his handgun into his holster. Several other officers ran toward him and Mr. Parker.

"We've got her," an unfamiliar male voice said over the phone. "She's been stabbed, and the two other guys who were with us are chasing the man and woman who did it. They ran into the forest."

Brentin crushed the phone in his hand. "Is she—can I talk to her?"

"She's lost consciousness. We'll do what we can, but get help up here—and the police—fast."

Brentin ran to the police, ran to the ambulance that turned into the parking lot, ran.

And prayed.

# Chapter 30

JUST BEFORE SUNSET FIVE DAYS later, the construction workers set the new sculpture into its cement slab outside the almost fully renovated Kotuku Inn. It was a simple addition, but to Mikaela, it transformed the inn's tumultuous influence into a new world of peace and hope. That was due in large part to Brentin staying there to take care of her when he should have returned to his job in Colorado days ago. Yet they still hadn't broached the subject of their relationship.

Mikaela adjusted her jacket so the zipper wouldn't brush against the stitches on her abdomen and slid her art book across the deck table into the light outside her shadow.

Her grandfather sat in the chair across from her. He glanced at her drawing. "A fitting title."

She wrote quote marks around the decorative words at the top: *An Eternal Bond.*

"Are you referring to the sculpture, the inn, or something else?" he asked.

Heat flew to her cheeks. She couldn't pretend she didn't know his *something else* actually referred to *someone else*. To Brentin. After all, how many men would not only miss their flight home but would also stay all night in the Redwoods helping the police capture Sara and Frank? Brentin had said it was the only constructive thing he could have done for her, but she suspected it was more than that. That he, like Mikaela, had needed to know Sara and Frank were in jail and could no longer harm her or her family. It was something a real friend would do—the forever kind of friend.

"Whichever you choose it to refer to," she said to her grandfather, "is the sculpture a good likeness?"

"It's perfect."

"I might have gilded it a little, but homes should be idealized, don't you think?"

He leaned his elbow on the table and, shifting left, stared toward the flower garden. "I do."

"Is something wrong?"

He exhaled, glanced at her, and focused again on the garden. "I wanted to wait until you'd had more time to recover, but since you've brought it up, I have two things I need to tell you." He took a newspaper from the inside of his jacket and set it on the table in front of her. "Read the headline."

"One-time Roturua Resident Found Dead at Kotuku Inn by Andrew Evans." At first Mikaela scanned the words. It was all there: Caroline's generosity, her move, and her subsequent murder by Noah Cooper. But the closer Mikaela got to the end, the more she focused on each word. Andrew had done as both she and Ms. Sabey had asked him to do; he'd left their names and their specific comments out of his report. Her grandfather's name too.

She swallowed and handed the paper back to her grandfather. "Andrew did a good job."

"He did."

"So what's the second thing?"

"I've decided to sell Kotuku Inn."

"What? You can't do that. Kotuku Inn means everything to you."

"Not everything."

Warm moisture stung her eyes, but she lifted her chin in a show of defiance. "You mean me."

"Yes. And your grandmother. I want to be close to her and to you."

"You don't need to take care of me anymore, Grandpa. I could have been married by now."

"But you aren't, and you're alone." His voice softened, but his words pressed like weights against her heart. She couldn't let him sacrifice his life for her again. It was her turn to sacrifice for him. "It's your property, your money. You have a right to enjoy it. And what about the doll? Will you be able to take it out of New Zealand?"

He lifted an eyebrow. "It looks like there are three things I need to tell you, or in this case, ask you. Would it be all right with you if I gave the doll back to the Evans family? That reporter—"

"Andrew."

"Andrew came to see you while you were in the hospital. You were asleep at the time. It was just after the doctor told us that if Sara had stabbed you any closer to your abdomen, you wouldn't have made it."

Mikaela glanced down at her side. Wounded but preserved. *Thank you, Heavenly Father.*

"Anyway, Andrew said he couldn't wait for you to wake up, so I spent a little time with him. He asked if he could buy the doll from me."

"I thought there was something up with him and that doll."

"The doll meant a lot to me, Mikaela, because Caroline gave it to me. I know I promised it to you, but a thing like that . . . If you don't mind, I believe it should stay with Caroline's family. The earring too."

"I agree, so if that's what you want to do, it's fine with me. Whatever you want to do—about the doll, the inn, everything. It's all fine. But before you make any drastic decisions, I need to tell you something too."

"You do?"

"I'd already decided, but I thought it best to wait to tell you until after I'd recovered a bit more so you'd believe me—so you wouldn't think I wasn't in my right mind because of the painkillers."

He smiled, and Mikaela clasped her hands together on top of the table. She looked him straight in the eyes. "I'm not going back to USU. I'm going to finish school somewhere else. So don't decide to sell Kotuku Inn because of me. I won't even be in Brigham City."

"Don't tell me you've finally decided to go to the University of Utah."

She placed her hand on top of his. "I'm glad I went to Utah State, but now, well, I need to set some of those memories aside. I need to make a new life for myself, and it will be easier to do in a new place."

"Running away won't give you what you want. You've got to face life—"

"Head on. I know. That's what I'm doing."

Brentin stepped outside the glass door onto the deck and held it open for Tui. She carried a thick, folded blanket. Mikaela's grandfather had spent several days trying to persuade Tui to return to Kotuku Inn, but it wasn't until he'd promised he'd never again bring that doll into the house that she agreed to return. After all, Kotuku Inn couldn't survive without her.

Brentin nodded at Mikaela. That was all, but it was enough—her cheeks blazed.

Her grandfather glanced between the two of them. "Colorado?"

Mikaela grimaced. Did he have to speak so loudly? "I don't know yet," she whispered. "I haven't known him very long. But maybe."

"Knowing a person for a long time isn't what keeps a marriage together, Mikaela. It's commitment. And from what I've seen, he has that. Do you?"

"What are you . . . I didn't say anything about marriage."

He patted her hand. If it were possible for expressions to dance, she'd have said that's what his did before he looked up to Tui and Brentin.

"It's getting cold out here," Tui said, "and I've just taken some bread from the oven. Come on in and have a cuppa chocolate with it, you two."

Mikaela's grandfather looked meaningfully at Brentin, sighed, and stood. "I can't refuse that kind of offer, but I'm afraid we'll have to indulge Mikaela for a few more minutes. She's not quite finished with her drawing."

Mikaela's face blazed hotter. She hadn't meant she had to talk about college and—and *other stuff* with Brentin now. They'd hardly spoken of their relationship since that night he'd kissed her—except for those first moments in the hospital when the doctor finally allowed her to have visitors. And then she'd been in too much pain to say much, and Brentin had simply kissed her on the forehead and told her not to worry about anything except getting well. Even the memory of that kiss made her heart pound so loud she feared everyone could hear it.

"Brentin, you don't mind sitting out here with Mikaela for a few minutes, do you?" her grandfather added.

*Not now. I haven't figured out what to say.* Mikaela dropped her gaze to her drawing and drew a completely unnecessary line on the base of the deck steps.

Brentin sat in the chair next to hers. "I'd be happy to."

Her grandfather patted his shoulder, and he and Tui went inside.

Her skin tingled where Brentin's knee bumped hers. He touched the corner of her art book. "An eternal bond?"

Their gazes locked. "Yes."

"Perfect," he said.

"My grandfather said the same thing." Mikaela drew three more unnecessary lines on the inn's roof and added a tiny flower next to the sculpture.

She heard him breathe. A breeze wafted an extra-strong scent of sulfur into the air, but somehow it too seemed perfect.

"It's nice out here," Brentin said.

Mikaela swallowed. She told her fingers not to tremble around her pencil, told her mouth to say *something*.

Brentin touched the back of her hand. "Your skin's cold. Let's get you inside."

"Not yet." Her grip viced around her drawing pencil.

Brentin slowly removed his hand from hers and settled back in his seat. She felt his gaze on her as she added more unnecessary shadows to her picture. Finally, he stood. "You're shivering, Mikaela. Let's—"

"Remember that night?" She looked up at him.

He sat again, holding her gaze, and though he didn't move closer, her skin trembled as if he had. "When I kissed you?" he asked.

"Yes."

He lifted his eyebrows, waited.

"I know I should have said something then, but I didn't know it at the time." She licked her lips. "The day we met was my best day too. And the truth is—"

A small smile lifted the edges of his lips, and this time he did move closer to her.

Mikaela's fingers quavered. "Out there in the forest, when I believed I was going to die, I thought of my grandparents."

He nodded.

"But I also thought of you. Especially you. How you were always, always there for me. On the phone, when I said—" had she known him long enough to say it?—"*I love you*, I was talking to both you and my grandfather."

His gaze widened, but his expression deepened. He leaned toward her.

Mikaela's heart thumped against her throat, her chest, her wrists—so hard she didn't know if she'd ever be able to breathe properly again.

Brentin wrapped his arm around her and, pulling her against him, pressed his lips to hers and held them there. She closed her eyes and leaned into the strength of his embrace until her pulse pounded through her senses and her breath blended in rhythm with his.

The back door opened.

"Oh my," Tui said just before she pulled it closed again.

Mikaela laughed. Brentin did too, but their lips didn't separate until Mikaela lifted her gaze to his. "It's not like she couldn't see us through the glass. Do you think she's still upset about you not choosing Amiria?"

He gently cupped his hand around her jawline. "Does it matter?"

"No. But I almost wonder if . . . Is this, our being together, too much of a good thing?"

"No way." Brentin pulled her even tighter into his arms and kissed her until every inch of her skin shivered.

# About the Author

RONDA GIBB HINRICHSEN LIVES WITH her husband on a small farm in northern Utah. They are the parents of three children and care for a few cows and goats. She has a passion for reading, writing, and music, though not necessarily in that order, and she enjoys traveling with her husband throughout the world. Through those travels, she's discovered she loves the mountains—a good thing since she lives at the foot of the Rocky Mountains. One of her most favorite countries to visit is New Zealand. *One Fell Down* is Ronda's fourth romantic-suspense novel.

To learn more about Ronda, visit her website at rondahinrichsen.com.